A
Deadly
Bouquet

A
Deadly
Bouquet

Janis Harrison

Thorndike Press • Chivers Press
Waterville, Maine USA Bath, England

This Large Print edition is published by Thorndike Press®, USA
and by Chivers Press, England.

Published in 2003 in the U.S. by arrangement with
St. Martin's Press, LLC.

Published in 2003 in the U.K. by arrangement with
Robert Hale Limited.

U.S. Hardcover 0-7862-5207-3 (Mystery Series)
U.K. Hardcover 0-7540-7206-1 (Chivers Large Print)
U.K. Softcover 0-7540-7207-X (Camden Large Print)

The text of this Large Print edition is unabridged.
Other aspects of the book may vary from the original edition.

Set in 16 pt. Plantin by Myrna S. Raven.

Printed in the United States on permanent paper.

British Library Cataloguing-in-Publication Data available

Library of Congress Cataloging-in-Publication Data

Harrison, Janis (Janis Anne)
    A deadly bouquet / Janis Harrison.
        p. cm.
    ISBN 0-7862-5207-3 (lg. print : hc : alk. paper)
    1. Solomon, Bretta (Fictitious character) — Fiction.
2. Women detectives — Missouri — Fiction. 3. Women
gardeners — Fiction. 4. Gardening — Fiction.
5. Missouri — Fiction. 6. Florists — Fiction. 7. Large
type books. I. Title.
PS3558.A67132D43 2003
  813'.54—dc21
                                  2003040708

This book is dedicated to three ladies who free up my time so that I may write. My thanks to Cathy Bartels, Sugger Gauchat, and Melissa Roberts.

Acknowledgments

As I write this acknowledgment, the words of a John Cougar Mellencamp song run through my mind. I've always lived in a "Small Town." I most definitely daydream in this small town. I probably haven't seen it all in this small town, but I've seen enough. I won't forget where I came from, and I won't forget the people who care about me.

On that note, I'd like to express my appreciation to the following:

Librarian Phyllis Jones and her board of directors for the wonderful book signings they've held in my honor.

Attorney John Kopp for attempting to answer my strange questions.

To the citizens of Windsor, Missouri — population thirty-two hundred. Thank you for allowing me to be myself in this small town.

Chapter One

"Death tapped me on the shoulder, so I figured my time was up." Oliver adjusted the strap on his overalls and looked at me. "Bretta, that heart attack nearly sent me to my grave." His eyes sparkled when he grinned. "But I'm still here. I've got holes to dig, only they aren't for my old body."

I touched the leaves of the golden spirea shrub Oliver was about to plant. "Old gardeners never die. They just *spade* away."

He chuckled. "Ain't it the truth. Fifty years ago, when I began my landscaping business, my only qualifications for a job were my love of plants and a new spade. This is that original tool." Oliver caressed the worn handle. "Whenever I touch this wood memories of bygone years flash into focus."

Oliver lowered his voice. "But I can't trust my memory like I used to. Since I came home from the hospital my old noggin goes out of kilter. I see things, remember things, but I don't always make the connection."

9

"Your body has been through a rough time."

"Yeah." Oliver nodded. "That's true." His grip tightened on the wooden handle. "One thing is for certain. I haven't forgotten how to plant a shrub. My father was a gardener pure and simple. 'Just as the twig is bent, the tree's inclined.' From an early age I knew what my course in life would be."

I watched Oliver ease the sharp tip of the spade into the soil. He was a nice man, and I enjoyed visiting with him, but I wondered if it was a good idea for him to be working. He appeared to be in fair health, but his heart attack had been just six months ago. His eyes were bright, his weathered cheeks flushed, but that could be from the warm sun shining on us.

River City Commemorative Park was a lovely place on this June morning. A gentle breeze stirred the oak and maple leaves and carried the sweet scent of petunia blossoms. Birds twittered with importance as they brought food to their newly hatched offspring. It was peaceful and should be an ideal spot for a wedding. Just how ideal would be proved a week from today when the Montgomery/Gentry nuptials put my flower shop's reputation on the line.

When Evelyn Montgomery first approached me with plans for her daughter Nikki's wedding, I'd seen the event as a way of stretching my artistic talents, as well as getting the word out that I was capable of more than sympathy and hospital bouquets. I'd visualized turning the park into a floral fantasy. My shop would get the kudos, and my River City floral competitors would choke on my creative dust.

If my husband, Carl, were alive, he'd have cautioned, "Bretta Solomon, when ego comes into play, the brain takes a holiday."

I hoped my little gray cells were stretched on some sandy beach soaking up sunshine, because the rest of this ego-ridden body had been trapped into making sure every floral detail of this wedding was perfectly executed. I would triumph if it killed me — and the way things were going, it very well might.

Since my initial contact with Evelyn, my doctor had treated me for a severe case of hives. I also had a persistent burning in the pit of my stomach that disappeared only when I was sure Evelyn was otherwise occupied. Too many times, I'd been surprised by her popping into the flower shop to have "a brief confab" over a detail we'd settled an hour ago.

Today's appointment was for ten o'clock, but it was only nine thirty. I'd come to the park early so I could look over the lay of the land and perhaps zero in on something that would soothe my ragged nerves. It had been my good fortune to find Oliver Terrell and his son, Eddie, hard at work on the plantings Evelyn had donated to the park.

As Oliver lifted another scoop of dirt, Eddie said, "Dad, take a break. I still think it was a lousy idea for you to come on this job. I could've handled it."

Eddie was around my age — forty-five — and had fabulous blue eyes. I was sure he had hair, though I'd never seen it. A cap bearing his company's name — Terrell Landscaping — usually sat atop his handsome head.

Oliver took a red handkerchief from his pocket and wiped his brow. "I'm fine. I need this work to get in shape for when we tackle Bretta's garden next week."

I flexed my fingers. "I can hardly wait. I plan on being right alongside both of you, pulling weeds, chopping stumps, wheeling mulch —"

"— smoothing Ben-Gay on your aching muscles," finished Eddie.

I grinned. "Probably, but I'm looking forward to the challenge. Being a florist is more cerebral than physical. I don't get much exercise toting bouquets."

Eddie dumped a wheelbarrow load of shredded bark on a tarp he'd spread near the shrubs Oliver was planting. "Surely, toeing Mrs. Montgomery's line has kept you in tiptop shape?"

I reached into my pocket and flashed a roll of antacid tablets at him. "Does this answer your question?"

Eddie grunted. "I should buy stock in that company."

"When Evelyn asked me to design the flowers for her daughter's garden wedding, I listened to her general outline, then calmly replied, 'Sure, no problem.' And there's been problems galore."

Eddie muttered something under his breath. I didn't catch his comment, but Oliver did. "A job is a job, son. We're here to please the customer." Oliver turned to me. "I haven't met Mrs. Montgomery, but from what Eddie has told me, it sounds as if she has more money than common sense."

Wasn't that the truth? I left father and son to their work and meandered down the path that led to the area of the park known as Tranquility Garden — the site of the upcoming nuptials. For weeks, I'd reminded myself that Evelyn Montgomery had a right to be persnickety. As mother of the bride, she wanted everything perfect for her daughter's wedding.

Nikki and her fiancé were on a tour of the United States with a ballet company from France. When the troupe hit St. Louis, they'd be a hop, skip, and a pirouette from River City. There would be a two-day layover before the dance company continued on with the tour.

Two days to be fitted for gowns and tuxedos, the rehearsal, and the main event. Thank heavens, I only had to make sure the flowers were petal perfect.

Only?

I stuffed another antacid tablet into my mouth and heard voices off to my left. The tone of one stood out from the other: Sonya Norris, wedding coordinator, had arrived. Brides paid dearly for her services because if a job had to be done, and done right, Sonya would see to it. She wouldn't physically do the work herself, but her instructions would be carried out.

The women came into view. Sonya was tall and thin and favored "power" suits, tailored blouses, and plain gold-hoop earrings. Her hair was dark and cut in a no-nonsense style. Today she was dressed in a teal-blue straight skirt and matching jacket. Her blouse was a lighter shade.

The woman with Sonya was Dana Olson, a River City caterer. I liked Dana. She was as sweet as the cakes she baked. Soft and pudgy, her figure was a testimonial to her prowess in the kitchen. For children's parties she not only decorated the cakes but also dressed as a clown. This added bonus had made her popular with frazzled mothers.

As the two women walked toward me, I had a mental flash of Dana in total clown regalia cutting the Montgomery wedding cake. The image made me shudder. Why had Evelyn given Dana, whose forte was birthdays and anniversaries, total responsibility for the food for such a lavish party? Perhaps Sonya was thinking along those same lines. Now that they were closer, I could make out their conversation.

"— can't bring all that food across this path to the tent. There's to be a display of flowers, candles, and hurricane lamps. Think, Dana," Sonya ordered sharply. "You'll have to hire extra help to carry your supplies from the other side."

"I already have three girls on the payroll.

I'd like to make a profit for all this worrying." Dana shook her head, and her brown curls bounced. "And to think I turned down four ordinary birthday cakes and a golden anniversary to cater this wedding."

"It will work," said Sonya. "My job is to spot a potential problem, but you have to follow my suggestions." She turned to me. "Bretta. It's good to see you here early. I hope everything is shipshape on your end of this gala?"

I only had time to nod before Dana started again.

"That's all well and good, Sonya, but where were you this morning when Mrs. Montgomery called to tell me to look at the sunrise?" Dana didn't wait for an answer. "Our mother of the bride wants me to match that particular rosy apricot color for the punch." A hot flush stained Dana's plump cheeks. "Who gives a flying fig about the punch when the cake has to tower six feet in the air?"

"Six feet?" repeated Sonya, frowning. "I thought the cake was to be spread over three tables with sugar bridges connecting the tiered layers. When was that changed?"

"Try eight o'clock last night. Mrs. Montgomery says Nikki has decided she wants a cake that will stand as tall as her six-foot fiancé."

"Oh my," said Sonya. "Not a good plan. The tent is to have a wooden floor, but as people walk about, the shifting of the boards might topple —"

"Don't even say it." Dana moaned. "I wish I'd never taken this job. I feel as if I'm being punished. Nikki will be in St. Louis. Why not have the wedding there?"

I added my two cents to the conversation. "I have to admit I'm surprised Evelyn would hold such an important event in a town she's called home for less than a year."

Sonya shrugged. "She's made more influential friends in the last eight months than I have all my life. You should see the guest list. The mayor is coming, as well as bankers, doctors, lawyers, councilmen, judges, and all of River City's elite. At last count there's to be five hundred people milling around this park."

"But why River City?" whined Dana. "Why us? Why —"

"Dana," said a woman coming down the path toward us, "will you stop that screeching? I could hear you clear out to the parking lot."

This new arrival looked like a sixties reject who had found her way back into style. She wore bell-bottom slacks and a tie-dyed shirt. A narrow band of cloth was fastened around her forehead and kept her stringy blond hair out of her eyes. She was as thin as a willow branch. Her arms were like twigs.

"You think you've got problems?" she said, pointing to a mammoth oak. "See that tree? Workmen are coming this week to build a platform so I can take aerial photos of this wedding." She tossed her head. "I've been ordered to dress as if I'm a guest so I won't be intrusive. Can you explain to me how I'm supposed to climb that tree in a skirt and panty hose while carrying a video camera and equipment?"

I shifted uncomfortably. All these last-minute changes bothered me. For the past twenty-four hours I hadn't heard a peep out of Evelyn. I turned to Sonya. "Exactly why were we asked to meet here this morning?"

Before Sonya could answer, another woman sprinted toward us. Her hair was a shrieking shade of green. Her eyes glittered like emeralds. She wore an orange uniform with a lemon-colored apron tied around her narrow waist. "Hi, guys. Am I late?"

"Would it matter?" asked Dana, star-

18

ing at the green hair.

"Nope. I've got a business to run, and Claire's Hair Lair has to come first. I can't be away for more than an hour. I'm on the trail of a hot piece of gossip, and Mrs. Dearborne is coming in for a perm. If I phrase my questions just right, she'll never know what I'm after, and I'll —"

"Claire, what have you done to your hair?" demanded the photographer. "All those chemicals aren't healthy."

Claire gave the woman's own limp hair a sharp study. "Cut, color, curl. The three C's will earn you a man."

"Like your track record makes me want one."

I laughed politely with the others, but had the feeling I was being left out of some private joke. While Sonya and I had a professional acquaintance, and I'd often sold Dana fresh flowers to decorate her cakes, the other two women were strangers.

I asked for an introduction, and Sonya quickly responded, "I'm sorry, Bretta. Since we know each other, I never thought you'd be left out of the loop. The woman with the broccoli-colored hair and contacts is Claire Alexander, beauty shop owner." Sonya turned to the other woman. "This is Kasey Vickers. She's a local celebrity. Her photo-essays have earned her national recognition in environmental circles."

I must have looked as confused as I felt. An environmentalist was shooting the photos for a wedding?

Sonya said, "I know what you're thinking. But regardless of the subject, Kasey's photo techniques will give Nikki a wonderful keepsake."

Impatiently, Claire said, "What are we waiting for? I have to get back to my shop." She lowered her voice. "After I talk to Mrs. Dearborne, I may have some news that will knock you all onto your fannies."

Sonya frowned. "You keep hinting at some great secret. Are you going to let us in on it?"

"Not till I get more information."

Sonya said, "It's no wonder you became a beautician. You thrive on gossip. What's going on?"

Claire shook her head. "I'm not saying another word."

"That'll be the day," muttered Kasey.

Dana turned to me. "Ignore their bickering. Our friendship goes back to high school."

I looked from one face to another. "You're all the same age? What year did you graduate?"

"Nineteen sixty-six," said Dana, fluffing her brown curls. "I'm the baby of the group."

While the others razzed her, I did some fast calculations. If they had graduated when they were eighteen that meant these women were fifty-four years old. Of the four, only Sonya looked her age. Dana's plump cheeks were wrinkle-free. I wouldn't have guessed the green-haired Claire to be past forty. As for Kasey, her skin was stretched so tightly over her bones my estimation of her age would've been way off the mark.

Claire thrust her hands into her apron pockets. "That's how we can get away with the insults. We've been friends too long to let a little criticism separate us. Besides, nothing any of us could say would be new." She studied her friends and softly chanted, "You can boil me in oil. You can burn me at the stake. But a River City Royal is always on the make."

Dana's mouth dropped open. Sonya stiffened. Kasey said, "No, Claire. You —" But then she stopped and bit her lip.

In the silence that followed, we heard Evelyn's voice. Her tone was sharp. "I want everything perfect, right down to the leaves on the shrubs."

Evelyn walked toward us with Eddie and Oliver trailing along behind her. When I met Eddie's gaze, my stomach muscles tightened. The man had fire in his eyes. Oliver's skin was mottled. His chest rose and fell with sharp, agitated breaths.

I looked back at Evelyn. She was a beautiful woman — blue-black hair and deep brown eyes, her complexion as smooth as a magnolia blossom, her makeup flawless. She possessed a figure a teenager would have envied. Pointed breasts, a narrow waist, and nicely rounded hips were displayed in a bronze-colored dress.

"As I've told Mr. Terrell," Evelyn said, coming into our circle, "my goal for this wedding is a tribute to an exquisite woman." She dazzled us with a smile. "Thank you for coming this morning. I thought it best to be on-site for this discussion. If you have any questions, suggestions, or complaints say them now. You'll have my undivided attention. Oliver and Eddie have heard what I want." She nodded to them. "You may both go back to work."

It was a cool dismissal, but Eddie had something else to say. Oliver tugged on his son's arm, but Eddie wouldn't move.

Evelyn ignored him and said, "All right,

ladies, who wants to go first?"

Claire stepped forward. "I have to get back to my shop —"

"That hot piece of gossip from Mrs. Dearborne won't wait, huh?" asked Dana.

Oliver stared at Claire. "Dearborne? Gossip? Who are you?"

Claire raised an eyebrow. "I'm Claire Alexander, owner of Claire's Hair Lair."

Oliver studied her face and shook his head. "I don't know you, but suddenly something is niggling at me." He gazed at the ground. "I wished I could remember."

Evelyn said, "Please, we have to discuss the fine points of Nikki's wedding."

Oliver closed his eyes and cocked his head as if listening to some distant sound. His hand moved up and down the handle of his spade. "So long ago," he murmured.

Eddie said to Evelyn, "Dad and I have done like you asked. We took out the euonymus shrubs, and we're planting the golden spirea. The look is natural. To spray the foliage with gold paint would be ridiculous."

"Spray the foliage?" I repeated.

Evelyn turned to me. "Yes, Bretta. The color of the shrubs is too yellow. I want Nikki to stroll down a gilded path."

"She also wants us to plant dead trees,"

23

groused Eddie. "Dead trees, mind you, so the bare branches can be draped with hoity-toity lights."

"I saw the idea in a magazine. The effect against the night sky was —"

"— not done by Terrell Landscaping," finished Eddie.

Oliver opened his eyes. "Where are the markers?"

Eddie shot his father a puzzled look, but said to Evelyn, "I've had it. Dad and I are done. Plant your own shrubs. Drape your own damned lights."

Evelyn's smile was cold. "Fine. Pack up your stuff and get out."

Eddie waved an arm. "It's a public park."

"Son?" said Oliver weakly. He stumbled forward. "Chest hurts. Heart."

Eddie whipped around. "Where's your pills?"

Oliver sunk to his knees. "Can't . . . get . . . breath." He gasped and fell forward.

Sonya used her cell phone to call 911. I knelt next to Oliver. "Help me turn him over," said Eddie.

Once we had Oliver on his back, he opened his eyes. Eddie found the pills, uncapped the brown bottle, and slipped a tablet under Oliver's tongue.

24

"Hang in there, Dad," he coached. "Give the medicine a chance to work."

Spittle drooled from the corner of Oliver's mouth. Eddie used his shirttail to wipe it gently away. Oliver gazed at his son. Love reflected beyond the pain he was enduring. He turned his head and stared directly into my eyes. Softly, he said, "Bretta . . . Spade."

Chapter Two

My flower shop has always been a safe haven, a place I can go to regroup and put my thoughts in order. I headed for that calming piece of real estate when I left River City Commemorative Park.

As a florist, I've helped bereaved families choose a fitting memorial for their loved one's service. On a personal level, I've had my own share of dealing with an unexpected death. But never has my name been on a dying man's lips. Never have I stared into his eyes as he drew his last breath.

I pulled into the alley behind the flower shop and climbed wearily out of my car. It felt as if an eternity had passed since the morning. As I went up the steps to the back door, I checked my watch, but my wrist was bare. The timepiece had stopped a few days ago, and I hadn't bought a new one. I entered the workroom and glanced at the clock. It was only eleven thirty. The shop closed at noon on Saturdays. My employees, Lois and Lew, were finishing a couple of last-minute orders.

"Oh, boy," said Lois, eyeing my grim expression. "I take it the meeting didn't go well. What does that woman want now? White doves released from gold-plated cages?"

Lew said, "More like trained seals barking 'Ave Maria' from the reflection pool."

I moved a tall stool closer to the worktable and sat down. Lois Duncan is my floral designer, and while I value her work, I treasure her friendship. Over the years, I've tried to analyze why we get along so well when we have so many differences.

Lois is taller than I am, and has the metabolism of a hummingbird. Her weight never varies even though she sucks down candy like a vacuum cleaner in an M&M factory. My hips expand when I so much as smell chocolate. She has five children. I have none. Her bouquets are flamboyant. Mine are conservative. Sometimes she's bossy, especially when the subject concerns my lack of a social life.

Lew Mouffit is my deliveryman and perhaps the most annoying male in River City. He has the answer to everything and pontificates with such pomposity that I'm often tempted to fire him. However, he has a following of well-to-do women who patronize my shop, so I bite my tongue again and again.

Before I plunged into the story of my morning, I looked around me, drawing strength from what was near and dear to my heart. Years ago, when I had to name my business, a cutesy title didn't cut it. I'd settled on the Flower Shop, which suited my practical nature. I ran a tight ship. I believed that everything should have a place, that an object should be where I wanted it when I wanted it.

Bolts of satin ribbon were neatly lined on shelves. From where I sat I could see the front cooler, displaying fresh, colorful arrangements. Next to the cash register was a vase of white carnations, their spicy scent an open invitation for my customers to make a purchase.

I took a deep breath, then released it in a sigh. "You can't begin to imagine what happened." I filled them in on everything. My visit with Oliver and Eddie. Meeting the other women involved with the wedding. Eddie's and Evelyn's disagreement, and finally, the morning's distressing finale.

"The paramedics arrived, but it was too late. Oliver had already passed away. Eddie was devastated. He jumped in his truck and tore out of the park."

"Poor guy," said Lois.

I glanced up, saw the concern in her blue eyes, and knew what she was thinking. Carl had died from a heart attack, too. Lois was worried that my morning's experience might send me into a deep depression.

I summoned up a smile to ease her fears, then turned to Lew, who was muttering under his breath. Lew was thirty-five and rapidly going bald. I've never seen him dressed in anything but well-pressed slacks, a shirt, and a conservative tie.

Against my better judgment, I asked, "Are you talking to us?"

Lew checked to make sure he had our complete and undivided attention. "If Oliver used his dying breath to whisper 'Spade' to you, then it must have been important." He added piously, "I've figured it out."

Lois rolled her eyes. I had to control an urge to do likewise. This was so typical of Lew. I'd skimmed through the account of my conversation with Oliver. I'd briefly explained his brush with death six months ago. I'd ended my story by repeating Oliver's dying words. I'd been there, I'd seen everything that had happened, and yet, *Lew* had drawn a conclusion.

I said, "Let's have it. Why did Oliver say 'Spade' to me?"

"If I understood you correctly, Oliver actually said, 'Bretta . . . Spade.' " Lew's balding head shone in the fluorescent light. "He was asking for your help. It makes sense. Bretta Spade."

When I didn't shout "Eureka!" or do a cartwheel across the floor, he demanded, "Don't you get it? Oliver was drawing a parallel between you and Dashiell Hammett's fictional detective — Sam Spade."

Well, that was stupid, and I would have said so, but Lois beat me to it.

"Get real. The man was dying. He could've been confused. Disoriented. Bretta told us he cherished that gardening tool. Maybe he was asking her to keep it safe for Eddie."

Lew's chin rose several degrees. "As my great-grandmother would've said, 'Balderdash!' If Oliver wanted his son to have the spade, he'd have said 'Spade' to him. According to Bretta, Oliver actually turned his head toward *her.* He spoke *her* name. He knew who he was talking to, and he knew exactly what he was saying."

Lois said, "You won't convince me that a man on the brink of death was playing some convoluted mind game."

Lew straightened his tie. "All right, how about this? Spades are the highest suit in bridge. What if Oliver used the word *spade* to denote an event that was of supreme importance to —"

I didn't let him finish. "I doubt that Oliver ever played a hand of bridge. Let's drop it. I'm too tired to discuss it further."

Lew frowned. "Too tired? I'm amazed you aren't hot on the trail of this latest mystery. Or is it because these theories came from me?" When I didn't answer, he turned on the heel of his well-polished shoe and stomped to the back room. "I'm taking these last deliveries. See you Monday."

"Thanks for the warning," said Lois under her breath.

After the door had closed, I said, "He's in a foul mood. What's his problem?"

"My first thought is that he isn't getting any, except he never does. I don't know why things are different today. He's been a grouch all morning, and he's taken to critiquing my bouquets." She grabbed a broom and swept the littered floor. In a haughty tone, she mimicked, " 'Red, purple, and yellow are so gauche, Lois. Must you always pick that combination for a hospital order?' "

I chuckled. "So what's been going on here, besides Lew being a bigger pain than usual?"

Lois shrugged. "Not much. Business is slow for a Saturday." She swept the flower stems into a dustpan and dumped them into the trash bin under her table. "If you don't need me to close, I'm going home." But she didn't look happy about it.

Last month, Lois had agreed to let her sister's daughter, Kayla, come live with her. Lois had raised five children, but all were finally out on their own. I didn't think it was a good idea when Lois talked it over with me. In Cincinnati, Kayla had been in trouble. Her mother thought a change of scenery might change the girl. That hadn't happened. Kayla, a junior at River City High School, was in trouble again. Lois hadn't told me the problem, which was unusual. She and I had few secrets.

"Is there anything I can do?" I asked.

Lois's smile was pinched. "No thanks. I assume we'll be putting in overtime on this wedding?" After I'd nodded, she continued, "I have a ton of dirty laundry, and I need to go grocery shopping."

I waved her on. She hung the dustpan on

its hook, then picked up her purse. Hesitating at the door, she asked, "You aren't going to let Oliver's death get to you, are you?"

"I'm fine. But I wish I knew what he tried to tell me. Not to agree with Lew, but it sure seemed like Oliver expected me to do something."

"Not necessarily true. His mind could've flipped back to your earlier conversation with him. He'd talked about the spade. He saw you leaning over him. Put it out of your mind. We have enough to deal with when it comes to this wedding."

I made a face, but Lois didn't see it. She'd already gone. I counted out the cash drawer, then glanced through the day's orders, but saw nothing interesting. I checked the walk-in cooler to jog my memory as to what fresh flowers were available for Oliver's upcoming funeral.

Would Eddie want red roses for the spray on the casket or something earthier, befitting a gardener? Bronze and yellow mums with an assortment of greens — ivy, variegated pittosporum, and some gold and orange croton leaves — would be appropriate for a man who'd made his living from loving plants.

I turned off the workroom lights and

strolled up front, where I flipped the lock and put the CLOSED sign into place. I particularly like being in the shop when the doors are shut to the public and the lights are off. The pressure eases, and I can relax and let my mind drift. I stared across the street at Kelsey's Bar and Grill and felt a need for an order of their curly fries.

Two years ago, after my husband, Carl, had passed away, I'd lost one hundred pounds. My struggle to keep the weight off is an hour-to-hour battle. With the stress I'd been under, I yearned for a plate of comfort. But I summoned up some willpower and turned my back on Kelsey's, staring instead at the shop's shadows.

This month was the second anniversary of my husband's death. It had taken every one of those days to accept the fact that he was gone and my life was forever changed. For twenty-four years, Carl had been at my side. I'd been married to him longer than I'd been alone. We'd been friends before we became lovers. I could tell him anything, talk to him about everything under the moon and stars, and he'd listened, really listened to what I had to say.

I hadn't known the true extent of his faith in me until he became a deputy with the Spencer County Sheriff's Department.

He'd trusted me with the facts of cases he worked on. Together we'd explored possibilities as to what might have happened. We'd made wild conjectures. I was a great one for taking that "shot in the dark." Carl had urged me to let my mind flow even if the picture seemed askew.

Carl's legacy had been a bountiful education, but the art of solving a mystery had been a fraction of his tutoring. From the first day I'd met him, he'd tried to teach me to trust and to forgive. I hadn't been a willing pupil. When your heart's been broken, it isn't easy to give those emotions another chance.

When I was eight years old, my father walked out of my life. For more years than I care to count, he was simply a name on a birthday card or a box of grapefruit at Christmas. This past December he'd come to River City for a visit, and I'd learned that you can't have trust without forgiveness.

I smiled sadly. It hurt that Carl wasn't here to see that I'd gone to the head of the class. The lines of communication with my father were open. In fact, last night I'd gotten a call from him. He'd said he had a fantastic surprise for me and that it would arrive this afternoon.

I wasn't particularly curious. He'd gotten into the habit of sending me trinkets. What I really wanted, he wasn't ready to give. I needed a detailed account of why he'd walked out. So far all I'd gotten was the old cliché — irreconcilable differences with my mother — which didn't tell me squat.

And neither did the words "Bretta . . . Spade."

What had Oliver meant? What was he trying to tell me? Lew had been right about one thing. If Oliver had used his dying breath to whisper those words to me, it must have been important to him. Of course, the man couldn't be sure he was dying. He'd fought death before and won. Only this time he'd lost the battle and had left me with a final plea.

Damn but I hated not knowing what was expected of me. By not doing anything, by not having an inkling of what I should do, I felt as if I was denying Oliver his last request.

Guilt was a great motivator. I grabbed my purse and started for the back door. I could go to the park, pack up Eddie's tools, and take them by his house. I wouldn't knock on his door. I'd simply leave everything in plain sight. It wasn't much, but it was better than —

The telephone rang. Irritated, I stopped and stared at it. Now that I had a plan, I was anxious to put it into action, but it's difficult to ignore a ringing phone. Two more jingles and I picked up the receiver.

"The Flower Shop. Bretta speaking."

"This is Claire. I met you this morning at the park."

"Yes, Claire. I remember." Green hair. Green eyes. How could I forget? "What can I do —"

"I've got to see you."

"If you have any questions about this wedding, go straight to Evelyn. I'm not about to second-guess what she wants."

"I can't discuss this on the phone. Can you come to my beauty shop? The address is 3201 Marietta Avenue. You have a reputation for getting to the bottom of suspicious doings. I can't make heads or tails of this information, but I'm not sitting on it."

"What information?"

"Just get here —" Claire's voice lost its excited tone. "Well, hi," she said calmly. "This is a pleasant surprise."

I frowned in confusion. Was the woman crazy? Perhaps all those chemicals she used on her hair had seeped into her brain. "What's going on?" I asked.

Instead of answering, Claire plunked down the receiver, but I could still hear her talking. "Just making an appointment. If you'll take a chair, I'll be right with you."

Oh. A customer had come in. Claire said, "Sure, I have time. Let me finish this call."

The receiver was picked up, and Claire asked, "You have the address, correct?"

"Yes. I'll be there in a few minutes."

"No hurry," she said quietly. "My pigeon just walked through the door." She hung up.

I replaced the receiver and went out to my car. Pigeon? That was a strange way to refer to a customer.

I made a left turn, headed for the park, but after a few blocks I detoured back the way I'd come. I was curious as to what Claire wanted.

Marietta Avenue was located in the old historic district, which sat on the limestone bluffs overlooking the Osage River. The area with its brick-paved streets was undergoing revitalization, which I was glad to see was progressing well. I had a fondness for this part of town, and had done a bit of research on its history.

In 1810 a man named James Horton and his wife, Hattie, had organized a group of people intent on finding a new land and new beginnings. On their trek west, these pioneers had gotten lost. Finding themselves on the bank of the Osage River, they had either lacked the will to travel forward or liked what they'd stumbled upon. For whatever reason, the settlers had put down roots in this soil, and River City, Missouri, had sprouted.

I traveled up Marietta Avenue, stopping often to let cement trucks go around me. The area was a beehive of activity. Scaffoldings were everywhere. Workmen called back and forth from rooftops.

The building that housed Claire's Hair Lair had already received its face-lift. The front was painted burgundy with gray shutters flanking the plate-glass window. Styrofoam heads topped with stylish wigs were on display, along with several bottles of enriching shampoo and cleansing rinses.

I leaned closer and read a sign: DON'T LET YOUR UNRULY HAIR MAKE YOU A SOURPUSS. CLAIRE WILL HAVE YOU PURRING WITH SATISFACTION IN NO TIME. For emphasis two stuffed lions had been added to the exhibit. One had matted fur, his mouth opened in a snarl. His companion sported a glossy, manageable mane.

Chuckling, I opened the door and

stepped inside, where my nose was assaulted by the smell of fresh perm solution. Fanning the air with my hand, I called, "Claire? It's Bretta Solomon."

"Just a minute," was the muffled reply from a curtained doorway at the back of the building.

"I know I'm early," I said, "but I decided to come by before I did another errand."

My answer was the sound of a toilet flushing. I peered at my surroundings and forgot my burning nose. Blue, red, green, and yellow stripes raced up and down the walls. The floor was covered with a vinyl pattern that screamed kindergarten finger painting. But it was the ceiling that grabbed my attention. I tilted my head and marveled at the sight.

Painted directly on the tiles was a ten-foot picture of a lovely girl who might have been fifteen years old. My gaze skimmed over her face, noting the closed eyes and gentle smile. She was dressed in a robe and looked angelic surrounded by an aura of light achieved by the shading of brush strokes. Her hair was a crowning glory of flowers, painted in meticulous detail, sprouting from her head.

I squinted at the blossoms. These weren't flower shop varieties. The pinkish purple daisylike flower was echinacea. An evening primrose curled seductively around the girl's left ear. The brilliant orange blossom of the butterfly weed was an exact replica of the ones that lived on the farm where I'd grown up. Rose mallow, milkweed, and elderberry were all Missouri wildflowers.

Standing just above the other flowers was another blossom that was a cluster of eight blooms on one stem. Each was yellow-green, tinged with purple. The individual flowers had five tubular hood-shaped structures with a slender horn extending from each.

I didn't recognize this last flower, but I was impressed with the overall appearance of the painting. "How neat," I said aloud. My voice echoed in the silence.

The absolute stillness of the building finally penetrated my preoccupation with the ceiling. Impatiently, I called, "Claire, if you're busy, I can come back later."

This time I received no answer. As I made my way across the floor to the curtained doorway, the soles of my shoes made tiny *tick-tick* sounds like I'd stepped in something sticky. I checked but saw nothing except wild swirls of color underfoot.

"Claire?" I called again, pushing the curtain aside. A strong herbal odor rushed out. I moved farther into the supply room. Here there was a total absence of color. The walls were unfinished Sheetrock, the floor bare concrete. Metal shelves held bottles of shampoos and such. The bathroom was on my right. I rapped on the door, then pushed it open. The room was empty.

I turned to my left, and my breath caught in my throat. Claire lay on her back. With a cry of surprise, I hurried to her side and carefully felt for a pulse. There was none. A pale green froth oozed from her mouth and nostrils. Near her body was an aerosol can of herbal mousse. A bit of green foam clung to the nozzle.

At first I couldn't comprehend what I was seeing. If Claire was dead, then who'd answered me when I'd first entered the beauty shop? Who'd flushed the toilet? I looked from the can to the watery foam that filled Claire's mouth and nostrils and nearly fainted as I put my own interpretation on these details. Someone knocked her unconscious, then squirted the thick foam into her air passages so she'd suffocate.

Slowly I dragged my gaze up to her

wide-eyed stare. Since I'd met her in the park, she'd changed her emerald contacts for ones that resembled a cat's eyes, with lentil-shaped, hyacinth-colored pupils.

Because of the lack of natural moisture on her orbs, the thin pieces of plastic were losing their shape. Even as I watched, one of the lenses curled, popped off, and landed on her cheek.

Chapter Three

Two dead people in one day were more than this old girl could handle. My chest hurt from the thumping of my heart. I clamped my teeth tightly together to keep them from chattering and stumbled out of the storage room into Claire's beauty shop. I couldn't leave the salon unattended with Claire's body in back. A phone was on the desk by the door, but I knew better than to touch it. I stood in the middle of the floor like a dolt, wondering if I should step out into the street and scream for help.

"Bretta?"

I whirled around to find Evelyn peering at me from the doorway. "I was just by your flower shop." She came farther into the room. "I've been tracking everyone down so I can apologize for the way I've acted. Nikki's wedding is important, but when I saw Oliver die —" She shuddered. "I've been a real nag, and I'm sorry."

"You can't come in here."

Evelyn's shoulders stiffened. "Good heavens, I said I was sorry. Surely you aren't going to get on some righteous high horse and back out of —"

"Do you have a cell phone?"

"Yes, but I —"

"Pass it over. I need to make an emergency call."

"What's going on?" She peered around the empty beauty shop. "Where's Claire? I have to talk to her, too."

I held out my hand. "Please. I need to use your phone."

Evelyn frowned but reached into her purse. "Here," she said, thrusting the gadget at me. "But there's a phone right over there."

She nodded to the desk, but I ignored her, punching in 911. Evelyn drew a sharp breath when she saw what I was doing. Her head swiveled as she looked about the room. Seeing the curtained doorway, she took a step in that direction, but I grabbed her arm and shook my head.

"This is Bretta Solomon," I said into the receiver. "I'm at 3201 Marietta Avenue, Claire's Hair Lair. I've just found the owner, Ms. Alexander, dead in the storage room."

Evelyn gasped and looked ready to keel over. I tightened my grip on her arm, but she shrugged off my helping hand. "I'm fine," she said. "But what am I going to do

45

now? The girls are expecting a beautician in residence at the park."

The helping hand I'd offered clenched into a knot at my side. I wanted to slap her. Did this woman think only in terms of the wedding?

"Yes," I said into the phone. "Yes. I know. Yes. Yes. Okay. Yes. I'll be right here." I disconnected and handed the phone back to Evelyn.

Absently, she tucked it into her handbag. "I'm leaving," she said. "I wasn't here when you found — uh — Claire. No need in me staying until help arrives."

"You have to stay. Your fingerprints will be on the doorknob. I used your phone to make the call. We have to stand right here and not touch anything."

Evelyn didn't like this, but whether it was my commanding tone or the command itself, I couldn't be sure. Her chin came up, and she glared at me. "My fingerprints will be here anyway. I've been in this shop before. I sat in that chair while Claire and I discussed the wedding. Besides, fingerprints are only important in a murder —"

I said nothing.

Her jaw dropped. Slowly, she closed it and turned to look at the curtained doorway again. "Oh, God. Murder? Is there blood? I can't stand the sight of blood. I think I'm going to be sick."

The wail of sirens overrode her need to upchuck. "I can't believe this is happening," she whispered. "What in the world will Nikki say? Her hairdresser murdered. Oh dear. Oh dear."

"Yeah, Claire's untimely death is a real inconvenience. If she were here, I'm sure she would express her regret."

"That isn't what I meant."

I took a steady bead on her. "I know *exactly* what you meant."

A River City patrol car arrived first. The officer took one look behind the curtain, then radioed for reinforcements. Paramedics soon arrived, followed by a Spencer County deputy and, finally, a Missouri Highway Patrol officer. It was a fashion show of uniforms. Khaki for the county. Blue for the MHP. Green and gold for our town's protectors. Jurisdiction fell to the city officials, but in the case of a suspicious death, it was all hands on deck.

I knew and was known to most of the men because of Carl's involvement with law enforcement. I was treated with respect, but nonetheless, Evelyn and I were hustled out of the beauty shop and were told to wait so our statements could be taken. I can only guess at what went on in that storage room, but I surmised plenty. The coroner was followed by Jean Kelley, River City's chief of police.

Jean is a willowy blonde who looks as if she ought to be on a runway, modeling chic clothes. She maintains a good relationship with her deputies, has earned every ounce of their admiration. Her mind is sharp, her need for thoroughness a mantra cited by her staff.

Jean nodded to me, then hurried into the shop. "Who was that?" asked Evelyn. The officer standing near us shook his head. "No talking, ladies."

Evelyn pursed her lips and glanced at her watch. "How much longer am I to wait? I have an appointment in half an hour."

"It'll keep," he murmured, watching a new arrival stride toward us.

I followed his line of vision and gulped. Sid Hancock, the sheriff of Spencer County, was on the scene. Sid and I had a tentative relationship, or perhaps it would be better called tenacious. Tentative in that our relationship tends to come and go depending on if I'm muddling in one of his cases. Tenacious because even though he disapproves of my amateur detecting, he's been Johnny-on-the-spot when I needed his help.

He was not very tall, about five foot eight or so, and slight of build. His hair was red, his complexion pale but freckled. A fiery temper and crotchety disposition summed up his personality. Seeing the glint in his eye, I knew I was in for a sampling of both.

"Holy crap," he said in greeting. "Why the hell am I not surprised? I heard that a body had been reported, and here you are."

He rolled his eyes and turned to Evelyn. His surly stare swept her in one fluid motion. Apparently, he liked what he saw. He squared his shoulders, and his mouth curved upward. "At least you're keeping better company, Solomon," he said to me, but held out his hand to Evelyn. "I'm Sheriff Hancock. And you are?"

Evelyn lowered her eyes, gazing up at Sid through thick, dark lashes. "What a pleasure, Sheriff. I'm Evelyn Montgomery. I moved to River City a few months ago, and I've heard nothing but wonderful things about your work in this county."

An enamored Sid was pretty tough to take. That the attraction was reciprocated was nauseating. Thank God Sid didn't shuffle his feet and stammer, "Aw, shucks, ma'am, 'tweren't nothing." But he might as well have. He thrust out his chest like a preening rooster. "I do my job," he said.

I cleared my throat. "Beauty shop. Body. Statements." I waved a hand at Evelyn. "She's in a hurry, and I —"

"Bretta, please," said Evelyn. "This man has important things to oversee. We'll have to wait our turn."

"But you said —"

"The dressmaker will understand when I explain that I've been unavoidably detained."

Sid's smile grew to a cheesy grin. "Damned fine attitude, Mrs. Montgomery. It's appreciated." He turned to me. "What the hell's been going on?"

"Are you taking my statement?"

"Not formally, but I want the facts."

"Fine. Claire called because she wanted to talk to me about some information."

"What information?"

"She was dead when I arrived, so I don't know."

"Didn't she tell you the nature of said information?"

"No. I'm not sure of her exact words, but she said something along the lines of

'Bretta, I've got to see you. You have a reputation for getting to the bottom of suspicious doings.' " I raised my voice to override Sid's nasty comment. " 'I can't make heads or tails of this information, but I'm not sitting on it.' About that time someone came into her beauty shop. I heard Claire greet this person, say something about it being 'a pleasant surprise' and that she had 'plenty of time.' I figured it was a customer. When Claire came back on the line to me she ended our conversation by saying, 'My pigeon just walked through the door.' "

"Pigeon?" said Sid.

"Yeah. I thought that was an odd way to refer to a patron."

Sid snorted. "Sounds to me like this Alexander woman was thinking along the slang version — someone easily deceived and gullible. Wrong assumption. Her meek little pigeon turned into a nasty bird of prey."

I shuddered. "When I arrived, I didn't sense a problem. I hollered that I was here. A muffled voice answered me."

Sid's attention sharpened. "You say someone answered you?"

"Yeah. The toilet was flushed, too. I think I was in the shop alone with Claire's killer."

"Have you told anyone this tale?"

"No one has asked — yet. We were hustled out here, and we've been waiting —"

Sid spun on his heel and stomped into the beauty shop. Evelyn eyed me. "That was really good. I'd have babbled like a fool. How did you know what to say and in what order?"

"My husband was one of Sid's deputies, and I've been involved in a few cases of my own. However, Sid doesn't like —"

The officer stepped closer. "Ladies, please. The sheriff doesn't like gabbing."

I sniffed. "That's exactly what I was going to say, Officer."

"Don't say it. Do it."

Evelyn smiled. "May Bretta and I have a conversation if the subject isn't the — uh — present situation?"

The officer lowered his eyebrows. "What?"

"My daughter is getting married a week from today, and Bretta is designing the fresh flowers, but I'm not sure if she has the manpower to plant and spray the shrubs."

Evelyn took a hurried breath and turned to me. "Spraying the leaves gold will take more time, but the effect in the candlelight will be just the look I'm after. I wanted to let you know that if you need help, I'm sure Sonya will have an extra person or two lined up."

The officer folded his arms across his chest. "I believe you've said all that's necessary. I don't want to hear another word out of you." He looked at me. "Either of you. Have I made myself clear?"

"Absolutely," said Evelyn, with a swift glance at me. "I think we've covered the territory."

This woman had more nerve than a cliff diver and possessed an annoying one-track mind. Claire lay dead — murdered — just inside the building, and Evelyn was worried about gold-sprayed foliage. Jeez!

I turned my back to her, looked up and down the street, and then wished I hadn't. The sidewalk across the way was lined with rubberneckers. The sirens were a calling card to a free show. Boldly, I met the gaping stares. I had nothing to hide, and yet their attention made me feel like a bug stuck on a pin under a microscope.

As I swept the crowd, I saw a tall figure in the shadow of an old drugstore. The front was covered with scaffolding. The bricks, weathered and worn by time's ruthless fingers, were scheduled for a fresh coat of paint. I scrunched up my eyes, trying to make out the man. Something about the way he held his head seemed familiar.

Before I could decide if I knew him, he turned on his heel and disappeared up the alley. It was the ambling walk that cinched it.

"Bailey!" I shouted. "Bailey! Wait!"

The man didn't pause. He didn't even turn his head. Was I mistaken? My heart had fluttered with hope, but now it fluttered with disappointment.

Back in April I'd made the acquaintance of Bailey Monroe, a DEA agent. Bailey had jump-started my engine, making my heart race. A floral convention was the last place I thought I'd find romance. And while the only kiss Bailey and I'd shared had been fleeting, his smile, his eyes, and his irritating manner had left a lasting impression.

When we parted ways, I was sure I'd hear from him, but it had been eight long weeks without a word. So I'd written him off as hopeless, and I was helpless to contact him since I didn't have a phone number or an address.

"Old fool," I muttered.

"Couldn't have put it better myself," said Sid, coming up behind me. "Who the hell were you yelling at? Let's get your statement so you can scram. We have enough of a mob without you inciting a riot. Judas Priest. I should've known better than to leave you in plain sight on the sidewalk. You could stir up trouble in a funeral parlor."

Since that was exactly what had happened last fall, Sid's face turned carnation red at the memory. He jerked his head at me. "Get going."

Evelyn and I were taken to separate patrol cars. It didn't escape my notice that I drew Police Chief Kelley as my inquisitor, while Sid escorted Evelyn into his car for a private tête-à-tête.

Chief Kelley settled herself in the backseat and pulled a notepad from her purse. "You know how to push all of Sid's buttons, don't you?"

"It's usually not intentional," I admitted, "but he can be the most infuriating man on earth."

Kelley studied me thoughtfully. "With so much emotion involved, some people would say there's an attraction between you."

I stared at her in openmouthed wonder, then gave over to a good belly laugh. "You're right. Hate is supposed to be close kin to love, but in this case the answer is no. I don't hate Sid, and I might like him if he wasn't so . . . so . . . Sid. I admire him. Sometimes, I even respect him. Carl classed him as a friend, but the idea of there being something more between us is as ludicrous as — uh — Claire getting up off the floor and walking out that door."

My words put a deep frown between the chief's eyes. "There isn't much chance of that happening."

"I know," I said soberly. "She was hit over the head, dragged to the back room, and her mouth and nose were filled with that green mousse."

"You've got it all figured out, huh?"

"I checked to see if she was still alive. She wasn't. I saw the can. The foam was losing its substance, becoming all watery and yucky, but there was enough of it left that I could draw a conclusion." I shivered. "Did Sid tell you I must have walked into the shop not long after she was killed? I think the murderer actually spoke to me."

"He told me, but I want to hear it from you. Start where you think it's the most relevant, then we'll tie up loose ends."

"If that's the case, I'll need to go back to about ten o'clock this morning, when I met Claire in the park."

The chief twisted on the seat to stare at

me. "Ten o'clock? I thought you came here — Nope. Never mind. Tell me."

And I did. I covered everything. I tried to repeat verbatim all the conversations I'd been privy to up and until I arrived at Claire's beauty shop. When I was finished, forty minutes had passed. Evelyn had been allowed to leave. Claire's body had been taken away.

Once I was out of the squad car and in my own vehicle, I switched on the engine. I should've gone home, but while events were fresh in my mind, I decided to go back to the park.

Chapter Four

I'd only gone eight blocks when I came to the conclusion that every one of River City's thirty thousand residents must be on the streets. Hoping to make better time, I caught the outer-loop highway that circled the metropolis. I bypassed traffic lights but got hung up in a snarl of slow-moving vehicles driven by people looking for entertainment on a Saturday afternoon. The entrance to the Westgate Mall was off the loop, as were three cinemas and the newly constructed Menninger Civic Center, which featured a weekend puppet show for kiddies.

I zinged in and out of traffic until I spied the exit sign for the park, then switched lanes once again, taking the off ramp into a quiet wooded area. After the roar of gas engines, the silence was welcome. I took my foot off the accelerator and coasted around the first of several lazy bends in the road. Filigreed tree branches laced overhead created a tunnel of shade. I rolled down my window and breathed deeply.

My shoulders ached with tension. I tried to relax, but images of Claire's body kept my muscles taut. To take my mind off that vivid picture, I thought about events leading up to her death. We'd been in the park. Oliver had died. A short time later, Claire was murdered.

Was there a connection between Oliver's heart attack and Claire's murder? He had said he didn't know Claire. Had his heart attack been brought on by the tension in the air? The situation between Eddie and Evelyn had been volatile, but Oliver hadn't seemed concerned about the landscaping for the wedding.

I frowned. But he had asked, "Where are the markers?" Had he been thinking about another job? Tree markers? Plant markers?

Oliver's heart condition was a fact. That he'd died at that point in time was a fact. I wanted to assume his death was from natural causes, but where murder is concerned, it would be foolhardy to assume anything. Maybe I should make a discreet inquiry.

My mind flip-flopped back to Claire. In the park she'd been fired up about some gossip. Beauty shops had a reputation for being the center of spicy gossip. But so did local taverns, church choirs, or any place where more than two people congregated. Should I make the assumption that

Claire's tidbit of news had something to do with one of her clients? There was Mrs. Dearborne. But if I understood Claire's earlier reference, she was using Mrs. Dearborne to confirm something she'd already heard or suspected.

My eyes narrowed. Hmm? Oliver *had* been interested in Claire's reference to the Dearborne name.

I caught up to a line of cars making their way between the stone pillars that marked the entrance into the park. The fifty-acre tract of land contained tennis courts, a swimming pool, bike and jogging trails, a three-acre fishing lake, and numerous shelter houses and playground equipment. The smell of roasting hot dogs and burgers overpowered the scent of flowers. The peace and quiet I'd noticed this morning was shattered by the shrill screams of children hard at play.

Tranquility Garden was secluded from the rest of the park by a line of cedar trees. The garden couldn't be seen until you passed that screen of vegetation and took the path Eddie and Oliver had been landscaping. I squeezed my car into a slot, locked the doors, and headed for that path.

An elder gentleman sat on a bench soaking up the sun. We traded polite nods.

He commented that it was a lovely day. Weatherwise it was perfect — warm, sunny, blue skies, and clouds sculptured like giant heads of cauliflower.

I hadn't eaten in hours, and the aroma of grilled food had made even the clouds take on the shape of sustenance. I would gather up Eddie's tools, deliver them to his house, and then head for home.

But all the tools were gone. The shrubs were planted, mulch layered at their bases. Amazed, I walked down the path, touching a leaf, raking the toe of my sneaker against some wayward wood chips on the bricks.

Spinning on my heel, I headed back the way I'd come. I wondered who was responsible for finishing the work, and stopped near the gentleman on the bench. "Did you see anyone over there?" I asked, indicating the area where I'd been.

"Just Eddie Terrell. Always knew he was a hard worker, but the man acted possessed, heaving tools into the back of his truck."

"Did he plant the shrubs and spread the mulch?"

"Sure did. Dust fogged the air as he worked."

I thanked him and went back to the path, taking it to the gazebo that would serve as the altar. The latticed structure was six-sided with a dual set of steps — one for the bride and her attendants, the other for the groom and his. Wood shingles covered the peaked roof.

Squinting, I envisioned the results of my hard work. Brass baskets filled with masses of white flowers were to be hung in the gazebo's arched openings. Extensive use of ivy, Boston ferns, brass and copper containers, helium-filled balloons, and yards of gold-shot white tulle were to dazzle the immediate surroundings. Highlighting the altar would be twelve large hurricane lanterns. The reflection pool in front of the gazebo was to have floating wreaths made of flowers.

Plans called for five hundred candles, under protective globes, to be placed in designated areas and lit at a strategic moment before the wedding ceremony. Thank heavens this chore fell under the heading of wedding coordinator. At last count, I'd heard Sonya had hired twelve people just to light wicks.

I went up the steps to the gazebo and stood at one of the arched openings. Staring down at the reflection pool, I should've been mentally concocting the wreaths, thinking about the mechanics that

I'd need to make them float. Instead my mind skipped back to Oliver's death and Claire's murder.

I waited for some revelation, but after twenty minutes nothing came to me except an overwhelming desire to eat.

Last October I moved from the house Carl and I'd shared to a mansion that we'd dreamed of someday owning. His life insurance had provided the down payment, which was a bittersweet turn of events. In those early days of ownership, I cared for my new home with all the maternal instincts of a proud mother. I saw my child's flaws — peeling paint, cracked plaster, and cluttered attic — but knew it would mature into a fine specimen if I gave it the loving attention it deserved.

That was the rub. When I first moved into the house, I'd worked myself into a frenzy renovating the downstairs. At that time I'd had a goal. I'd scheduled my flower shop's annual Christmas open house to be held in the stately mansion, and I'd wanted everything impeccable. I grimaced. What I'd gotten was murder and an inheritance that wiped my debt for the house clean.

I owned it. I lived in it. But I didn't love

it. My original plan had been to turn it into a boardinghouse. I'd wanted people around me. I'd wanted to come home from work to lights and conversation, not darkness and my own spiritless company. But those holiday catastrophes had squelched my enthusiasm for the restorations that needed to be made before I could rent the first room.

The lane up to the mansion was a quarter mile long. Majestic pine trees lined the drive and would have embraced me with a warm fuzzy feeling that I was home if I'd let them. I couldn't. It had been months since I'd discovered the history of this land, and I still hadn't come to terms with my findings.

Hoping to bolster my waning interest in the house, I'd put painting and plumbing on hold and had plunged into a rejuvenation of the overgrown garden. It had taken less than a week to see I needed professional help. There were so many different species of plants that I couldn't tell a weed from a flower. Brush needed to be hauled off, trees had to be trimmed or removed. That's when I'd called on Eddie and Oliver to discuss what I wanted done.

I'd supplied them with pictures from gardening magazines of fancy stepping-stone paths, lattice arbors, arched bridges, statues, and a tire swing like the one I'd played on as a child. I wanted a secret garden where I could go to wile away a few spare minutes. I wanted beds of bright annuals that I could tend. I wanted well-kept trees and rosebushes bursting with color.

To my left, past the furthermost edge of my property, was a cottage. At one time it had been part of this estate, but when I'd bought the mansion and land, that piece of property had been excluded from the sale. The structure was empty. I'd made numerous offers to buy it, but so far my bids had been ignored.

I wanted that cottage because it would square out my holdings. But most of all, the cottage — with its vaulted ceilings, hardwood floors, and fireplace — would make an ideal chapel. By coupling the chapel with my garden plans, I hoped to replace the wickedness this land had once seen by holding weddings on my property.

I pulled my car into the garage and climbed from behind the steering wheel. Before I'd taken two steps, the door leading into the house opened, and DeeDee stuck out her head.

For the first time in what felt like hours, my lips spread into a genuine smile.

Twenty-three years old, DeeDee was my housekeeper. Today she wore her dark hair straight to her shoulders. Her prominent eyes were brown. Her cheeks were rosy. I'd never had a child, but this young woman filled that void in my life. Overprotective, overindulgent parents had home-schooled her. By rights she should've been an obnoxious brat. She was caring, loyal, and when I'd needed her the most, she had always been there for me.

"W-what's w-wrong?" she stammered.

DeeDee's stuttering was the reason her parents had kept her out of public schools. They'd sheltered her to the point she'd almost stopped speaking when we first met. Elocution lessons and the responsibility of an entire household had built up her confidence. Her faltering speech was evident when she didn't concentrate on what she wanted to say or when she was excited or worried.

I had no intention of going over the events of my day before I'd stepped foot in the house, but her sharp brown-eyed stare had ripped away any attempt I'd made to appear composed.

I forced a cheerful note into my voice. "Nothing's wrong," I said. "I'm just tired."

"Nope. Won't f-fly."

I rolled my eyes as I brushed past her and into the house. She trailed me like a curious kitten, batting at my arm, imploring me to dump my worrisome load on her slender shoulders.

I hung my purse on the doorknob to the back staircase, then headed for the kitchen. With my head in the open refrigerator, I said, "Is there any more of that gazpacho left? Cold vegetable soup isn't my first choice, but I'm starved."

"I have f-fixed a v-very nice s-s-supper, B-B-retta."

DeeDee had discovered that she loved to cook. She watched the food channel on television, took note of the fabulous recipes, and turned them into low-cal treats that kept my weight stable.

DeeDee tugged on my sleeve. "Look."

I turned and followed the direction of her finger. Through the kitchen doorway I saw the dining room table set with my best china, crystal, and flatware. Sprigs of English ivy cascaded from a vase and twined over the burgundy linen tablecloth.

"Pretty fancy for us," I commented before counting the place settings. There were five. I closed the refrigerator door. "I'm not in the mood for company, DeeDee. I've had one helluva day. All I want is food, a hot bath, and a good book. Maybe then I can forget my —"

The doorbell rang.

DeeDee galloped away.

"Damn it. Damn it. Damn it!" I would've stomped my foot in frustration, but I recognized the voice coming from the foyer and mellowed out.

Avery Wheeler and I had met during the Christmas open house fiasco. A florist and a lawyer make a dubious team, but we'd pooled resources, escaped a harrowing experience, and carried between us a secret we'd sworn never to reveal.

I crossed the polished oak parquet floor and listened to him tease DeeDee. His tone was melodious. Once I was closer, I saw his eyes twinkle with humor. As his lips moved, the salt-and-pepper mustache under his bulbous nose twitched.

"— your cooking is only surpassed by your delightful company," he was saying to a blushing DeeDee. "My evening meal usually consists of lukewarm soup and a dry contract. I've anticipated this repast all afternoon." He touched DeeDee's hand, then turned to me. His bristly eyebrows shot up. "Oh," he said. "Been one of those days, has it?"

I grimaced. For those who know me

well, there seems to be no area of privacy. The eyes are the mirror to the soul — or, as in my case, an invitation to invade my solitude. I waved a hand. "I'm fine. You're the first guest to arrive, but from the places set in the dining room it looks as if we have more to come."

DeeDee mumbled something that sounded like julienne and sauté. I watched her disappear through the kitchen doorway. "She's a real treat, Avery. The best thing to happen in my life in a long, long time." I turned to him. "So how have you been? When I left this morning there was no mention of a dinner party. What developed in the last few hours?"

Avery leaned heavily on his cane. "Might we have a seat? My old legs aren't as forgiving as they used to be."

"I'm sorry. Let's go into the library." I started to lead the way, then stopped when the doorbell chimed again. "This must be the second member of our dinner party."

Avery glanced at his watch and frowned. "Shouldn't be. I was to have at least thirty minutes alone with you."

"Why? What?"

The bell pealed again.

Sighing, I swiveled on my toe and headed for the door. Before I could reach for the knob, the oak panel swung open. My father stood on the veranda.

When he saw me, he threw out his arms and yelled, "Surprise!"

I looked past him and saw a cab parked at the end of the sidewalk. My heart sank. The driver was unloading what looked like a mountain of luggage.

Trying to keep my expression composed, I focused on my father. He was a handsome man in his seventies. His hair was thick and gray, his eyes blue. In his younger days he'd been lean and wiry. Age had added pounds, particularly around his middle. His joints were stiff, and sometimes he carried a walking stick, which wasn't evident at the moment.

"Gotcha, didn't I?" he said. "Bet you thought I'd mailed you another dust collector to set on a whatnot shelf." He awkwardly patted my shoulder. "Bretta, we can't rebuild our relationship with all those miles separating us. I've burned my bridges in Texas. I've come back to Missouri for good." He leaned close and whispered, "I've got plans. Big plans, and I'm fired up to put them into motion."

He directed the cabbie to set the suitcases in the foyer, then ignoring Avery, who was standing not more than five feet from us, took my hand and towed me toward the library.

I mouthed "Sorry" as we passed the old lawyer, then made an attempt to curtail my father's barrage. "Dad, please," I said, applying the brakes. "You're going too fast — both physically and mentally. Besides, I have another guest. When you were here at Christmas, you met Avery Wheeler. Avery, you remember my father, Albert McGinness?"

My father scarcely acknowledged the introduction. "I've kept my plans bottled up for the last two months." He dropped my hand and did a clumsy two-step jig. "We'll make a great team, Bretta. You have a way of attracting trouble, and I have a problem-solving mind. Look at all the money I made with that cattle-branding tool I invented. It's one of a kind, just like us. We'll sweep this town of its crime."

I shook my head. "What are you talking about?"

"You still don't get it?"

"Get what?"

"A detective agency." He frowned. "We have to get in sync if we're going to be a team. I'm having the sign painted." He swirled his hand in the air. "Can't you see

71

it? McGinness and Solomon Detective Agency."

When he leaned closer, I sniffed to see if he'd had one too many on the flight from Texas. I wrinkled my nose. Garlic. Whew! I turned my head, but I didn't miss what he said.

"Fact is, I have our first case. You know that cottage at the edge of your property? Well, someone is there. When I talked to DeeDee earlier, she said it was empty. I thought I'd set up shop close by until I find an office downtown. Before I came to your house, I had the cabbie drive past the cottage, and there was a truck parked under the trees. It wasn't out in plain sight, but back where some bushes camouflaged it."

He paused for a breath, but he was far from finished. "It looked damned suspicious, Bretta. It's up to us to find out who it is and report him to the local authorities. It could be drugs. What better place to make a drop? It's out of the way. No close neighbors. And you're at work all day."

In his younger days my father had been a painter, a poet, and a freethinker. He was artistic and creative, and I'd attributed my design talents to him. As I watched him rub his hands together, already anticipating the notoriety that would surely

72

come his way after nosing out this nefarious drug ring, I added another trait — wild imagination.

This wasn't a bad thing. My imagination had helped me solve some pretty tough cases, so there was a time and a place when it could be useful. Other times it hindered clear thinking. I was firmly grounded by my mother's no-nonsense upbringing. I eliminated the chaff from my father's mental fantasies, looking for the whole kernel of truth.

Out of the corner of my eye, I saw Avery glance at his watch. Two things struck me. Avery wanted thirty minutes alone with me before the next guest arrived. My father said someone was at the cottage. Professionally, Avery had complete control over that cottage, but so far neither he nor the owner would take my offer.

I met Avery's gaze, and his eyes shifted uneasily away from mine. Disappointment brought a lump to my throat. I'd never pressed him. Not once had I demanded a decision. There were hard feelings toward me from the owner, and I'd hoped that if I bided my time, those old wounds would heal. But that hadn't happened. My intention to be a good-hearted, understanding person was about to be flung in my face.

The doorbell rang. Anger replaced my frustration. I crossed the foyer, but I didn't open the door. Instead, I turned my back to it so I could tell Avery just what I thought. From the look on his face, my words were unnecessary.

"I assume this is my new neighbor," I said. "You knew I wanted that land because it's part of the original tract. And now you expect me to make this tenant feel welcome? To sit at my table and eat my food?" I gulped. "Gosh, Avery, I didn't think my day could get much worse."

I swept open the door and gasped.

Bailey Monroe stood on my doorstep. Since I'd returned from Branson, he'd haunted my thoughts. I almost reached out a hand to touch him, to see if he was real, but I quickly checked that impulse. "Bailey?" I whispered. "What are you doing here?"

The glance he traded with Avery said it all. I'd coveted the land. I'd coveted the man. Now both were tied together in one neat package.

Chapter Five

Since I'd last seen Bailey it would've been heartening to learn I'd magnified his fine points, exaggerated his good looks. No such luck. Six feet, two inches of muscle. Eyes the color of unpolished copper. Dark hair feathered with gray at his temples. When his lips slid into a lazy smile, my body reacted in a disturbing manner.

Carl had been as comfy as my house slippers — cushy to my soul. Bailey was that pair of stiletto heels you admire in a store window. Common sense says not to buy them — don't even bother trying them on — but the allure was there.

Feeling the need to say something, I repeated, "What are you doing here?"

"Who won the floral contest in Branson?" he said.

My eyes narrowed. He and I'd had a couple of these rounds where I'd ask a question and he'd answer with another. This was a different time and place, so perhaps it was only a coincidence. I tested him. "Won't you come in?"

The well-mannered response could have

been "Thank you, Bretta." Or "Lovely home, Bretta." Or "Nice to see you, Bretta."

Bailey said, "Will I be a bother?"

I couldn't resist. "Are you usually?"

Bailey brushed past me. "Have you heard something I haven't?"

I gritted my teeth but fought foolishly. "Is this conversation going somewhere?"

Bailey didn't pause. "Life is trying, isn't it?"

I gave up. "But not as trying as you."

Avery and my father gaped as if they'd viewed a complicated vaudeville skit and hadn't gotten the punch line. No way was I going to explain.

"Let's eat," I said, waving the men into the dining room. I headed for the kitchen, where I could catch my breath. DeeDee looked up from the pot she was scraping.

"Is everyone here?" She turned her question into an explanatory sentence. "Everyone is here."

"Ha, ha," I said, grabbing the platter of grilled pork chops. "We'll discuss your part in this calamity later."

"Th-there's nothing to d-discuss. Avery is your f-friend, and it isn't m-my p-place to d-deny your father a meal."

"And Bailey? Where does he fit in?"

DeeDee met my gaze. "Wherever you let him."

Dinner passed rather well with my father monopolizing the conversation, telling about his flight from Texas. Under Bailey's artful questioning, I along with everyone else learned that my father had sublet his condo, had sold his interest in the cattle-branding tool manufacturing company, and was here to stay. Where he was going to live brought us to the hot topic of the evening — Bailey's takeover of the gardener's cottage.

We had moved into the library and were sipping coffee. DeeDee clattered dishes in the kitchen. My father lounged in one of the wingback chairs; Avery occupied the other. Bailey sat on the sofa with his arm flung across the upper cushion. If I were to sit, he'd either have to move his arm or I'd find it draped across my shoulders. I stayed where I was, which was across the room near the fireplace.

Avery twisted around to stare at me. "Bretta, come sit down. Let's get this situation ironed out."

I moved to the sofa and perched on the arm. "What's to iron out? Seems to me every wrinkle is permanently set."

Bailey chuckled softly.

I turned my cool gaze on him. "What's so funny?"

"You're bent out of shape, and you don't know the details."

"Are you living in the cottage?"

"Yes."

"Are you buying it?"

"The contract is signed."

"So it's a done deal. I don't need to hear the details because they won't make any difference."

Bailey sighed and stood up. "If that's the way you want it. Thanks for dinner. I'll see myself out." He strode from the room. His footsteps clunked across the foyer. The front door opened, then closed with a sharp snap.

"Well," I said, "I don't know why he's upset. I'm the one who's gotten the short end of this situation."

Avery drummed his fingers impatiently. "This hasn't worked at all the way I had planned." He shook his head at me. "Which would you rather have in that cottage? Bailey Monroe or Fedora's Feline Care and Grooming Center?"

"You had *my* offer."

"But the owner wasn't going to take it regardless of the amount. I've warned you not to get your hopes up over buying that piece of property, but you ignored me. She doesn't want you to have it, and she doesn't want any ties here. I was given orders to find a buyer. I had two offers at the stipulated amount."

Avery raised his hands with the palms turned up. He lifted his right hand. "Here is Bailey, a retired federal agent. He wants a quiet place to write a book on his twenty-odd years of work." He lowered his left hand. "Here we have Fedora. A nice lady, but a fanatic when it comes to cats. I visited her home and was appalled at how she let her pets have free rein."

His hands seesawed. "Quiet man. Cat woman. You weren't in the equation, Bretta. I made my decision, and it's the right one." He smoothed his collar, then settled back in his chair. "If you think about it, you'll see I've done you a tremendous favor. You're planning a garden. Do you want cats running amuck over your seedlings?"

I pursed my lips, then finally said, "I guess not. Did Bailey tell you we'd met before?"

Avery nodded. "That's why he was out this way. He was hunting your address and saw the cottage. His inquiries brought him to my office. That piece of property was going to someone, other than you, and as I see it, Bailey was the best choice."

My father hadn't asked for an explanation but had apparently caught the main theme of what was going on. "I'll offer five thousand over Monroe's deal. With my name on the deed, who'll know —"

"I will," said Avery. "It's over."

"But if I —"

"No. I don't operate in that manner." Avery heaved himself out of the chair. He nodded to my father. "It was a pleasure meeting you again," he said, though his huffy tone sent a different message.

Avery's expression softened when he turned to me. "I worry about you in this rambling old house with only DeeDee for company. Put that cottage out of your mind and concentrate on finishing the rooms upstairs. Your plan for a boarding-house is sound. Stick to it. Diversification is the right step for some people. You have plenty on your plate with the flower shop and this house. Don't be led into more than you can handle."

He gave my father a sharp glance before moving toward the door. Of course, Avery was referring to the idea of my becoming a partner in a detective agency. At the moment that plan was the last thing on my mind. I was exhausted. The day had been an emotional roller coaster with monumental valleys and peaks.

"Did you know Oliver Terrell?" I asked Avery as I opened the front door.

"Yes. I heard he'd passed away." Avery's walrus mustache twitched. "I also heard you were there, and a short time later you discovered a body in a beauty shop."

"How come you didn't say something?"

"I had my own agenda for this evening. The last thing I needed was you reliving your disastrous day when I was about to pile more on top."

"Did you know Claire Alexander?"

"I go to a barber, not a beautician."

"What about a Mrs. Dearborne?"

Avery stroked his mustache. "Would that be Doreen, Sharon, or Lydia Dearborne?"

"I don't know. What about the name Spade?"

"I can't know everyone in River City. Why? Are these people connected to that alleged murder?"

"There's nothing alleged about it. Claire Alexander was hit over the head, her nose and mouth filled with herbal foam so she'd suffocate."

Avery shuddered and stepped out into

the warm night air. "I don't want to hear another word, Bretta. I need a good night's sleep."

He gave my arm a squeeze and warned me to keep my wits about me. I waited until he had his car started and was headed down the drive before I closed the door and went back into the library.

While I'd seen Avery out, my father had made himself comfortable on the sofa and fallen asleep. His snores were a sonorous accompaniment as I spread an afghan over him. I stared down at him and shook my head. What was he thinking when he'd concocted the foolish notion that I would want to be part of a detective agency? I enjoyed dabbling in solving mysteries, but to make it a day-in-and-day-out job wasn't of interest to me. Like Avery said, I had the flower shop, and I had this house and the garden — minus the cottage.

"Bailey." I breathed his name softly. He was so close and yet so far away, held at arm's length by my frustration and disappointment at not being able to buy the cottage.

Sighing, I gathered up the used coffee service and headed for the kitchen, where DeeDee was putting away the last of the dishes. "Here's some more," I said, setting the tray on the counter. "You can leave these things till morning, if you want. I'm going to bed."

"I heard Avery say you f-found a b-body today. W-whose was it?"

"Her name was Claire Alexander. She had a beauty shop located in the old section of town."

"Claire's Hair Lair? That's where my m-mother g-goes."

"You knew Claire?"

"N-not really."

"Does your mother have a friend by the name of Dearborne?"

"L-Lydia Dearborne."

I opened a drawer and took out the phone book. After flipping through the pages I saw a number of Dearbornes, but all were male. "Do you know her address?" DeeDee shook her head. "Could you call your mother and find out?"

"I-I guess." She glanced at the clock. "She'll be getting r-ready for bed."

I pressed. "It won't take a second. I'd like to have this information to give to the police."

Her tone was droll. "You don't think th-they can get it on th-their own?"

I gestured to the phone. "Please call."

Reluctantly, DeeDee did as I requested.

Ten minutes later she replaced the receiver. Her slender shoulders slumped. Her head drooped with despair.

I'd eavesdropped the first few minutes, then busied myself washing up the coffee cups and saucers. I'd heard only one side of the conversation, but DeeDee's answers had clued me in. Her mother was being her usual annoying, overbearing self.

"I'm sorry, DeeDee," I said. "I keep thinking your mother will change. That she'll see how independent you've become, and stop being so domineering."

"W-won't h-happen, B-Bretta. I can take most of it until she asks if I'm w-wearing clean underw-wear. Then I l-lose it. L-Lydia lives on C-Catalpa R-Road. Out b-by that g-garden c-center. M-Mother can't recall the n-name."

DeeDee's stuttering was always worse after a conversation with her mother. I wanted to kick myself for putting her through — Garden center? There wasn't any garden center on Catalpa Road, but there had been a gardener.

Again I grabbed the phone book, although it wasn't necessary because I knew what I was going to find. Yes. There it was. "Terrell Oliver 18807 Catalpa Road." I flipped back to Dearborne. "Dearborne

84

Harold 18809 Catalpa Road."

With this bit of trivia cluttering my brain, I said "Good night" and went upstairs to my room. So Oliver and Lydia were neighbors. How did that piece of the puzzle fit into the scheme of Claire's murder?

I tried to think about it after I was settled in bed, but I kept seeing Avery's blue-veined hands weighing his choice for the new owner of the cottage.

I dropped off to sleep with the image of those hands rising and dipping. But in my dream I removed Bailey and Fedora from the formula. Avery's hands were replaced by an old wooden teeter-totter. A faceless Mrs. Dearborne straddled one end of the plank, with Oliver balancing her weight at the other. They seesawed back and forth like a couple of kids at a playground. Then, like the zoom lens on a camera, I took a closer look at the middle support.

Mrs. Dearborne and Oliver were teetering over Claire Alexander's body. Claire's green hair grew like tentacles, twisting and tightening its hold over Oliver and Mrs. Dearborne. I reasoned this was a ridiculous dream. I had only to open my eyes and the horror would fade, but those slithering tendrils were mesmerizing, drawing me in.

Chapter Six

The ringing of a bell prompted swollen buds to emerge from the tendrils of Claire's hair. Another shrill ring and those buds burst into a multicolored display of blossoms. Like the painting on the ceiling of the beauty shop, the flowers flourished around the girl's head. Only this time the girl was Claire.

"Bretta? There's a c-call for you."

I came awake in a rush of confusion. Sunlight shone through my bedroom window. DeeDee stood in the hall doorway, motioning to the telephone on my nightstand.

"What time is it?" I asked, wiping the sleep from my eyes.

"Seven on S-Sunday morning."

I made a face and picked up the receiver. "This is Bretta."

"Why didn't you call me about Claire?"

I recognized Sonya's voice though it was rough with grief. Sitting up, I swung my legs over the edge of the mattress. "I'm sorry, Sonya, but I never thought —"

"I heard the news from Evelyn. She said you found the — uh —" She stopped and blew her nose. "I can't believe Claire is dead. We were like sisters, staying at each other's house, walking to school. I've let my business take over my life. She called a month ago to see if we could meet for lunch, but I've been booked up. I should have called her back, but I knew we'd be seeing each other as we worked on this Montgomery wedding. I thought it would help renew our friendship. Now it's too late."

"Do the others know?"

"I told them, and they're as shocked as I am. What happened? Was she robbed?"

"I don't know."

"How was she — uh — killed?"

I dodged her question. "Don't think about that. Think of the good times. Claire remembered them fondly or she wouldn't have recited that poem in the park. Something about Royals being on the make? Sounds like the male population back then didn't stand a chance against the four of you."

Sonya's tone was distressed. "I have work to do." She hung up.

I put down my receiver. I'd mentioned the poem because I'd wanted to divert her from asking about the murder — a subject I'd been warned not to discuss. But I'd also been curious. Sonya, Dana, and Kasey had all seemed bothered when Claire had recited it in the park. I wondered how the other women would respond to my referring to that poem now that Claire was dead.

I looked up Dana's number. She answered after several rings, sounding as if she had a severe head cold. When I identified myself she let me know she'd been crying nonstop, which accounted for her stuffy, nasal tone.

"Why Claire?" asked Dana. "She was good, kind, and generous. Did you know she spent her days off at local nursing homes washing and curling the residents' hair? Or that for the senior prom she styled the hair of any girl who couldn't afford a trip to a beauty shop?"

"No. I didn't know that. I'd never met Claire until yesterday at the park, but I could tell she had a sense of humor. That poem she recited was — uh — cute. Something about the Royals being on the make, wasn't it? Is that part of a school song or something?"

Dana gulped. "Why are you bringing that up?"

"Just curious, I guess. Claire must've had a reason. Perhaps good memories were

88

associated with it?"

"She shouldn't have said it. I have to go. I have a — uh — cake in the oven." Dana hung up.

Next I looked up Kasey Vickers's phone number. When I dialed it, the line was busy. I got out of bed and made a trip to the bathroom. I washed my face, brushed my teeth, and wondered why I was exploring the reactions of three women about a poem that most likely didn't have any relevance on any level.

But if I didn't think about the poem, I'd have to think about my father's arrival and his plans for a detective agency. Or about Bailey's purchase of the cottage and his close proximity to my house and my life.

I wanted to know both men better, but I'd been thinking small doses, not the chug-a-lug portions I'd gotten. I'd hoped for a quiet talk with Bailey — a time of discovery — who he was, what he liked, how the past had shaped him into the man he was today.

As for my father, a lengthy and honest discussion was in order. After said discussion, I assumed he would go back to Texas, and I could digest the information at my leisure.

In my room, I plopped down on the bed

and dialed Kasey's number again. This time she answered.

"This is Bretta Solomon. We met yesterday in the park."

"Oh. Hi."

Not a promising beginning. "You've heard about Claire?"

"Yes."

"I was wondering about that poem she —"

"Dana warned me that you might call. Drop it. She's dead. Everyone is dead." Kasey's voice hit a hysterical note. " 'Wherefore I abhor *myself*, and repent in dust and ashes.' " She slammed down the phone.

I hung up, rubbing my ear. "Whew," I breathed. "That woman has some serious issues." In fact, all three women seemed strangely moved by that simple poem.

I picked up a pencil and paper and tried to remember Claire's exact words. When I was finished, I studied what I'd written:

> You can boil me in oil.
> You can burn me at the stake.
> But a River City Royal
> Is always on the make.

The words seemed innocuous. The kind

of song a kid might sing while skipping rope. What I needed was an impartial viewpoint. I picked up the phone once again, but this time I dialed Lois. She answered in a dull monotone.

"Are you all right?" I asked.

"Not really. Kayla and I had a terrible fight."

"Are you ready to discuss the problem?"

Lois sighed. "Out of fairness to my sister, I'd better talk to her first, but thanks."

"I won't bother you," I said quietly. "I'll see you in the morning — or if you need time off, just give me a call."

"Speaking of a call, why did you?"

"Forget it. We'll talk tomorrow."

Lois chuckled. "Go ahead, Bretta, tell me. Is it another detail about this wedding?"

"No. I haven't heard from Evelyn."

"That's a blessing. The Lord does work in mysterious ways."

"I think I had a Bible verse quoted to me this morning."

"It *is* Sunday."

"True." Then I spilled the whole tale. When I'd finished, Lois clicked her tongue. "That's one helluva story. And the dream you had is frightening. I'm looking at my English ivy in a totally new light. It's growing awfully fast. The tendrils trail a good three feet. Maybe I should take it out of the house in case it has lethal tendencies."

"Not funny."

"I know, but I've learned that in the face of adversity, it's better to laugh than to bawl."

"I suppose so. But what about the poem? Don't you think it's odd that all three women seemed put off by my reciting a portion of it? Kasey was nearly hysterical." I gave Lois the gist of what I could remember of the verse Kasey had quoted. "Do you recognize it?"

" 'Ashes to ashes and dust to dust' is well known if you've attended a funeral, but you said Kasey said 'dust and ashes,' so I haven't a clue. As for the rest, my opinion is they're justifiably distressed. Their childhood friend has been murdered. That would freak anyone. Why are you harping on this poem business?"

"Harping?" I repeated. "Mmm. I guess I am, but it's easier to think about something distant than what's going on under my nose."

"And that would be?"

"I have a new neighbor and a houseguest. Bailey and my father."

Lois's tone brightened. "Wow. I hope Bailey is the houseguest, and while we're having this useless conversation he's in your shower washing away a night of passion."

"Useless conversation is right. I'm hanging up."

"I need details. I need juicy gossip. I need —"

"Bye, Lois. See you tomorrow." I dropped the receiver into place, cutting off her bawdy cackle.

Speaking of gossip. My hand hovered over the telephone. I wanted to call Mrs. Dearborne and ask a couple of questions, but I knew if Sid found out my goose would be fricasseed. Feeling as if I was leaving an important stone unturned, I dressed in a pair of jeans, sneakers, and a T-shirt.

My plans for the day involved puttering around the house. Makeup wasn't called for, but with Bailey nearby, I applied my weekday regimen of powder, blush, and mascara. I was combing my hair, grimacing at the nearly all-gray strands, when a chain saw roared to life outside.

I strode to the window to see what was going on. Eddie's truck was parked in the driveway. I craned my neck and caught a glimpse of him in the garden. Muttering under my breath, I left the bedroom and hurried down the back staircase.

He saw me as soon as I'd opened the terrace doors and stepped out onto the paving stones. His chin rose defiantly, but he kept sawing at an old apple tree we'd said needed removing. The chain saw's engine dipped and rose in pitch as the blade bit into the decaying wood.

From the terrace the main focal point of the garden was a concrete water lily pool. The water was long gone, but a crusty scum fringed the cement walls like a lace collar. I walked closer, but stayed well away from where Eddie worked. Four brick paths led to separate areas of the garden. The house was at my back — to the north. The east path ended in what had once been a formal setting with statuary, stone benches, and an abundance of perennial plantings. The west edge of the property was covered with dense-foliaged trees. Nothing much grew under them except ferns, astilbe, lily of the valley, and a few stubborn bleeding heart plants.

The section of the garden that set my creative juices flowing was where Eddie was working at clearing away the apple trees. Oliver had taken me beyond the rotting orchard to show me how the land gently sloped to a creek. We hadn't walked very far because of his heart problem, but through his eyes, I'd seen the possibilities. Before I'd talked to Oliver, the garden had looked like a mass of rampant-growing vegetation that could only be tamed by an experienced hand. Hearing the way Eddie gunned the chain saw, I wondered how knowledgeable his hands would be without Oliver to guide him.

The area below the terrace needed more brawn than brains to give it order. Rambling roses had grown unchecked for years. The thorny branches had caught weeds in a stranglehold, binding them together seamlessly like a woven cloth. Mingled among the dried thatch was a new growth of plants trying to make headway. It was in this area that I'd depended on Oliver for guidance.

I looked back at Eddie. He was bent over his task, ignoring me. As I watched, the final cut was made, and the tree crashed to the ground, reduced to a heap of brittle branches. Eddie hit the choke, and the chain saw spluttered and died.

Before I could say "Good morning," he spoke. "If you don't want me here just say so, but I can't stay at home. Everyone is bringing food to the house." He grimaced. "As if a casserole is going to make Dad's passing any easier."

"People want to show their support. Taking food to a bereaved family is a gesture of love and respect."

He kicked the pile of wood. "I know it, but I don't have to like it. I need to work."

"Fine, but at some point you're going to have to deal with Oliver's death and the people affected by it."

Eddie's handsome jaw squared, and his blue eyes narrowed. "I don't need any lectures. I've already had my quota from my wife. Molly says I should be honored that Dad was so well liked." He grabbed a pitchfork and stacked the broken limbs. "This wood is too rotten to burn in your fireplace. The branches will have to be hauled off. Just another mindless job for me. I told Dad we should hire more people, expand our business. But he wanted to keep it in the family — a mom-and-pop operation. Mom is gone, and now Dad. Surprise. Surprise. Guess who's left?"

Eddie's attitude wasn't a good sign. Hurt or even anger would have been healthier. I didn't want Eddie to be bitter at Oliver's memory or his shortcomings. "Your father did what was right for him. Now you can do what you want."

"Oh, sure, like I have the capital to make major changes. Dad didn't have a business sense. When Mom was alive, she kept the books. She bid the jobs because Dad charged what he thought the customer could afford, not what the work was worth."

I faked a wide-eyed gaze of alarm. "You mean he didn't gouge people? He didn't take advantage of their ignorance? Gosh, Eddie, that's terrible."

"You don't get it. We're scrounging along. Dad was brilliant. He'd forgotten more facts about plants and shrubs and trees than I'll know in a lifetime. He could've cashed in on that knowledge, but he chose to be more of a handyman than a true landscaper."

Eddie leaned on the pitchfork. "He knew instinctively which plants were compatible, which ones needed shade, sun, more moisture or less. He wasted his talent. He could've been famous like those guys on PBS. He could've been rich."

"Let me get this straight. You think Oliver wasted his life because he wasn't on television or wasn't wealthy?"

Eddie didn't answer, but then I didn't give him much of a chance. "Your father was a sweet, generous man. You came here today, not because of the food that was being brought to your home, but because you couldn't stand hearing people tell you what a wonderful man your father was. You're resentful, Eddie, and probably jealous, too."

Eddie had a short fuse, and I was prepared to duck if he decided to throw that pitchfork. To my surprise, he blushed. "Yeah. I'm jealous of Dad's ability. I'm also mad because he should've placed a higher value on his talents and made people pay for his services."

I waved my arm, indicating our surroundings. "Who came up with the bid on my garden?"

"Me."

"According to what you're saying, I'm going to pay dearly for this work?"

"No. I wouldn't do that to you, Bretta."

I raised an eyebrow. "Really? And why is that?"

"Because it'll be a pleasure putting this area back to its original beauty. Dad said that in its heyday this estate was one of the most beautiful private gardens in Missouri. Once I get these trees cut and hauled out,

I'll do a controlled burn to get rid of the thick layer of weeds and grass thatch that's been allowed to grow. Plants that have struggled to survive will be set free to reproduce and, I hope, to flourish."

He smiled. "Then I can get at the true spirit of this land. Taking advantage of what nature has lain out is what landscaping is all about. Once I get this useless vegetation out of the way, you won't believe the change."

"So you're doing this work because you want the satisfaction of a job well done and not just for the money?"

Eddie jerked around to stare at me. "Molly's good, but you get the gold star. You've made your point — loud and clear. Just for the record, I will make money on this project or I wouldn't be doing it. Dad would've done it for free."

"Oliver mentioned something along those lines to me, but I told him I could afford the bill."

Eddie rolled his eyes. "And that's *my* point."

He reached for the chain saw, but I forestalled his action. "Eddie, did the coroner rule Oliver's death was from natural causes?"

"Of course. Massive coronary." Pain flashed across his face. "I could have given

Dad the entire bottle of pills and it wouldn't have made any difference."

I breathed a silent sigh of relief. I was sorry Oliver was gone, but if there had been a hint of foul play connected to his death it would have been devastating.

Eddie made another move toward the chain saw, but again I stopped him. "Before Oliver passed away, he looked up at me and said, 'Bretta . . . Spade.' Did you hear him?"

"Nope. I had other things on my mind."

"What do you suppose he meant?"

Eddie lifted a muscular shoulder. "I don't know."

"Do you have his spade with you?"

"Yeah. It's in my truck."

"Can I see it?"

"Why? Do you think Dad was giving it to you?"

I could tell he didn't like that idea. "No. The spade is unequivocally yours, but I'd like to see it again."

Eddie strode across the garden to his truck and opened the passenger cab door. I hid a sad smile. For all of Eddie's tough talk, he'd given Oliver's spade a place of honor up front instead of rattling around in the truck's bed with the other garden implements.

I took the spade and stood it upright. It was about my height, coming almost to my shoulders. I ran my hands down the handle. Years of heavy use had refined the wood to a satiny sheen.

Eddie said, "I'm thinking I'll take the spade to the cemetery and use it to put the first scoop of dirt on Dad's grave." He glanced at me. "Do you think that's sappy?"

It took me a moment to find my voice. "No, Eddie, I think Oliver would have liked the idea."

"Dad did it whenever someone close to him passed away, so I guess he'd approve if I do it for him." Emotion made Eddie's voice husky. He tried to clear his throat, but tears filled his eyes.

Embarrassed, he grabbed the spade out of my hand and spun on his heel. His long strides took him back into the garden. After a few minutes, I heard the chain saw start up.

Oliver had said, "Just as the twig is bent, the tree's inclined." It was heartening that Eddie's grief hadn't killed his love for the work he and his father had shared. My garden project was the best thing for him right now.

I moved toward the house, leaving Eddie

to vent his anger and frustration in the best way he knew how. I, on the other hand, wasn't sure what to do with my day. Slowly, I climbed the veranda steps, making plans, and eliminating each as uninteresting or uninspiring.

The front door was locked. I'd brought my hand up to press the doorbell when, from behind me, Bailey said, "Bretta, I'm gonna talk — and you're gonna listen."

Chapter Seven

I froze at the sound of Bailey's voice. I couldn't move, but my stomach lurched. My feelings for Bailey were confusing. I was upset that he owned the cottage, but the attraction I'd felt for him in Branson was as strong as ever. He'd come to River City looking for me. While this thought was exciting, it was also frightening. It meant that he was interested in me, interested enough to purchase a home that made him my closest neighbor.

Slowly I turned and faced him. He was dressed in blue jeans and a plain white T-shirt. Each time we'd met, I'd been impressed by his good looks. But it was more than his appearance that had kept him in my thoughts these last few weeks. He possessed an air of knowing what he wanted and having the ability to go after it. Nothing seemed to daunt him.

But he sure confused me. "Bailey," I said, "how nice to see you. Isn't this a beautiful morning?"

"I'm not playing that game."

I raised an eyebrow. "What game?"

"Twenty questions." He came up the walk and settled on the steps. Patting the space next to him, he said, "Sit here and listen. It's time to even the score."

"Even the score" sounded like revenge, and I wasn't in the mood to match wits with him. Fact was, I'd probably be out of my depth before the first insult was hurled. And anyway, revenge for what?

"No thanks. I've got things to do." Before I could do the first — press the doorbell for admittance into my own home — Bailey grabbed my ankle.

"Nothing is more important than what I have to say."

The solemnity of his tone carried more weight than his hold on my ankle. After two years of doing as I pleased, coming and going as I saw fit, I didn't like being ordered about, especially on my own front porch. But curiosity has always been my downfall. I gave in as gracefully as an independent woman could.

"This better be good," I said, plopping down. I put four feet of porch between us. "And for the record, I didn't know there was a score to even."

Bailey, having gotten his way, relaxed and stretched his long legs out in front of him. He folded his arms across his chest.

"Your mother's name was Lillie McGinness. Your father is Albert. He left you and your mother when you were eight years old. It wasn't until last Christmas that you renewed your relationship with him. You were brought up on a farm near a small town called Woodgrove. You never had children, but you were married for twenty-four years to Carl Solomon. He has a brother and a mother in Nashville, but you never see them. You own your own business — a flower shop. You have many friends, one of whom is the current sheriff of Spencer County. Sidney Hancock doesn't miss a chance to belittle your talents for meddling, but I think he has a high regard for you."

He cocked an eyebrow at me. "Shall I go on?"

Because of Bailey's career, I didn't question how he'd gotten this itemized account, but the *why* made me glare. "You forgot my weight and IQ."

Bailey chuckled. "I have it on good authority that I'd better not mention the former. As to the latter, I know from past experience that you're damned smart."

"Am I supposed to be impressed that you've taken the time to look into my background? Don't expect me to swoon from the attention. Frankly, it's an invasion of my privacy, and I don't like it."

"Ah, but that's where evening the score comes in. I know all these details about you. I'm ready to bring you up to speed on me."

To say I was interested was an understatement, but I played it cool. "I'm sure you've led a fabulous life."

Laughter rumbled in Bailey's throat. "Subtlety is definitely your style. You're a clever woman. I admire that." His tone grew serious. "I'm too impatient to fool with some convoluted male/female flirtation. I'm laying it on the line. I'm attracted to you. I came specifically to River City with you in mind. We had the beginnings of something special in Branson, but my job called me away. That part of my life is finished now. I'm ready to begin another."

His words made my skin prickle with excitement. What was he proposing? My pulse raced. He was free. I was free. We were of an age to do as we wished, and yet my upbringing reared its fundamentally moralistic head.

I couldn't leap into bed with this . . . this stranger, no matter how handsome and intriguing he was. Besides, I had all those ugly stretch marks that crisscrossed my body like a road map. Before I disrobed, I had to make sure the man I was with wouldn't take one look and run screaming from the room. My ego couldn't take such a beating. Neither could my heart.

But I was getting ahead of myself. Bailey had merely said he was attracted to me. "Just what are you suggesting?" I asked.

"How about a date? We can go to whatever restaurant you like. Or you can come to the cottage for dinner. I'm a good cook, though not too fancy. When my wife died, I had to learn my limitations the hard way."

"And this would be your first wife?"

Bailey smiled. "My one and only wife. That line I fed you in Branson about having three spouses was part of the plan to get information from you."

"As I remember, it didn't work particularly well."

"Depends on how you view the outcome. I'm here, and so are you. Dinner tonight? Say six thirty?"

He was rushing me. I wasn't sure how to take this sudden bout of honesty. I was suspicious, and my guard was up. Maybe everything he said was true, but what if he was in River City for a different reason? What if he wasn't retired from the DEA?

What if he was feeding me another line?

He'd bought the cottage. I still hadn't gotten used to the idea that it would never be mine. But was the title of that piece of property more important than getting to know him?

I could tell him to dry up and blow away, but I'd wanted the chance to get to know him better. Here he was, offering me that chance. I'd be a fool not to take it. Or was I a fool for considering it?

Bailey said, "I can hear the wheels turning in your head. Are you willing to take a chance?"

I was startled at his use of the very same word I'd been thinking. "I . . . uh . . . guess dinner wouldn't be a bad idea."

His coppery eyes teased me. "Love your enthusiasm. I'll try to live up to your expectations."

I glanced sideways at him. "You have an advantage. You've had time to think this all out, but I haven't." Something had been nagging at me since he'd started this conversation. Now seemed a good time to check the degree of his candor. "I saw you yesterday — in the old part of town. I called out, but you walked away. What's the deal?"

"No mystery. I was taking a drive,

looking over River City. I saw a crowd and stopped to see what was going on."

"How long have you known Claire Alexander?"

"Isn't that the name of the woman who was murdered?" Bailey's full lips turned down. "You're trolling for something, but I'm not biting."

He pushed up off the steps and stared at me. "I'll have dinner ready at six thirty. I can eat it alone or I can eat it with you. If you decide to come to the cottage, please leave your suspicions at the door. I've spent the last twenty-seven years screening every word I say. In my line of work, I had to be circumspect or it could mean my life or the life of my partner. I'm tired of it. Take me at face value, Bretta, or don't take me at all. The choice is yours."

With that, Bailey walked off. As I watched him go, I was mad, then I was sad, and finally I was resigned. The next move was mine, but thank goodness I had the rest of the day to make my decision.

Sundays are usually laid back, unless I have to go to the flower shop to do sympathy work for a Monday funeral. In the newspaper's area obituaries, I'd learned that Oliver's graveside service was to be

Tuesday morning at ten o'clock. That left today free to do as I wished. It could have been pleasant except for two things — my father and Sid Hancock.

It was mid-morning when Sid arrived. I'd gone to the garden to give Eddie a message from his wife, Molly. She thought it was time for him to come home, but first she wanted him to order the flowers for his father's casket. Eddie liked my idea of assorted foliages with just a few flowers. Once I'd seen him on his way, I went back into the house to find my father and Sid chatting in the library. Or rather Dad was chatting. Sid was doing a slow burn.

"— no such thing as a private investigator's license in Missouri." Dad delivered this bit of wisdom with a so-there attitude. "I'll locate office space, have business cards printed, and it's a done deal."

Sid heard my step in the doorway and swiveled around. "Well, if it isn't Ms. P.I. herself. Is it your goal in life to send me to an early grave?"

I smiled sweetly. "Right now my goal is food. DeeDee has refined her talent in the kitchen. How about scrambled eggs, sausage, and a biscuit topped with homemade strawberry preserves and a glob of butter?" I was in no mood to entertain Sid, but if his stomach were full, perhaps he'd be less inclined to be obnoxious.

"Trying a new tactic — stuffing my arteries with cholesterol and grease?" Sid grimaced. "Make that two biscuits and you've got yourself a victim."

I found DeeDee in the kitchen squeezing oranges for juice. When I told her there would be three for breakfast, her face lit up.

"Can do. I've got the b-biscuits in the oven. Won't take but a s-second to s-scramble more eggs." She flew into high gear, and I reluctantly went back to the library, where a stony silence greeted me.

I looked at my father. Our relationship was still at that "getting to know each other" stage. I was glad he was back in my life, but I wasn't sure I was ready to find him in my house each morning when I came downstairs. Opening my home to strangers, who were paying for their accommodations, would be easier than having a relative under my roof.

This morning my father wore a pair of mocha dress pants and a plaid sports shirt. His wavy gray hair gave him a distinguished look. The mulish gleam in his blue eyes gave me a bout of queasiness.

I settled next to him on the sofa but directed my comment to Sid. "Breakfast is on me, but it's gonna cost you. For the next half hour let's have pleasant conversation. No nasty remarks or harsh accusations." Out of the corner of my eye, I saw Dad open his mouth. I hurried on. "I know you have a reason for driving out here, but unless it's an emergency, it'll have to wait until we've eaten."

Sid struggled to hold in his usual caustic remarks. He finally muttered, "No emergency, but I never eat breakfast. I'll call this lunch."

And with that, the mood was set.

When DeeDee announced "B-brunch is s-served," in her most dignified manner, we filed silently into the dining room. To say this was a friendly occasion would be an out-and-out lie. Sid's business with me or his need for food must've been powerful because he behaved rather well. "Pass the jam" and "Anyone got dibs on that last sausage?" was hardly titillating conversation, but at least there was no open hostility at the table. At least not until Sid wiped his mouth and tossed the linen napkin on his grease-smeared plate.

"Thanks," he said, gesturing to the leftovers, which were scanty. He looked at my father. "You're excused. Close the door on your way out."

Dad bristled. "You, sir, may be a law enforcement officer, but you don't know peanuts from pecans when it comes to getting information."

"And you don't know shit from Shinola. You'd better make sure you don't step out of line in my county. I'll be watching you so close you'll think you're casting a double shadow."

"Whoa," I said. My head wobbled back and forth as I stared at the two men. "Did I miss something? What's with you guys?"

Dad regally rose from his chair. "The sheriff and I understand each other, Bretta. When he arrived, I offered him our services in his latest case — the murder — but he tossed that offer back in my face."

"I never tossed nothing," said Sid. "I laughed. I thought he was joking. But hell no. He's having a sign painted. Haven't you heard that's the first qualification for going after a killer?" He turned a fierce glare on me. "Put an end to this nonsense, Bretta, but do it later. I want to go over your statement. I've got a couple of questions."

I gave my father a placating smile and nodded to the door. He took my suggestion, but he had the last word. "This is an election year. If we decide against the detective agency, perhaps I'll look into the sheriff's position." He swept Sid with a contemptuous stare. "The *qualifications* surely aren't too rigorous."

He walked quietly out of the room, pulling the door closed behind him. I shut my eyes, praying for a giant hole to open so I could painlessly disappear. The floor remained firmly in place, even as Sid noisily scraped his chair back from the table. I took a deep breath and faced him.

"Well," I said, not quite able to meet his gaze. "DeeDee's cooking skills have improved. She can caramelize with the best of them. She made a chiffon cake the other day that was —"

"Cut the food review. I want to hear again why you went to that beauty shop. Why did this Alexander woman call you? If you only met her that morning, why'd she pick you to confide in? Why didn't she call a crony?"

"Look, Sid, all I know for sure is what she said to me. I can draw conclusions, but you hate that. Right?"

"Right. Draw a couple anyway."

I couldn't hide my amazement. In the past Sid has overemphasized that if I didn't know something to be God's own truth, I was to keep it to myself. Yet here he was inviting me to give him my theories. Maybe Bailey was right. Perhaps Sid did have a high regard for me. However, he hid it well behind a face flushed with anger.

He whirled his hand in a "get with it" motion. I settled in my chair and gave him my best uneducated guess.

"Claire made the comment that I have a reputation for getting to the bottom of suspicious doings. Yeah, yeah. Don't give me that look. You asked. Something was bothering her. At the park she made reference to a hot bit of gossip. She hoped Mrs. Dearborne would confirm what she suspected. If I were in your position, I'd ask Lydia Dearborne a few pointed questions."

"Been there, done that."

"What did she say?"

"A bunch of gobbledygook that's insignificant."

"How do you know that? You're still missing a big piece of the puzzle — the motive behind Claire's murder. Tell me what Lydia said, and maybe it'll trigger something."

Giving information wasn't easy for Sid. He acted as if he were choking on a chicken bone. He hacked a couple of times and consulted his notebook. "According to Lydia Dearborne, the topic of conversation while she got her hair done was nostalgia."

"Nostalgia for what?"

"A time when people were friendlier, when life wasn't so fast-paced."

"That's strange. I got the impression from what Claire said in the park that she had a particular subject in mind. There must have been more to their conversation."

"I wouldn't know. Lydia wasn't in the right frame of mind for doing any heavy-duty remembering. When I arrived at her house, she'd already heard about the murder. She'd called her doctor for a sedative, as well as a horde of relatives to hold her hand. It wasn't easy getting anything out of her. She kept saying she hadn't known Claire long, but she'd been a nice lady, though perhaps a trifle wild in her younger days."

"Maybe that's where the nostalgia comes in. Maybe they discussed some of Claire's adventures."

"The victim didn't have a record. I checked that."

"You saw Claire's hair and her contact lenses? Your average woman isn't prone to parading around town with green hair and strange eyes. When I see someone with a bunch of tattoos or body piercings, I always wonder what they're trying to compensate for in their lives. I didn't know Claire. Does she have a husband? Children?"

"Five ex-husbands, but no kids."

Now I understood Kasey's remark about Claire's track record. "That's interesting. Are the men still in town?"

"Nope. All are out of state except one, and he's serving time for criminal assault and armed robbery."

"What number was he?"

"Five."

I sighed. "None of this is helping, is it?"

"Nope." Sid came slowly to his feet.

I followed his lead and walked toward the dining room door. "I'll keep thinking on it. Can I talk to Lydia?"

Sid made a face. "You know where she lives?"

I nodded and would have opened the door, but he put a hand on the wooden panel.

"One more thing," he said softly. "Keep that father of yours in check. If you get the chance, send him back to Texas. He's a rich, bored old fart out to impress his daughter. That's a bad combination. He

117

informed me that he's been a subscriber to the *River City Daily* newspaper since he left Missouri. Your snooping has made the front page, and he's aware of your . . . uh . . . luck."

Sid shrugged. "Poke around. Ask your questions, but keep me informed. Don't make me look bad. I want another term as sheriff in this county."

Abruptly, he opened the door, and my father nearly tumbled into the room. Dad recovered with aplomb.

Sid scowled. "This is the kind of crap I'm talking about," he said, stomping past my father. Sid crossed the foyer, but before he opened the front door, he looked over his shoulder at me. "Do what you gotta do." He slammed the door with such force the windows shimmied in their frames.

Dad harrumphed. "That man has the personality of a rock and the manners of an alley cat."

"Dad, we have to talk." I led the way to the library, and once we were seated, I said, "You can't antagonize people because you think you're helping me. They're my friends. Offering to top Bailey's bid for the cottage was very kind, but it was offensive to Avery. He has too much integrity to make what would've amounted to an underhanded deal."

"But you were disappointed about that cottage, and so was I. It would have worked as a wonderful location for our detect—"

I had to put a stop to this once and for all. "There isn't going to be a detective agency, Dad. At least none that will have my name attached to it. And I'd rather you didn't do it, either."

"Figured you was going to say that. You've let the sheriff bully you."

I perched on the edge of my chair. "No. Regardless of what Sid says, I'm my own woman. I make up my own mind, and I don't want any part of an agency. Besides, I have the flower shop. I love my work. There isn't room in my life for another vocation."

"Or room for me?" he asked in a morose tone.

"There's plenty of room for you in this old house."

He gave me a sad smile. "That isn't what I meant, and you know it."

He wanted reassurance from me, but I couldn't say the words. To lighten the mood, I said, "I can stir up enough trouble on my own. I don't think this town could handle the two of us."

He waved his hand to our surroundings. "I can't sit around here all day. I have to do something."

He was used to leading an active life, and besides, if he were busy he'd be out of my hair. I thought a moment. "How do you feel about overseeing the renovations of the rooms upstairs?" When he perked up, I added, "Let's take a tour, and I'll point out some of the things I want done. I have the names of some contractors, and you can —"

The phone rang, interrupting us. I said, "DeeDee, I'll get it." I stepped across the room and picked up the receiver. "Hello?"

A male voice edged with impatience asked, "You the one who found Claire?"

"I beg your pardon?"

"I said, are you the one who found Claire's body?"

"Who is this?"

"A simple yes or no," he said sharply.

"I'm not answering your question."

A deep, rough chuckle sent shivers down my spine. "I'll take that as a yes," he said. "So you're the florist. Maybe I should send flowers to her funeral. Didn't send them when she was alive, but what the hell? How much would a dandelion cost?"

"I don't know who you are, but I'm hanging —"

"Don't bother, lady. Claire was scared. Looks like she had good reason. History has a way of biting you in the ass. Everything can't be saved. It became extinct just like she is."

His laughter was cut off as he hung up the phone. I pressed the disconnect button, released it, and got a dial tone. I hit the numbers for the return call option. A recording identified the number as coming from within the state penitentiary at Jefferson City.

Sid had said one of Claire's husbands was serving time. I'd just been reach-out-and-touched by a man convicted of criminal assault and armed robbery.

Chapter Eight

I hedged my father's questions by saying the caller had been a newspaper reporter. He accepted this explanation dubiously before I switched his focus back to the house.

"I'm proud of the downstairs, Dad, but whenever I think about all the hard work and the headaches I had to go through, I lose interest in finishing the upstairs. When this house was originally built it didn't have the garages or the servants' wing. DeeDee is happy in her rooms next to the kitchen. I have the master bedroom, which is in fair condition, but the rest of the upstairs is in need of some heavy-duty work. Plastering, painting, cleaning, and of course, installing a couple of extra bathrooms." I sighed. "There are so many details that need attention."

"I'll have plenty of time. Where do you want to start?"

A balcony circled the upper floor with each of the seven bedrooms opening off it. I gestured for my father to take his pick, and trailed along behind him. My mind wasn't on the virtues of wallpaper versus paint, or if the hardwood floors under the old carpets would be worth refinishing. All I could think about was Claire's death.

From what Sid had said, I wanted to give Lydia Dearborne another day to recover. Perhaps by then the sedative the doctor had prescribed would have worn off and her relatives would have moved on.

Dad opened the door to the room that held the most potential. I'd dubbed it the Mistress Suite after its former resident.

"You should get a nice price for this room," he said, looking around. "It has its own bath, and this little sitting area is a good addition. It's larger than your room, daughter; don't you want it?"

Daughter? I frowned. Addressing me as such seemed rather formal, but his tone was kind, almost tender. "No. I like being able to see the front drive as well as the garden from my windows."

"I'd like to name each room. You know, the Green Room, Blue Room, but more inventive. Otherwise, we'll have to identify them by number, and that seems too much like a hotel."

"Good idea," I said absently. Who could I talk to about Claire? Dana was my most likely candidate. She'd always struck me as being gabby. I broke into Dad's commentary on the wonders of polyurethane. "I have to run an errand."

His face creased with a frown. "I thought we were going to make plans."

"Write down your ideas, and we'll go over them later. I won't be gone long."

"I could go with you, and we'll talk in the car."

"That would be nice, but you need time to get a feel for each room."

"True. True," he said, eyeing a crack in the ceiling like a doctor contemplating a seriously ill patient. "We've got a tough road ahead of us. These cracks could stem from a structural difficulty. A quick cosmetic cover-up will only hide the problem. What we want is long-term repairs."

He patted my shoulder awkwardly. "If that's the case, we're looking at a hefty chunk of cash. It's a good thing your old dad is here."

He looked at me expectantly, but again I couldn't say what he wanted to hear. So I teased him. "You'll have so much to oversee, you'll wish you were still in Texas."

"Won't happen, daughter." He rubbed his hands together briskly. "You go do your thing, and I'll do mine. I have to hunt up a measuring tape and some paper and a pencil."

"DeeDee can get whatever you need. I'll see you later."

I hurried downstairs, stopping in the kitchen to give DeeDee a brief explanation as to what my father was up to. "Keep an eye on him. I don't want him climbing any ladders." I took off down the hall.

From the kitchen doorway, DeeDee called after me. "Who's k-keeping an eye on you?"

I halted my retreat. "What's that supposed to mean?"

"I've s-seen that look. You might as w-well have a sh-shovel in your h-hand. You're d-digging for information on that m-murder."

Shovel — Spade.

Digging? Was that what Oliver had been trying to tell me? That I needed to dig for information? Claire had been murdered *after* Oliver had passed away. What had been on the dying man's mind?

"I'll see you later," I said, going out the door.

Dana lived on Mossy Avenue. I hadn't taken time to look up a house number, but I hoped her catering van would be parked in plain sight at the curb. Luck was with me. The van was in the garage, but the

125

door was up. On the concrete pad, a man tinkered with a lawn mower. I parked and got out of my car.

"Hi," I said, coming up the drive. "Is Dana home?"

"She's in the kitchen. Go around back and knock on the door. Step light," he warned. "She has cakes in the oven."

I nodded and took the well-worn path around the side of the garage. I lifted the gate latch on a chain-link fence and stepped into the backyard. The front of the house had been bland, without personality. Here the place came alive. An above-ground pool dominated the area with a number of brightly colored deck chairs that invited a relaxing break from a hectic schedule. A gas grill stood near a picnic table covered with a red-checkered cloth. A couple of glasses and an almost empty pitcher of what looked like lemonade had attracted a swarm of insects. Flies buzzed happily as they sipped the nectar. The air smelled of grilled meat, chlorine, and some profound baking going on nearby.

I rapped on the screen door.

"You don't have to knock, Jonah," said Dana over her shoulder. "Just don't come clopping in here and make my cakes fall."

"It's me, Dana."

126

She whirled from the sink, soapsuds dripping off her hands. "Bretta? You startled me." She tiptoed across the floor and opened the door. "Come in, but walk easy. I've got my first batch of wedding cakes in the oven."

"Getting a head start?"

"With so much to do, I have to. Once these have cooled, I'll freeze them. No one will know they're eating week-old cake." A look of horror crossed her plump face. "Don't tell Evelyn. If she knows I'm doing this, she'll throw a fit. I'll be baking the day before the ceremony."

"My lips are sealed."

She pointed to a chair. "Have a seat. I can use a break. I'll fix us a glass of lemonade." She glanced out the window at the picnic table. "Oops. I forgot to bring in the pitcher. How about iced tea instead?"

"Don't go to any trouble. I'm not staying long."

Dana bustled around, brewing tea, filling two glasses with ice cubes. The legs of her blue jeans were dusted with flour, and her face was flushed from the heat that radiated from the dual stack ovens. The kitchen had been remodeled to accommodate her catering business. The refrigerator was monstrous. Mixing bowls were oversized, as were the pots and kettles that hung from hooks above an island.

By leaning back in my chair I could see into a formal living room that impressed me as being more froufrou than comfortable. The furniture was Queen Anne chairs and a sofa that looked as inviting as an oak log. Table lamps had shades trimmed in beaded fringe. The farthest corner caught my eye. A megaphone imprinted with the River City Royals' logo sat on a shelf. Near it were framed snapshots of Dana in a cheerleader's uniform. Blue and gold pompoms clashed with the room's formal decor, so I assumed this corner meant more to her than maintaining a fashionable theme.

"I thought my daughter and her family were coming for dinner," said Dana, "but Kyle, her youngest, has the sniffles, so it was just me and Jonah. I put steaks on the grill. It's an easy meal, and his favorite. He'll mow the yard, and I can clean up my mess. Tomorrow I'll bake another batch of cakes. And the next day another. By Wednesday, I should have them done, and I'll start on the main course menu."

She glanced at the refrigerator. "The shrimp arrived by special courier yesterday. I've cleaned them, and they're marinating. I'll drain them this evening and put them in the freezer." She shook her head. "Evelyn wants me to deep-fry them at the park. She's even brought me a special cooker. Everything has to be freshly prepared. I've never seen anything like it, or her, for that matter."

"She has specific ideas, that's for sure."

"What about the flowers? Can you do any early preparations?"

"Not a lot. We'll have the containers ready by cutting the floral foam to size. The bows for the corsages are made. But working with flowers is like working with food. Both are perishable, and it's the last-minute rush that's a *killer*."

It was a sly way to introduce the subject of my visit, and I hoped it would jar Dana's preoccupation with the wedding. The word had the desired effect. Apparently, Claire's death wasn't far from her thoughts. Dana's hand trembled as she set my glass of tea on the table. Liquid slopped over the rim.

She grabbed a paper towel to mop up the spill. "I still can't believe Claire's dead. If she'd been sick —"

"But she wasn't."

Dana pulled out a chair and sat down. "Maybe it was a random killing," she offered hopefully. "The paper didn't mention a motive."

"It's a safe bet she was killed for a reason. She knew something. You heard her in the park. She had a 'hot piece of gossip' she wanted confirmed. How many people do you think she teased like that?"

Dana propped her elbow on the table and cupped her chin. "Knowing Claire, it could have been her entire clientele or no one. When I saw her green hair, I should have suspected something was going on."

"Because it was green?"

"Not so much the color but that her hair had been changed. If Claire was upset or out to prove a point, she'd try a new style, but I've never known her to go for weird colors."

"Do you think the green was significant?"

"I doubt it. This hair business goes back to when we were sophomores in high school. Claire had the most beautiful auburn hair. It hung to her waist in gorgeous waves. When she discovered girls weren't allowed to take shop class, and boys weren't allowed to take home ec, she went to the administration and told them they were discriminating. According to Claire, young men needed to know how to cook and sew on a button. Young women needed to know how to change a tire, use a hammer, or anything else that would make them self-sufficient."

"That's sensible. Did she win them over?"

"No, and Claire was furious. In retaliation she whacked off her hair and took to wearing boys' jeans. From the back she looked like a guy."

"And how was this supposed to help convince the administration to change their school policy?"

"Remember, I'm talking about the sixties. Radical actions were the order of the day. Free love was the rage, along with bell-bottom trousers, miniskirts, and Beatles' haircuts. On a more dramatic note, we had the Vietnam conflict, riots, and demonstrations. Acid, not antacid, was in heavy use, and yet we were a naive society. We still thought we could save the world."

"I suppose that's true. I was about eight or ten, but I remember the hype. Save the rain forests. Save the whales. Feminist groups. Power to the people. Flower power." I grinned at Dana. "I must have been influenced even at that tender age." I expected her to give me an answering smile, but she stumbled to her feet.

"My cakes are about ready to come out of the oven."

131

As if on cue, the buzzer sounded. She waited for me to move, and when I didn't, she stepped to the ovens. She turned off the timer, twisted a couple of dials, and then opened the doors. A rush of hot, vanilla-flavored air wafted out.

Instead of reaching for a hot pad, Dana faced me. "I have work to do. You'll have to excuse me."

"Had you talked to Claire recently?"

"Just on the phone, the night before I saw her in the park."

"And she didn't say anything about knowing something that might have devastating results?"

"If she had, I'd have warned her to be careful. Claire wasn't always cautious. She wanted to right wrongs, to compensate for any injustice, and she was good at it. She had this built-in radar. She instinctively zoned in on wickedness."

"Her radar must have hit a snafu on the day she was murdered. Or maybe she thought she had the upper hand?"

Dana's face crumpled. "Please. I don't want to think about Claire anymore. I just want to do my part of this wedding and have it over."

I could relate to that. I stood up. "Did you know any of Claire's husbands?"

"Just Howie. He's in prison."

"Howie Alexander?"

"Oh no. Claire always took back her maiden name after each of her divorces. Howie's last name is Mitchell. His mother is my granddaughter's Girl Scout leader."

Mrs. Mitchell. The name was another thread in the tapestry of people who had a connection to Claire. I thanked Dana for the iced tea and left the house. I drove to the flower shop, where a quick hunt in the phone book revealed eight River City residents with the name Mitchell. I dialed the first three numbers without success but hit a bull's-eye on number four.

"Mrs. Mitchell?" I asked hopefully. "Are you a Girl Scout leader?"

"Yes, I am. What can I help you with?"

"My name is Bretta Solomon. We've never met, but I'd like to stop by your house and talk with you."

"Is this about one of my Scouts?"

"No, ma'am." She sounded nice, and I wasn't going to lie. "Your son, Howie, called me today. He said some rather . . . uh . . . unpleasant things."

Her voice trembled. "My son is thirty-seven years old. I'm not responsible for his actions or what comes out of his mouth."

"I understand, but I'd still like to speak

133

with you. I can be there in about five minutes."

Mrs. Mitchell's tone lacked enthusiasm. "Very well. You have my address?"

I told her I did, and we hung up. Before I left the flower shop, I grabbed a bouquet from the cooler. I'd made the arrangement several days ago and had included three lavender roses. The blooms were past the bud stage, which meant salability was chancy at best. But the roses still had a wonderful fragrance. Since I have a hard time tossing discards into the Dumpster, I hoped Mrs. Mitchell would appreciate the unexpected gift, and cooperate.

What I wanted from her still wasn't clear in my mind when I rang her doorbell some eight minutes later. The house was small — a two-bedroom bungalow dating back to the early fifties. The windows next to the porch were open. A breeze filled the lacy curtains. When they billowed away from the screen, I got the impression of a tidy living room with several silk arrangements and a floral-patterned sofa.

Good, she likes flowers, I thought to myself as I pressed the bell again. This time the chimes set off a riotous barking from inside. The timbre wasn't the annoying *yip-yip* of a lapdog but a deep *woof-woof* that carried the threat of bodily harm.

I shuffled my feet. I'd done enough delivering for the shop to have an aversion to house dogs. Most guarded their property with aggression. Lew kept a big stick in the van and carried pepper spray with him at all times. I had neither.

The door opened a crack. A pair of brown eyes peered at me through the screen door.

"Mrs. Mitchell?" I shouted above the din. From what I could see of her, she was about my height with dyed brown hair and exaggerated penciled eyebrows. One was arched higher than the other, giving her a perpetual look of skepticism.

She nodded primly, then turned and bellowed, "Down, Aristotle. Stop that racket or I won't give you a puppy morsel."

Puppy? The dog sounded like a mammoth canine with years of experience ripping flesh from bones. Instead of quieting the animal, her command provoked him. He hit the wooden door panel with a solid thud. The impact slammed the door in my face. I should've taken it as an omen to leave. I leaned closer to the windows, listening to Mrs. Mitchell admonish her pet for having "a nasty temper tantrum."

After another moment, she wrestled the

door open to a six-inch gap. "I'm sorry. I don't understand what's wrong with him. He usually isn't so —" She saw the flowers in my hand. "Oh. That's the problem. He hates anything with a floral scent. Goes positively berserk when he smells roses."

Raising my voice, I said, "I'll put the flowers in my car."

"But you'll still have their scent on you. I can't wear perfume. I can't spray a room deodorizer, but he's as docile as you please when we go for a" — she quickly spelled — "w-a-l-k."

The barking had quieted, but deep menacing growls raised the hairs on my neck. "I'd really like to speak with you. Could you step outside for a minute or two?"

She glanced down. "I don't know. He seems quieter now. I can try."

She opened the wooden panel farther, giving me my first glimpse of the dog. His black-and-brown head was massive. His eyes were filled with evil intent. Lips curled back to expose fangs that dripped doggie drool. While I gave him a quick appraisal, he did the same to me. His expression seemed to say, "A snack is only a screen door away."

I shuffled the bouquet behind my back, then checked to see if he was fooled. Aristotle took a step closer and dropped to a crouch. I tore my gaze away from him and suggested to Mrs. Mitchell that we go to a restaurant. I added my own personal incentive: "I'd be glad to buy you a cup of coffee and a piece of pie."

Her eyes brightened at my suggestion. "I don't get invited to go out —"

The moment she said "out" Aristotle leaped at the screen. My high-pitched squawk of alarm intensified to an unadulterated scream of terror. The flimsy screen gave way. Aristotle's head and shoulders were suddenly on my side of the door. Snapping and snarling, he lunged, trying to widen the opening. His sharp toenails scratched and clawed the aluminum panel. He wanted a piece of me, and I wasn't about to accommodate.

I heaved the bouquet, hit him square on the head, and ran lickity-split to my car. I didn't have the notion that I was being chased, and once I had the door open, I glared at the house. Aristotle had made his escape, but he'd lost interest in me. He chomped on the flowers like they were a carcass to be devoured. Mrs. Mitchell stared down at her pet, shaking her head.

She looked so forlorn I was moved to say, "I'm sorry."

"So am I." She gestured to the dog. "He's named after the Greek philosopher Aristotle, who believed that reason and logic are what separates humans from animals. My pet has a high intelligence, and if my son hadn't mistreated him, I think I could have taught him rudimentary logic."

"Mistreated him how?"

"Howie doused Aristotle with perfume, then tied him to a rosebush without food or water. I was gone for three days. By the time I got home, Aristotle was dehydrated and almost starved. The chain had gotten tangled with the brambles, driving the thorns into his skin. That happened five years ago, but if I run my hand over his shoulders, I can still feel the scars under his fur."

"That's terrible," I said, staring at the dog with newfound understanding. If Aristotle had gone after his human tormentor with the same malice as shown him, he'd have been put to sleep. With no other recourse, the dog had sought revenge by transferring his hate to an inanimate object — the rose.

Mrs. Mitchell said, "That emotional trauma rules his life. When he smells any floral scent, he proves his namesake's theory. Logic and reason are beyond his capabilities."

I might have sympathy for the dog, but not an all-out forgiveness for his scaring me half to death. I ducked to get into my car, but Mrs. Mitchell's next words stopped me.

"I don't know what Howie said to you. It wouldn't matter if I did. I can't explain him. I've often thought my being involved in Scouts should've given me a special wisdom when dealing with youths, but that could be hubris."

"Hubris?"

"Excessive pride." Pain twisted her face. "I'm no psychologist, but I've had plenty of experience studying adolescent emotions and behavior. Even so, I couldn't help my own son."

I leaned on my car, staring across the rooftop at her. "What was Claire like?"

"Needy."

"In what way?"

"All ways. Claire followed her desires against reason and more often without logical forethought. Her marriage to my son is ample proof of that. But in the last few months I'd noticed a change. Everyone wants to feel special, unique. Claire dyed her hair and wore those strange contacts. Everyone wants a sense of being useful. She lavished attention on anyone who walked through the doors of her beauty shop. She donated her time and talents wherever they were required. Everyone needs to feel an emotional bond. We need to have a sense of belonging in this world."

Mrs. Mitchell shook her head sadly. "From what I understand, Claire's earlier years were spent eliciting attention. What she got was a reputation for being a rabble-rouser."

Aristotle had finished massacring the flowers. He stepped to the edge of the porch and stared at me.

Mrs. Mitchell grabbed his collar. "You'd better go."

I didn't have to be told twice.

As I drove away, I looked in my rearview mirror. Amid the flower stems, petals, and chunks of floral foam at her feet, Mrs. Mitchell hunkered down to the dog, her arms wrapped around his neck. Aristotle's thick pink tongue slurped her face with adoring kisses.

I might have smiled. On the surface it was a charming picture — a woman and her faithful companion. I shook my head and pressed on the accelerator. Aristotle wasn't the only one in that household who carried emotional scars.

Chapter Nine

I drove up my driveway, keeping my eyes straight ahead. I would not look over at the cottage. It wasn't any of my business if Bailey was home. Besides, I'd know soon enough if I decided to join him for dinner.

If? Who was I kidding?

Since I'd met him in Branson, I'd tried picturing him going about his daily life, but it was hard forming a mental image when I didn't have a shred of information. Would we have things in common? Did he listen to the radio while he drove? Were the lyrics important to him — that unique phrase that can strike a chord, bring forth a passionate thought? Was he a sports fanatic? Did he like walks in the woods? Was he content to lean against a tree to marvel at nature?

I knew the cottage and could imagine him in this setting. The vaulted ceiling with its rough-hewn beams seemed like it might suit him, as did, perhaps, the multi-colored braided rug on the glossy hardwood floor. Would he use the fireplace? Or see the necessity to cut wood and clean ashes from the hearth as a tasteless chore?

I had hundreds of questions, and if I'd understood Bailey correctly, he was willing to answer them. Anticipation made my stomach quiver. I felt as giddy as a schoolgirl about to go on her first date.

What was I going to wear? My weight had stabilized, but only because I was prudent and DeeDee cared enough about me to not keep high-calorie snacks under my nose. It wasn't a blue jeans evening, but nothing too dressy. I had that pair of black slacks. I could top them with a shirt and my favorite vest. Catching sight of my expression in the rearview mirror replaced my enthusiasm with guilt.

"I'm sorry, Carl," I said as I pulled into the garage. I shouldn't feel guilty. I hadn't gone looking for someone. I still wasn't sure I was doing the right thing, but spending one evening with Bailey was an opportunity I didn't want to pass up.

I'd been gone from home longer than I'd planned. Had my father found something to occupy his time? In the hallway, I stopped. White particles danced and swirled, cloaking the air like a fine mist. At first I thought it was smoke. I sniffed, but only smelled something cooking in the kitchen.

A crash from above brought my head up. I charged into action when my father yelled, "Stand back! There's more gonna fall!"

"What's going to fall?" I demanded as I took the stairs two at a time. I was about halfway up the steps when another loud crash rocked the house.

On the second floor the dust was like a fog. "Dad? DeeDee? Where is everyone?"

"Bretta?" answered my father, stepping into the hall from the Mistress Suite. An embroidered dresser scarf was tied over his mouth and nose. He carried a fine ebony walking stick topped by a pewter knob. He brandished the staff like a classy bandit about to rob me.

"You hadn't been gone fifteen minutes when I discovered we've got one hell of a problem. But I've remedied it. That wasn't just an ordinary crack in the ceiling, daughter. I poked at it with my stick, and a huge chunk of plaster fell. It hit the light fixture, and we had fireworks. Sparks were shooting out like it was the Fourth of July. DeeDee replaced the blown fuse. She's a smart young woman. Can't figure out how she knew what to do, but she did it. While I caught my breath, we did some evaluating over diet-style slices of key lime pie.

When we came back upstairs I put in a new bulb, and everything is in working order."

I went past him, but stopped at the doorway. DeeDee was on the far side of the room. Her eyes were like two pee holes in the snow. I couldn't speak, but stared in utter confusion at the chaos.

Three quarters of the ceiling had been reduced to rubble on the floor. The falling pieces of plaster had hit a lamp, and it lay smashed. A curtain had been ripped from the window. A marble-topped table had one corner broken. But what rocked me back on my heels was the dust. I could feel it in my nose, my eyes, and my mouth. The white grit sifted over everything, coating the interior of the house as effectively as pollen stuck to a bee's belly.

My gaze traveled from the floor to the twelve-foot-high ceiling. "How did you get up there?" I asked.

"DeeDee said you don't have a ladder — which is on my list to buy — so I improvised." Dad rapped his knuckles on a wooden highboy. "They don't make furniture like this anymore. I used the open drawers for steps and climbed up."

He stared at the ceiling with a small smile, as if reliving some great adventure.

"Just before you arrived, I knocked down the rest of the ceiling. That corner over there is being stubborn, but I'll get it. We'll have this fixed in no time."

My temperature shot to a dangerous level. Three quick thoughts — He's an old man; he's trying to help; he's my father — kept me from combusting. "We'd better get this cleaned up," I said, trying not to clench my teeth.

"H-he meant w-well," said DeeDee, picking her way across the floor. "I'll go get some cardboard b-boxes from the g-garage."

"I know this is upsetting, Bretta," said Dad, "but you have to tear down before you can fix up. I remember the time we papered the living room at the farmhouse. We had to peel off eight or ten layers of old stuff before we could put on the new." He chuckled weakly. "Off with the old. On with the new."

"But I didn't plan to do any major plastering. The contractor had spotted the crack and said he'd take care of it."

"You didn't mention that."

"I didn't know you were going to poke it."

"True. True. We're both at fault."

I nearly choked. "Let's not talk.

Breathing this dust can't be healthy."

My father gestured to the cloth that covered his face. "Shall I find you a mask?" Using the toe of his shoe, he rooted in the debris. "Seems like I saw another one of these doohickeys on a table."

"Here comes DeeDee with the boxes." She handed me a large carton, and I picked up pieces of plaster. My father continued a running review on his afternoon. I let his words flow around me, but I didn't pay any particular attention.

I filled one box, left it sitting where it was, and then filled another and another. We were making headway, but the bulging cartons were in the way. I bent to heft one and groaned. I couldn't budge it. DeeDee was trying to drag a box across the carpet.

I straightened, rubbing my back. "We've done all we can. I'll have to call in a cleaning company. Even if we got these cartons downstairs, I don't know what I'd do with them." I waved a hand. "Let's call it quits. I need to shower and change. I have a dinner date at six thirty."

"You do?" said Dad. "I thought we'd spend the evening together."

It wasn't an unreasonable idea, but I wanted to wail like a banshee at the added pressure. He expected me to conform to his agenda, and I had my own. Even when Carl was alive I was free to come and go as I pleased. If I needed a break from the frantic pace of the flower shop, I could buzz off to Springfield without any pangs of guilt. If Carl's schedule let him, he'd go with me. If it didn't, I went on my own.

I liked that freedom, and I realized I'd been guarding it zealously. I'd made it clear to DeeDee, when she took the job of housekeeper, that I might be home or I might not, depending on my mood.

Maybe the curtailing of my freedom was another reason why I'd put off renovating these rooms. People in the house could tie me down. Make me feel that I had to put in an appearance. Having my father here was even more complicating. With strangers, I could be the eccentric land-lady. My father expected to be included in my life, and with each passing hour I felt the pinch of responsibility in a relation-ship.

"I've g-got to stir the b-bouillab-baisse," said DeeDee. "The ingredients are too exp-pensive to let scorch. I'll b-be r-right b-back." She dashed out of the room.

"Who are you having dinner with?" asked Dad.

"Bailey."

He cocked an eyebrow. "Oh, really. I didn't get the impression the two of you were friends."

"We have a few things to straighten out." I looked at the antique clock on a dust-shrouded table. We hadn't been cleaning as long as I thought. There was still plenty of time to get ready. Then I remembered the fireworks. "How long was the electricity off?"

Dad glanced at the clock, compared it to his wristwatch. "Looks like about thirty minutes. What time is Monroe picking you up?"

"He's not picking me up. I'm walking over to the cottage."

"Hmm. A private dinner party. Monroe's a good-looking man, and his former life could be viewed as glamorous — righting wrongs, rubbing out drug deals. I could see where a woman would be attracted to him, but discretion might be the better part of valor. Don't you think it would be more sensible to go to a restaurant or come here? DeeDee has that pot of fish soup simmering on the stove."

"No thanks. I can take care of myself."

"Carl's been dead, how long?"

I was rapidly losing my cool. "It's been two years, but I don't see —"

"I *do* see. You're lonely. You'd like to find someone to . . . uh . . . spend time with." He tugged off the mask to expose a crimson face. "Are you ready to take this step?"

With a studied effort, I kept my tone even. "What step? I'm having dinner with him. I'm not promiscuous, Dad. I never was, and you'd know that if you'd been around. Now, if you'll excuse me, I have to wash away this dust."

Alone in my room, I forced myself to take a couple of deep breaths, then I treated myself to a hot bubble bath. I shaved my legs, plucked a stray hair or two from my eyebrows, and did the things women do when they want to impress a man. I added a lavish spray of cologne, and I was ready. The black slacks were snug in all the right places. The blue vest brought out the color of my eyes.

"This is as good as it gets," I said as I turned away from the mirror. I opened my bedroom door and hurried down the front staircase.

DeeDee stepped out of the kitchen. "You l-look nice," she said. "Have a g-good time."

I grabbed a jacket out of the front hall

closet. "Gotta rush. I don't want to be late."

DeeDee glanced over her shoulder. "It's not quite s-seven-th-thirty."

I froze in the act of slinging the jacket over my shoulders. Slowly I turned. "What did you say?" When she opened her mouth to repeat it, I said, "Never mind. Where's my father?"

"He t-took a cab into t-town. He's th-thinking about b-buying a car."

My expression must have been frightening, because DeeDee's stuttering intensified. "W-what's w-wrong? He's t-trying to f-fit in. H-he s-said if h-he h-has h-his own v-vehicle he w-won't be a b-burden to y-you."

I opened the front door and stepped out on the veranda. I could see the cottage driveway if I went to the farthest end of the porch. By stretching my neck and peering around a grouping of pine trees I saw Bailey's black-and-silver truck was gone.

"I'm only an hour late," I said, going back into the house. "Doesn't the man have patience? Doesn't he know that stuff happens?" Stuff like an interfering father. But maybe Dad hadn't done it on purpose. Yeah, right. He knew he was giving me the wrong time, and then to make matters worse, he skipped out so he wouldn't have to take the heat when I discovered what he'd done.

I draped my jacket over the stair railing. In the library, I plopped down in a chair and folded my arms across my chest. After a few minutes, DeeDee peeked around the doorway.

"I'll be eating here tonight," I said. "Bring me whatever is left of that key lime pie, and you might as well haul out the crème brûlée. It's going to be a long, long evening."

DeeDee has a stubborn streak that often flares up when I try to eat something that I shouldn't. I didn't get the pie until after I'd eaten a bowl of the low-cal bouillabaisse. The fish was succulent, the shrimp plump and pink.

At regular intervals, I called the cottage armed with an explanation. Over and over, I rehearsed what I was going to say. Sometimes I thought I should be formal, not give a specific reason, but an ambiguous "I lost track of the time." In the next instant, I decided to tell the truth. That I had an overprotective father who was proving to be a pain in the tushie.

At a quarter after ten, my father still hadn't returned, but Bailey finally answered his phone. When I heard his voice, I blurted, "I would've figured a drug agent had a world of patience. I was only an hour late."

For a minute all I could hear was his breathing, then he said, "Ex-agent. I'm retired, remember? So what happened? An emergency call for flowers?"

"No, it's a bit more complicated than that. The electricity went off, and the clocks weren't set with the right time."

"I didn't lose power over here."

"This was an in-house catastrophe." I sighed. "You wouldn't believe me even if I told you."

"Try me."

So I gave him a spirited account of what I'd found when I came home. His laughter put the irritating event into a different perspective. "It wasn't funny at the time," I finished with a smile. "If you aren't doing anything, you can come see for yourself."

I'd thrown out the invitation with no real hope of his accepting. When he replied "I'll be right there," I was surprised. As good as his word, he rang the doorbell in less than three minutes. I was ready. I opened the door and we stared, looking quietly into each other's eyes. Not once did he make a move to touch me, but his expression told me he was thinking about it.

Suddenly shy and unsure of what I wanted, I broke eye contact and moved toward the staircase. "I'll give you a quick tour, then we'll go to the kitchen. DeeDee always keeps the cookie jar full for guests."

As I led the way up the stairs I could feel Bailey's eyes on my backside. I fought the urge to tug at my slacks. Perhaps they were too tight in the derriere department. I glanced back at him, and he winked. This was no playful eye maneuver. It was stimulating and damned sexy. I gulped and scampered up the remaining steps, talking a mile a minute.

"I'll have to call in a cleaning company to get rid of the mess. In fact, I'm wondering if they'll need to clean the entire house. The dust was unbelievable. I'm sure it's penetrated every nook and cranny." I opened the Mistress Suite door, thinking that in my irritated state I might have overplayed the details. Nope. It was bad.

Bailey's whistle was low and sharp. "And your father did this with only a walking stick and a chest of drawers? I'm impressed."

His quirky comment made me giggle. Before long I was doubled over with laughter. When I could speak, I said,

"Thanks. I needed that."

Bailey took my hand and kissed it. Goose bumps the size of ostrich eggs puckered my flesh. "I aim to please," he said.

Oh, yes, I breathed to myself. Please . . . please me.

Out loud I gasped. "Cookies."

He raised an eyebrow. "I beg your pardon?"

I eased my hand out of his and hurried toward the stairs. "I offered you cookies and here I am going on and on about —"

Bailey had caught up with my mad dash. He put a hand on my arm and turned me on the stairs to face him. "Cookies are fine — if that's all I'm being offered. But if I had my druthers" — he bent toward me, his eyes steady on mine, his lips a scant inch away — "I'd rather have a kiss."

"Oh," I squeaked. "Well . . . uh . . ."

I closed my eyes. Every sensory organ in my body was primed for his touch. My nose was filled with his scent — something woodsy and clean. His hand on my arm was warm and provocative. His breath was sweet and smelled of peppermint. His lips —

Where the hell were his lips?

I moved my head to the left and then to the right. Nothing. Opening my eyes, I found Bailey's attention had wandered. Not a good sign.

"What's wrong?" I asked. "Changed your mind?"

He brushed a quick kiss to my cheek, then galloped down the stairs. "Can't you hear it?" he called over his shoulder. "Something's going on outside."

I couldn't hear anything over the rapid beat of my heart. But now that he mentioned it, there was a hullabaloo out on my drive. Horns were blaring.

Horns? Car horns?

It had to be my father.

Trying not to whimper, I shuffled down the stairs and out on the veranda. Parked in the driveway were five vehicles with their headlights aimed at the house. Nearly blinded by the glare, I brought my hand up to shield my eyes. Bailey stood on the porch. I yelled, "What's going on?"

"Looks like a car show. Damned fine assortment, too. That's a Dodge Viper on the end. I've always wanted to see one up close." He leaped the steps and made for the yellow car on the far left.

"Viper?" I shivered. Sounded too much like a snake to me.

The horns stopped and peace reigned. Four men, whom I took to be salesmen, stepped from their vehicles. My father climbed out of a silver something or other. I didn't have a clue what make or model it might be, and frankly, I didn't care.

"Well, Bretta," said Dad, coming up on the porch. He waved his arm expansively. "What do you think?"

"Nice," I murmured, my eyes on Bailey. I was envious of that yellow car. He caressed the upholstery with a slow, lingering touch. I watched his chest rise and fall as he sighed wistfully.

"Take your pick, daughter. You can have whichever one you want."

Being called "daughter" was wearing on my nerves. It implied a closeness that just wasn't there. And being offered a car only agitated me more. I didn't want a car. I didn't need one. But I had been gypped out of Bailey's kiss.

Resentment and disappointment bubbled in me like Alka-Seltzer in a glass of water. Before I got carried away on an effervescent tide, I turned on my heel and went into the house.

Chapter Ten

I arrived at the flower shop Monday morning with the feeling I was running fast and furious from home. Turning down Dad's offer of a new car hadn't been as difficult for me as it had been for him. He couldn't accept the fact that I didn't want expensive gifts.

When I repeated my previous request for a heart-to-heart conversation about the past, he'd stalked into the library. I'd followed, but only to suggest that he take my room for the night. He'd replied that the sofa was good enough for him. He didn't mind living out of a suitcase.

This morning I found his signed blank check on the carpet outside my bedroom door. A notation stated that the money was to be used for cleanup. Since he was still asleep on the sofa, I'd placed the check on the end table next to him and left for work.

I took a swig of coffee. He wasn't getting it, and I didn't know how to be more explicit. Fancy cars or money wasn't going to buy my love — or my benevolence.

Footsteps coming from the alley entrance interrupted my thoughts. I turned, expecting to see Lois or Lew. But it was Evelyn who marched toward me. Frowning, I asked, "What are you doing coming in the back door?"

"You haven't unlocked the front, and I don't have time to wait."

Her attitude — that what concerned her had to be of utmost importance to me — really bruised my petals. I said, "We've been over each and every detail of your daughter's wedding until they're ingrained on my brain."

Evelyn smiled. "Let's hope so. I'm not here about Nikki's wedding. I want to place an order for flowers to be delivered to Oliver's funeral. He was a gentle, thoughtful man, and I want a fitting tribute sent from me."

She brought out her checkbook, dashed off the information, and then ripped out the slip of paper. Handing it to me, she said, "He believed in nature's own beauty. Keep my bouquet simple but elegant."

I shook my head in amazement. This from a woman who wanted foliage sprayed gold.

As the back door closed behind Evelyn, I looked down at the check. "Two hundred dollars?" I said aloud. "How much does she think 'simple but elegant' costs?"

The alley door opened again. This time it was Lois. "Hi," she said as she came into the workroom. "Did I see Evelyn leaving? Kind of early for a rout with her, isn't it?"

"No rout. At least, not this time." I studied Lois. Usually she bustled in babbling about something that had happened at home before she left for work. Today her shoulders drooped; her smile trembled around the edges. Was Kayla still causing problems?

Hoping to perk Lois up, I showed her Evelyn's check, explaining that it was for Oliver's funeral. "Got any ideas about what would please her?"

Lois didn't pause to think. "I'm uninspired. What's on for today?"

We discussed the orders. Lew arrived. The phones started ringing, and our day was off to a fast start. While we worked, I kept an eye on Lois. Twice I saw her dab at her eyes. Desperate to pique her interest, I brought up the subject of Bailey and how my father had sabotaged our dinner plans.

Her bland comment, "That's too bad," stabbed me with anxiety. Whatever was going on with her niece really was serious if Lois didn't have a speck of advice to give about my social life.

Lew had followed my account, and when Lois didn't offer any wisdom or insight, he put his own spin on the situation. "You and your father are too much alike," he said in that know-it-all tone.

I stiffened. "What's *that* supposed to mean?"

"Whether you like it or not, you have a combination of your mother's and father's genes. Perhaps the things about him that annoyed your mother are annoying you. He, on the other hand, sees your mother in you. He's trying to pacify you, maybe even make amends with her in the only way he has left."

I asked Lois. "What do you think? Is Lew right? Do you think my father —"

Lois picked up her purse. "I have to leave for an hour."

"What's going on?" I asked.

In a gloomy tone, Lois said, "I have a meeting with Kayla's principal. School is out, but the problem hasn't been resolved. I know we're busy. I should've said something when I came in this morning."

I glanced at the clock. It was after eleven. I looked at the orders that needed to be done. Some were for patients at the hospital, others for Oliver's funeral. I made a quick decision when I saw the distress on Lois's face.

I put two phone lines on hold. Picking up my purse, I said, "None of these deliveries have to be made right away. I'll take you to the school."

"You can't do that."

I touched her shoulder. "You're in no shape to drive, and besides, I'm the boss. I can do as I please."

Giving Lois a minute to compose herself, I told Lew to hold down the fort. Taking my friend's arm, I walked her out the back door and into my car. We were silent on the way to the school. I parked in the lot and turned off the ignition.

"You don't have to stay," said Lois. "Noah is joining me. He'll drop me off at the shop when this mess is cleared up."

Noah was Lois's husband. I was glad she wasn't facing this problem alone. "That's good," I said, then grinned sheepishly. "I brought you because I wanted to, but I also had another reason. Claire Alexander graduated from River City High School in nineteen sixty-six. I thought I'd nose around."

Lois reacted to my explanation like her old self. She snorted. "Lately my life has been topsy-turvy. Thank God I can depend on you. At least you never change."

"That's a compliment, right?"

Lois rolled her eyes, and we got out of the car.

Inside the school, the lingering odor of vegetable soup, sweaty bodies, and disinfectant layered the air. A bell rang. The sound triggered a rush of adolescent emotions that made my stomach flutter. For an instant I was once again that shy, unsure teenager, looking for acceptance among my peers. Irked, I shook off the image, but I was amazed that at my age, the clanging of a school bell could rouse such memories and make me feel vulnerable.

Aristotle, Mrs. Mitchell's dog, had gone berserk when he'd caught a whiff of the roses I'd taken to her. Oliver had said, when he touched the wooden handle of his spade, "Memories of bygone years flash into focus."

The school bell had triggered my reaction. The roses had set Aristotle off. Had the spade stimulated a remembrance that was so important it had stayed in Oliver's mind while he'd had his heart attack?

I left Lois at the door to the principal's office, then wandered down the hall. River City High School showcased its students' achievements with photos, trophies, and banners displayed on walls and in glass-fronted cabinets.

The awards were in chronological order, with the latest near the front of the building. Since information on Claire was my goal, I skipped recent decades, looking for 1966 — the year she and her friends had graduated.

From the amount of pictures and awards, the class of '66 had been out-standing in both athletics and academics. Bold captions depicted the highlights: RIVER CITY HIGH SCHOOL TRACK TEAM ENDS SEASON WITH HONORS.

Above a picture of young men in football uniforms were the words WE WERE DETER-MINED, TOUGH AND FINE . . . ROUGH AND READY ON THE LINE. Conference champs in 1966. I grinned but kept reading and searching.

Candid photos of River City cheer-leaders were next. I looked for Dana, but she wasn't there. That's odd, I thought, then shrugged. Perhaps she wasn't at school the day they took the picture.

DEBATE CLUB NAILS OPPOSITION. I searched the photo for Claire but found Sonya's name as a member, only she wasn't in the group picture. BOTANY CLUB MEMBERS PLANT TREES — WIN CITY'S BEAUTIFICATION AWARD. All four women — Sonya, Dana, Kasey, and Claire — were named as members, but none were pictured.

Peculiar that all four girls were missing the day photos were taken. Randomly, I picked three students, who seemed to be overachievers since they were in all the snapshots. A close inspection showed that in the Botany Club photo the two guys wore short-sleeved shirts. In another they had on V-necked sweaters. A girl named Tina had gone from a brunette to a blonde. Sweaters could be added over a shirt, but I was sure Tina hadn't gone for a dye job between photo sessions.

I meandered farther down the hall, looking in classrooms, but all were either empty or in session. Since I didn't have a specific question in mind, I gave up and went out to my car.

Driving across town, I kept wondering why all the girls had been absent each time pictures had been taken.

It was food for thought. Since I could chomp on this morsel and not gain a pound, I gnawed away like a frustrated dieter eating a celery stick. I'd found a bit of nourishment, but it lacked substance. What I needed was a glob of pimento cheese for my stalk of celery. Translation: I needed more information.

Chapter Eleven

When I returned to the flower shop I found a pile of new orders. The work was expected, but Evelyn seated on a chair wasn't. Before I put my purse up, I dug out an antacid tablet. The chalky, fake-fruit taste made me grimace. Lew caught my expression and sidled over.

In a low tone, he said, "I needed her help. She answered the phone and took orders while I waited on customers. It was a madhouse for a while, but she did a great job. Besides, what was I to do? I thought you would drop Lois off at the school and be right back."

"I'm here now." The smile I gave Evelyn was mere lip action — no warmth behind it. "Thanks for helping Lew. What can I do for you?"

"If I remember right, you said Nikki's fresh flowers would arrive today. I want to look them over."

This wasn't a good idea. Flowers were shipped without water. The foliage would be limp, blossoms tight. The flowers needed to be conditioned — stems cut and put in warm water. "The delivery is running late," I said. "I can call you after we've unpacked the flowers and they've had time to take up water."

Evelyn leaned back in her chair and crossed her legs. "If you don't mind, I'll wait."

I minded very much. Watching a florist struggle to get her work done isn't a spectator sport. I tried another tactic to get her to leave. "We're very busy. No time for chitchat."

Evelyn gestured to the ringing telephone. "I'm well aware of that. Shall I get it?"

"No thanks." I picked up the receiver. "The Flower Shop. Bretta speaking."

"I just talked to Mrs. Mitchell to see if she knew when Claire's funeral service would be, and she says you're asking questions about Claire."

"Dana?"

"Why can't you leave things alone? Don't tarnish Claire's memory."

"Tarnish it with what? We all have areas in our life we're not proud of. Are you thinking about a specific event?"

"I shouldn't have called," she said, gulping back a sob. "A wedding and a funeral. I'm not thinking straight."

166

I tried a soft, subtle approach. "Dana, something is bothering you. I'm trying to help. Tell me what it is. It often helps to talk to a stranger, someone unbiased, unconnected to the present circumstances."

"Time's supposed to blur the memories, not make them clearer. We were so young and so full of — I have to go. My cakes are burning."

"Dana, wait. Don't —" But she'd already hung up. I replaced the receiver and turned to find Evelyn smiling.

She nodded to the deliveryman who was unloading four big boxes from the alley. "My daughter's flowers have arrived," she said, clasping her hands. "Isn't that wonderful?"

God, but this woman was exasperating.

The day went down as the longest on record with no time for food to soften the edges. It was one o'clock before Lois came back to work. With Evelyn at our elbows, we didn't do much talking. It was three before the wedding flowers were processed and the mother of the bride had departed. The day's orders were finished and delivered around four o'clock.

By the time we'd cleaned the shop and I'd locked the doors and counted out the cash drawer, it was after five. The others had already gone. I schlepped out to my car with my tail dragging, only to find Sonya waiting. She didn't waste time with niceties.

"You've lost your focus, Bretta. The Montgomery wedding should be your prime objective. I understand from Dana that you're asking questions about Claire. Leave it be."

"She was murdered."

Sonya winced but didn't lose momentum. "That isn't your problem."

"Then why did she call me? Why didn't she call you or Dana or Kasey? After all, the three of you were her friends."

"We don't have your reputation for amateur detecting. But in this case, you should leave the investigation to the professionals. Your skill as a florist is on the line. Surely you don't want any unfavorable comments about your work?"

"I could ask you the same thing."

Sonya peered at me. "Explain that statement."

"You came all the way over here to put me in my place, so your mind isn't entirely on the wedding either." I gave her a tight smile. "Why are you really here? Is it because I might be close to discovering what happened all those years ago?"

Of course, I didn't know jack. I was bluffing. Dana's words "We were so young and full of —" were fresh in my mind. I used that as the basis for my bamboozling.

Sonya's eyes narrowed. Her lips thinned into a grim line. I'd pricked her composure, but with her experience at placating neurotic brides, Sonya had all the stress-reducing tools close at hand.

She flashed me a firm smile. "This conversation is going nowhere. Let's start over. I understand the flowers have arrived and are absolutely gorgeous. Evelyn is very pleased."

"That's good, because at this late date, there's not much we can do."

Sonya glanced at her watch. "And speaking of late, I really must be going." She went around to the driver's side of her car, but before she got in, she looked back at me. "Claire's death is a tragedy, but it can't interfere with our obligation to Evelyn and her daughter. Nikki deserves the best because that's what her mother is buying."

"Have you met Nikki?"

"No, but I'm looking forward to it. From her picture she's a lovely young woman. Working with a beautiful bride makes my job and yours easier. Anything we do will only enhance the final picture."

"That reminds me. I was at the high school this morning, and I saw that you were a member of the Debate Club in nineteen sixty-six. But you weren't in the picture of the team. And Dana wasn't in the picture of the cheerleaders. All four of you belonged to the Botany Club, but none of you were in the photo. What's the deal? Mass influenza?"

"That's right," snapped Sonya. Without saying good-bye, she got into her car and drove off.

I smacked my hand against my forehead. "Dummy!" I'd given her an easy out.

Boy, this questioning thing really sucked. If I was too blunt, I hacked people off. If I was too subtle, I didn't get anywhere. I had to find a happy medium, maybe adopt my own persona. With Sid, a suspect knew exactly where he stood if he didn't come across with the truth.

I climbed into my car. I didn't want to be as belligerent as Sid, and besides, I didn't have a badge to back me. Carl had switched between the direct method and the "I'm your buddy" approach. Both had worked for him. He'd tried to teach me how to recognize which one to use in different situations. I'd practiced interrogating him at our kitchen table or in bed, but that usually ended in a strip search with the lesson abandoned for more important activities.

I reached for the ignition but didn't turn the key. Bailey's way had been to fabricate giant tales that might elicit an emotional response. Making up all that stuff took too much brainpower. If I got befuddled, I'd never keep the facts straight.

I licked my lips. He'd also held my hand, stared deep into my eyes, and kissed me. Not exactly a formula he could employ every time he needed answers, but he'd sure gotten my attention.

"Are you okay?"

I jerked upright at the sound of Bailey's voice. Turning, I saw him leaning against my car. "I'm . . . uh . . . fine. What are you doing here?"

"Are you going to ask me that each time I see you?"

I shook my head. "Is something wrong?"

"Questions . . . questions. You sure have a bunch."

Bailey leaned closer. The coppery color of his eyes had stayed in my mind all these weeks. It was an effort to meet his gaze because I had so many emotions tugging at my heart, and yet, it was harder to look away.

"Have dinner with me," he said quietly.

I didn't need to think about it. "My car or your truck?"

"Come with me. You look too tired to drive."

I was, which probably meant it showed. I glanced in my rearview mirror and groaned. My nose was shiny. My hair was a mess. I'd known we'd be busy at the shop, so I'd worn a comfortable pair of sneakers and blue jeans that were too big.

Bailey opened my car door and held out his hand. "Come on. I can see you're having second thoughts."

"Where are we going? I'm not dressed very well."

"You look fine to me."

"Oh," I breathed. Suddenly I didn't care that my jeans were baggy. I slipped my hand in his and watched his fingers curl around mine. His touch was strong and warm and comforting. He held my hand all the way to his truck, where he opened the door so I could get in.

For a moment, I hesitated. If I turned and looked up at him would he kiss me? I wanted him to, but I was shy, and I was afraid. His lips on mine could unleash a passion I wasn't ready to handle. So I climbed into his truck and watched him close the door, hoping I hadn't missed an opportunity.

Bailey pulled out of the alley. "What are you hungry for?"

I gulped. "Whatever you want."

"Mexican? Oriental? A juicy steak?"

"Steak sounds good. But nothing fancy. Okay?"

Bailey nodded and drove to a restaurant that advertised family dining. It wasn't romantic, but the informal atmosphere put me at ease. We sat across from each other in a booth. After a waitress had taken our order, I said, "Even the score."

"Where do I start?"

"No particular place. Tell me whatever pops into your head."

Bailey settled back, one arm on the table, the other at his side. He glanced around the restaurant and suddenly smiled. "See that kid? The one giving his mom trouble?"

I followed his gaze. A boy I guessed to be eight or ten was arguing with a woman. She thumped his bulging jeans' pocket and then pointed to the table. With a disgusted expression the boy pulled out a fistful of sugar packets.

"But they're free, Mom," he said in a loud voice.

"Free to use. Not free to steal."

"But I was going to use them — at home."

Bailey said, "That's me, umpteen years ago. I always had something in my pockets, and my mother was always making me empty them. That woman is lucky it was only sugar packets. My mom was confronted with wooly worms, earthworms, toads, frogs, and once, a garter snake."

The waitress put our salads in front of us. I picked up my fork but didn't take a bite. "Did your mother make you toss out the snake?"

"No. She let me keep it at the barn. Along with a crippled rabbit, three turtles, a horse, and an assortment of cats and dogs. The number changed often. We lived on a gravel road that was a convenient place for people in town to dump their unwanted pets. In my younger days I saw myself as a healer and a protector of those animals. But sometimes they were beyond my help, and we couldn't afford to take them to a vet. Mom didn't have the heart to put them down. Dad didn't have the time. So the chore was left up to me."

"That's a pretty heavy load for a kid."

"It was the only humane thing to do. I could shoot a rifle as soon as I was big enough to hold one. The kill was quick and clean." Bailey's expression darkened. "Unlike some."

"Tell me what you're thinking."

"This isn't pleasant dinner conversation."

"Please?"

Bailey hesitated, then spoke quietly. "My brother was hooked on drugs by the time he was eighteen. He suffered as a human never should. He served time for dealing. He was in rehab more than he was at home. He was my brother, and I loved him, but I couldn't do a damned thing to help."

"Is that why you became a DEA agent?"

"To avenge my brother's death? To fight the bastards who used his weakness for their gain? It sounds heroic and noble, and if I was trying to impress you, I'd say sure, but it wouldn't be the truth."

"Is something wrong with your salads?"

We looked up at the waitress. Our steak dinners were on her tray, but she hesitated setting them down.

"Can you make our meal to go?" asked Bailey. He turned his gaze on me. "I need fresh air."

The waitress frowned. "I guess I can wrap everything in foil."

Bailey removed a money clip from his pocket and handed her a folded bill. "That should cover our tab. The rest is yours. We'll wait up front."

Five minutes later we walked to his truck with two foil-wrapped packages. Bailey opened the passenger door and stashed our dinner behind the seat. When he turned to me, his eyes were troubled. "Are you all right with this?"

"Leaving? Yes. Let's put the windows down, turn up the music, and just drive."

He ran a finger down my cheek and across my lips. "Thanks," he said before moving back so I could get into the truck. He shut the door and went around and got behind the wheel. "I was listening to this CD when I stopped by the flower shop. I hope you like Kenny G." He poked a button.

I grinned as the first notes of a familiar instrumental song filtered from the speakers. "I have this same tape in my car. He's bad. B-b-b-bad to the bone."

Bailey chuckled as he put the truck in gear, and we headed out of the parking lot.

We traveled up one street and down an-other, commenting about a house or a yard. Our conversation was easy and comfortable — no earth-shattering revelations or emotional remembrances. Our rambling took us to the outskirts of town, where the heat from the pavement was absent and the air cooler.

"This is nice," I said, taking a deep breath. "I haven't been this relaxed in days."

"Something bothering you?"

"I have a big wedding at the end of the week, but I don't want to think about that right now."

Bailey nodded that he understood, and turned onto a gravel road that edged the limestone bluffs that overlooked the Osage River. I feasted my eyes on the view. The multitude of trees swayed as if a chorus line of beauties vied for my attention. A June breeze fluttered the leaves, giving the impression of feathery plumes on elaborate chapeaus.

Bailey turned off the music. "I left you up in the air at the restaurant. You went along with my need to get out of there without question. I'm ready to finish my tale."

"Only if you want to."

"It's part of evening the score," he said. "I was one of those guys who went to college because he didn't know what else to do. I played with the idea of becoming a veterinarian, but after the first semester my grades were terrible. I knew I wasn't cut out for the medical field. For my second term, I enrolled in classes where I thought I might succeed. One was a firearms course. I aced it, and my skill caught the instructor's interest. He told me I should get a criminal justice degree. It seemed as good a major as any other, so I did as he suggested. I graduated college. Got a job as a security officer in the federal building in St. Louis. I changed jobs but stayed within the system. Federal work interested me, but I wasn't sure which branch to pursue."

"You became a drug enforcement agent. Some people would say that subconsciously you were striving for that goal all the time."

Bailey flashed me a lopsided smile that made my knees quiver. "Have I ever told you that you're too smart for *my* own good?"

"Not yet, but I'm sure you will."

"How about if I told you that we're being followed?"

I didn't look around, but accepted what he said as fact. "Really? When did you notice?"

"When we left the restaurant parking lot."

"You're kidding." I looked at his dashboard clock. "But that was over an hour ago."

"I know. He or she is persistent but not skillful. A tail doesn't drive a cherry-red SUV. Nor does he stick like glue to your bumper even in heavy traffic. Out here, he could have dropped back, but he's eating our dust." Bailey cocked an eyebrow. "What do you think? I can try to get a look at the license plate" — he tapped his chrome cell phone, which was on the console between us — "and call it in. Or we could confront our stalker."

"Let's confront. This tailing business sounds like something my father might do. It would serve him right if we embarrassed him. Turn left, and then right. The road dead-ends at Make Out Point."

Bailey waggled his eyebrows. "That sounds interesting."

"It's also known as Kegger Canyon and Drug Bust Bluff. He'll have to turn around, and we can nab him — or at least make an ID."

Bailey followed my directions to a deserted tract of land that was a sinner's paradise. Trash was caught in the brush at the edge of the road. The dirt lot was littered with bottles and cans that had been tossed out car windows. A rustic rail fence was the only barrier between wide-open spaces and us. Bailey pulled his truck around, parked parallel to the fence, and cut the engine. Out my window was a fantastic bird's-eye view of the treetops.

Bailey unbuckled his seat belt. "Here he comes."

I didn't bother turning. This was humiliating, but my father had to be taught a lesson.

"What the hell?" shouted Bailey. "He's gonna ram us."

My mind was still tracking on my father. "He wouldn't —"

I looked past Bailey, and my eyes widened. The SUV veered toward the back end of the truck.

Bailey grabbed my hand. "Hold on, sweetheart."

The SUV plowed into the rear fender. The impact whipped the lightweight truck bed into the fence. The back tires dropped, touched nothing, and the truck flipped like a tiddly-wink chip.

Bailey's hand was jerked out of mine. The front of the truck took a nosedive. The air bags inflated. Windows shattered.

Metal screeched with outrage at the abuse. The truck careened down the embankment and then came to an abrupt stop that rattled my teeth and jarred my bones.

My body had taken a beating, but I was secure in my seat belt, cushioned by the bag of air.

Seat belt.

The word shot through my brain like a piercing arrow. Bailey had unfastened his seat belt so he could confront the driver of the SUV. There hadn't been time for him to secure it again before we were hit.

"Bailey!" I screamed, clawing at the bag that protected me but blocked my view. "Bailey!"

The air bags were deflating. I pushed the wad of material out of my way. The driver's door had been wrenched off its hinges. Bailey was gone.

Chapter Twelve

I was dizzy and nauseous, like I'd been on a carnival ride gone berserk. My hands shook so badly it took several tries before I could unsnap my seat belt. I blessed the safety apparatus that had saved me, but cursed the fact that Bailey hadn't been wearing his.

The console lid had popped up, and the interior of the truck was littered with CDs, maps, papers, and notebooks, as well as leaves and twigs. Filling the air was the overpowering aroma of the grilled steaks we hadn't eaten.

I gagged and tried my door. It wouldn't open. Swallowing the bile that rose in my throat, I worked my way over the console, pushed aside the driver's air bag, and climbed from the truck.

I saw the giant tree that had stopped the truck's descent, then looked beyond it into nothingness. The sight made me puke. When I was finished, I leaned weakly against a crumpled fender and used the tail of my shirt to wipe my mouth.

I ignored the bumps and bruises that throbbed all over my body. Turning my back on what might have been, I searched the hill above me for Bailey. I called his name, but there was no answer. The truck had mowed a path down the slope. Bent almost double from the steep incline, I worked my way up, trying not to cry, trying not to imagine the worst.

The sight of Bailey's chrome cell phone, lying on some leaves, gave me a ray of hope. I picked up the phone absently, still searching. Then I saw him, and nearly strangled as panic gripped my throat. He was so still.

I flew to his side and dropped to my knees. I was afraid to touch him. Afraid of what I'd find. I looked him over. He was on his back, eyes closed; one leg, twisted at an odd angle, was obviously broken. Blood oozed from a gash on his forehead.

I leaned over him, peering into his face, willing him to be alive. Slowly I lowered my head to his chest and heard soft, shallow breathing.

I dialed 911 and begged them to hurry.

"Are you Mr. Monroe's next of kin?"

The doctor stood in front of me, his hands thrust deep into the pockets of his white coat. I focused on the stethoscope that hung around his neck, and licked my dry lips. "If it's bad news, you have to tell me."

We were in the waiting room at River City Memorial Hospital. I'd been checked over, my cuts had been treated, and I'd been released. I'd spoken with two Missouri Highway Patrolmen, giving them a description of the SUV that had followed us and rammed Bailey's truck.

My mouth tasted like caffeine-flavored vomit. I'd gotten some coffee from a vending machine and had waited and waited. Information concerning Bailey's condition had been sketchy up till now. This was the first time I'd been approached by anyone who might have answers. I wasn't sure I could deal with the news. "Next of kin" sounded too ominous, too foreboding.

The doctor sat in a chair next to me. "My name is Dr. Watkins, and I'm going to be honest with you. Mr. Monroe is in critical condition. We set his broken leg, treated his abrasions and contusions, but he hasn't regained consciousness. The blow to his head has left a portion of the brain swollen."

"Oh, no," I said softly. Tears filled my eyes. I tried to blink them away, but was unsuccessful.

"Now, now," he said. "Mr. Monroe is in good hands."

"Can I see him?"

"He's in the unit where only family members are permitted."

"I *could* be his sister."

The doctor eyed me. "Yes, you could. Since I'm not acquainted with Mr. Monroe, I can't dispute your claim." He nodded down the hall. "Tell the nurse at the desk that you have my permission to visit Mr. Monroe. Keep it short. Five minutes — tops. Don't be afraid to touch him. Talk to him, but be calm and reassuring. Let him know that he's going to be fine."

"But you said he was unconscious."

"That's true, but sometimes comatose patients can hear, and they're often aware of what's going on around them even though they can't respond. In this case, I think it might be helpful if Mr. Monroe heard optimism in your voice."

I thanked him with a smile that wobbled around the edges. The nurse didn't question my request to see Bailey after I'd mentioned Dr. Watkins's name. She looked at some papers on her desk and said he was in Cubicle 7b.

"Cubicle? Doesn't he have his own room?"

"This is the Critical Care Unit," she explained. "No walls, no doors, just curtained cubicles and seriously ill patients. Don't be alarmed by the tubes and wires. Each has a purpose and is important. You may go in, but keep your visit to five minutes."

I found 7b and pushed the curtain aside. I hesitated for only a moment before I took a deep breath and walked to the bed. Bailey's arms were straight at his sides. His right leg was in a cast, and a bandage wrapped his head. A crisp white sheet was smooth over his stomach. His chest was bare except for electrodes attached to a machine that kept up an encouraging *beep, beep, beep.*

I touched his hand. "Bailey, it's Bretta. You're going to be just fine." Tears threatened, but I forced myself to talk quietly. "You have to come back to me. We have too much to do. I want to sample your cooking. I want to slow dance with you. I want you to meet my friends."

I kept my eyes on the monitor as I leaned closer. "I want you to hold me in your arms." Saying those words made my own heart's rhythm increase. Did his? I scanned the peaks and valleys on the screen.

"What are you doing?"

I turned to see a nurse standing at the foot of Bailey's bed. My cheeks felt hot. "Dr. Watkins said I should talk to Bailey. So I am. Is that wrong?"

She looked from me to him to the electrocardiograph. "Mr. Monroe's heart changed rhythm, and we were alerted at the nurses' station."

"Changed in a bad way?"

"No. Just a hiccup in the pattern."

"Should I go?"

Again, she studied Bailey's handsome face. "No. If the doctor told you to talk, that's what you should do." She lowered her eyebrows. "Just watch what you say. Don't make any promises you aren't prepared to honor." She left the cubicle chuckling lightly.

Gingerly, I picked up his hand. Speaking softly, I said, "Looks like I'd better not try any more rousing experiments. But you get better, and we'll —" I dropped my voice to a husky whisper and said something that deepened my blush.

I looked at Bailey's heart monitor, then glanced behind me. No one appeared in the doorway, but his fingers curled ever so gently around mine.

"It was not a muscle spasm," I said to

myself. I limped back and forth in front of the hospital, waiting for my ride home. It was late. The parking lot was deserted, which gave me freedom to vent my frustration. When I'd felt Bailey's fingers move, I'd rushed to the nurses' station with the encouraging news. After he'd been examined, I'd been told there wasn't any change and that it was time for me to go.

I'd left the Critical Care Unit, but had gotten only as far as the nearest phone. My car was parked behind the flower shop in the alley. I couldn't drive it anyway. My purse was in Bailey's truck, which had been towed away and impounded for an evidence search.

I'd thought about calling Sid, but I didn't have the stamina to face him. I'd thought about calling Lois, but she had enough on her mind. I'd thought about calling DeeDee, but I didn't want her out on the roads at this time of night. I had settled on my father.

When he answered the phone, I'd simply said I was without a car and needed a ride home from the hospital. He'd promptly replied, "I'm on my way." Twenty minutes after my call, he rolled into the parking lot.

Leaning across the seat of his new blue truck, he pushed open the door. "Are you all right, daughter?" The dome light accentuated the wrinkles on his face and the concern in his eyes.

"I'll be fine once I get into bed. I'm exhausted." I started to climb in but saw my purse on the seat. I touched the familiar bag. "Where did you get this?"

"A deputy brought it out to the house. He said there had been an accident, but he assured me you were all right. I've been waiting by the phone, hoping you'd call."

"Accident?" I muttered, as I settled on the seat. I slammed the door with more force than necessary. "It wasn't an accident. We were rammed by an SUV."

"Rammed?" My father studied me. "Why would anyone ram your car?" His eyes narrowed. "We? Who was with you?"

"I was with Bailey in his truck."

"Ah," said my father. "That would explain it. I'm sure Bailey Monroe has made plenty of enemies over the years. A drug dealer who's been brought to justice would have irate customers wanting to even the score."

I winced at my father's choice of words — "even the score." They brought back happy memories of the first part of my evening with Bailey. The last half had been disastrous.

As we pulled away from the hospital, I said, "Please, take me by the flower shop. Since I have my purse and keys, I'll drive my car home. I'll need it in the morning."

"You're still shaky. Tomorrow you'll be stiff and sore. I'd be glad to take you to work."

"Thanks, but I'd rather have my car so I can come and go as I please."

"Always the self-sufficient one, aren't you?" Under his breath, he added, "You're so like your mother — intimidating and damned frustrating."

I stared at him. "What do I do that intimidates you? More importantly, what did *she* do?"

"I'd rather not discuss it."

"How did Mom intimidate you? I don't remember any fights. There weren't shouting matches. You simply took off. Why?"

"How is Bailey? Was he hurt?"

"Talk about frustrating. You could give lessons on the subject." I shook my head. "Bailey is in critical condition. He's in a coma."

We stopped for a red light, and I felt my father's steady gaze on me. "So your heart's bruised as well as your body," he said quietly.

My chin shot up. "My heart? Good heavens, no. Bailey is just a friend."

The light turned green. Dad didn't comment, just pressed on the gas pedal. We rode in silence. The lie I'd told hung in the air, begging me to recant it. But I couldn't find the courage to speak about my feelings for Bailey to my father. The subject was too personal.

After a moment, Dad said, "When I was in Texas and you were here in Missouri, I took comfort in the fact that the same sun that shone on you was shining on me. I wanted to see you. I missed you until the ache in my heart was almost too much to bear, but I stayed away. Sometimes, you have to be cruel to be kind."

I turned to him, relieved at the subject change. "What was kind about leaving me?"

"I'm not talking about the leaving. I'm talking about the staying away."

"I don't get it. Either explain what you mean or drop it."

"I knew when I left without saying goodbye your heart would be broken, but I also knew it would mend. Time does that, you know. It heals all wounds."

I hugged my purse to keep from trembling. "That's a crock."

191

"No it isn't, Bretta. You had your mother. You had school and other activities to keep you occupied. As time passed, the hole I'd left in your life would grow smaller and smaller."

I fought tears that were close to the surface. "What you don't understand is that you left me with all the reminders. You went on to a new and different life. But everywhere I looked, I expected to see you. Coming in the back door. Sitting at the dinner table. Holding me on your lap and reading me a story. Once I was older, I'd think about conversations we'd had. I kept looking for something I'd said that would keep you from picking up a phone and calling me."

"But if I'd called you, it would have renewed our relationship."

"But that's what I wanted. That's what I needed."

"I know. But it wasn't something I could handle. I couldn't chance talking to you. I couldn't see you. The sight of your face, the way your smile lights your eyes —" He sighed. "I would've been back in your life — and your mother's."

We'd come full circle. I still didn't understand, and I was too tired to pursue it. A block later, I pointed to the alley entrance. "Turn there," I said, searching in my purse for the keys. They always settled to the bottom.

"Oh, my Lord," said Dad. He slammed on the brakes.

I pitched forward, and the seat belt dug into my bruised shoulder. I moaned at the pain. "Dad, that hurt," I said, frowning at him. He stared straight ahead.

I followed his gaze and caught my breath. My car had been vandalized. Tires slashed. Windows smashed. Fenders battered.

Dad's theory about a drug-related hit was shot all to hell when his truck's headlights picked out the writing on the driver's side of my car.

"STRIKE 2!"

Chapter Thirteen

My father got a flashlight out of his truck, and while we waited for the police to arrive, I inspected my car. I was careful to not get very close, but I couldn't stop staring. I'd been too upset since the SUV rammed Bailey's truck to give thought as to why it had happened. My father's explanation had sounded viable, but to realize I'd been the intended victim was mind-blowing.

The devastation to my car made me heartsick, but the message painted on the driver's door panel shocked me. "STRIKE 2!" The unwritten words crept through my brain — strike three, and I was out.

I played the beam over the interior, wondering if I'd left anything in the front seat that I might need. Amid the twinkling bits of glass, I saw something lying near the accelerator. Leaning closer, I stared at a small bundle of flowers and leaves tied together with a piece of orange twine.

"Look at that," I said.

My father took a step forward and peered over my shoulder. "What is it?"

"It's a tussie-mussie. It's a custom that

dates back to pre-Victorian times. From what I've read, people didn't bathe regularly, so the women carried these little bouquets made from fragrant leaves and flowers to mask body odor. In later years the language of flowers evolved, and blooms and foliage were given individual meanings. The tussie-mussie was sent to a special person to convey a message of love. Each leaf, each flower, even the way the blooms were placed in the bouquet had a meaning, and they were all tied together with a piece of twine."

I frowned. "But I doubt this combination means I have an admirer. That dried white rose represents death. I wish I had a camera. Someone more knowledgeable than me will have to identify each leaf and the placement of the flowers."

"Why don't we take it? The police won't know anything about a tussie-mussie, and you'll have —"

"I can't do that. It's evidence — and important, too."

"Why so important?"

"Not just anyone would know how to construct a tussie-mussie. That in itself is a clue."

"I don't have a camera, daughter, but I could make a sketch."

"There isn't time —" I stopped speaking when he ignored me and went to his truck. He came back with a tablet and a pencil. With swift, sure strokes, he etched in the general outline of the nosegay. When I saw the bouquet come to life under his expert hand, I leaned closer to the car so I could better aim the flashlight at the floorboards.

"Make each leaf as accurate as possible, Dad. Isn't that a milkweed bloom in the center?"

"Could be," he mumbled, leaning through the broken window. "Smells funny in here. Pungent."

I sniffed, but a squad car pulling into the alley drew my attention. "Are you about done?" I asked.

"Need a few more minutes." He took the flashlight out of my hand and made another quick study of the tussie-mussie before he turned off the light. As he stuck the flashlight into his back pocket, he said, "Stall."

"How?"

"Hysteria might work."

I rolled my eyes, but moved away from my car and down the alley. Before the officer had climbed from behind the steering wheel, I was wringing my hands. I put on a good act — or was it an act? The fear and confusion came awfully damned easy.

Last night I'd said a sad farewell to my car as I watched the police tow it away. This morning I was behind the wheel of a cherry-red SUV, not unlike the one that had plowed into Bailey's truck.

When my father had offered to arrange transportation, I'd gritted my teeth and accepted. Only this time I'd given him a description of what I wanted. I didn't know motor size, make, or model, but I knew big and red.

My new set of wheels outclassed me in the color department. I was dressed in black. Oliver's funeral was at ten o'clock, and I planned to attend. But first, I made a trip to the hospital. I asked at the desk if Bailey was conscious and learned that his condition was unchanged.

My mood was glum when I arrived at the flower shop. Lois had the doors unlocked, the lights on. I didn't have to ask how she was doing. She gave me a quick grin as she carried a bucket of flowers to her workstation.

"I've taken another order for Oliver's service," she said. "The bouquet is to be in a large basket, so I guess you won't be able to haul it in your car. Lew can —"

"I've got plenty of room."

Lew strolled in. "Who owns that hunk of hot metal in the alley?"

I waved a hand. "Dad bought it after my car was vandalized last night."

Lois looked from me to the back door. "I wanna see what you're driving, then you can tell the tale."

"I don't have much time, and neither do you if you're going to do an arrangement for Oliver."

She nodded and took off. In a flash, she was back. "Wow. Why didn't you get a tank? That thing's as broad as it is long. Are the highways wide enough?"

I admitted that it was huge but that it drove like a dream. "Or a nightmare, if the wrong person is behind the wheel. I don't want to go into detail, but Bailey and I were rammed last night by an SUV that looked like the one in the alley. His truck went over Make Out Point with us in it. I had my seat belt on, and I'm fine. Bailey is still in a coma."

Accustomed to the task, Lois's hands flew as she designed the bouquet. "Rammed. SUV. Make Out Point. You're fine, but Bailey is in a coma." She tossed the order form at Lew. "Type the sympathy card." She handed me a bolt of yellow ribbon. "Make me a bow."

I drew the satin ribbon through my fingers. "Is that all you've got to say?"

"Are you kidding? I'm about to explode with questions. You didn't mention how or why your car was vandalized." She shot me a frown. "Though, since I know you so well, the why is obvious. You've been poking into that beautician's murder."

"The few inquiries I've made hardly warrant the type of destruction that was done to my car. It was bashed and battered."

"By a vengeful hand," said Lew.

I didn't comment, but folded the ribbon back and forth, creating even loops. "Vengeful hand" was an apt description.

Right now the big question was — did I back off? My shifting emotions ran as hot as my new car and as cold as a well digger's ass. Anger surged through me each time I thought about the devastation to my car, but the thought of Bailey lying in that hospital bed because I'd been the intended victim was enough to freeze me in my tracks.

I reached for a pair of scissors and saw Lois watching me. "You aren't telling us everything, are you?" she said.

"You've been pretty tight-lipped yourself. How's it going? Are you ready to talk about Kayla's problem?"

Lois gave me an exasperated glare at the subject change, but relented and spilled the beans. "Raising children can be rewarding, but it's also nerve-racking." She cut the stalk of a yellow gladiola. "I'm sorry for my sister. Kayla is a brat, but now she's my responsibility, and I'm not going to shirk it."

"Send her back to Cincinnati," I said.

Lois shrugged. "I could, but I know I can make a difference in her life. I just have to find the right approach."

"What did she do?"

"My niece and two of her new friends thought it would be a great joke if they put a mud turtle in the principal's aquarium." She poked the gladiola stem into the floral foam. "Cute, huh?"

"Where'd they find the turtle?"

"Does it matter? Suffice it to say they picked the nasty thing up on some road. It had crud and leeches on it, but my finicky niece put it in her backpack and took it to school."

"So?" said Lew. "What's the big deal?"

I ignored him to ask, "Was it a large aquarium?"

"Fifty gallons."

"Expensive fish?"

"Oh, yeah, to the tune of three thousand dollars."

"I still don't see the problem," said Lew, typing fast and furious. "A turtle can live in water, especially if it's a mud turtle."

A clueless Lew was awesome. If we'd had more time, I'd have played on his ignorance, but Oliver's funeral was in forty-five minutes. However, I couldn't resist putting Lew's own brand of pomposity in my tone: "A mud turtle can live in water, but it has to eat. I'm guessing that old reptile had a rich banquet."

"Oh," said Lew as understanding dawned. He rolled the card out of the typewriter and carried it to the worktable. "You say this was the *principal's* aquarium?"

Lois took the finished bow from me and attached it to her arrangement. She plucked the card from Lew's fingers and pinned it to the ribbon. "That's what I said. The principal is thoroughly pissed. Two of the fish she raised herself. She'd had the others for ages, and they were like family to her. I wanted to tell her to get a life, but figured that wouldn't help the situation. We've been waiting for her to decide the girls' punishment."

I picked up my purse and removed the keys. "Now you know?"

Lois stood back and stared at the arrangement. "I'm done. Does it look okay? My mind wasn't on what I was doing."

I assured her the bouquet was fine, and then asked, "So? Tell us what's going to happen to Kayla, but make it the condensed version."

"During the next school year each girl has to earn a thousand dollars without a parent or guardian contributing so much as a dime. The money, once it's earned, is to be donated to an animal rights organization."

"That's not so bad," said Lew.

I agreed and picked up the bouquet, ready to head out the door.

"There's more," said Lois.

I stopped and waited.

"When school begins this fall, Kayla and her friends will start the year with ISS — in-school suspension — for the first six Saturdays." Lois sighed. "It could have been worse. The principal had the right to expel the girls, which would've gone on their permanent records."

Oliver was laid to rest in a small country cemetery that was about eight miles from where he'd lived on Catalpa Road. It was a beautiful day to be alive, and I silently gave thanks, sending up an additional prayer for Bailey's speedy recovery.

Across the road prairie grass waved in the breeze like an undulating tide. A wrought iron fence enclosed the cemetery. Cedar and pine trees sparked the hope that life was everlasting. Carrying the bouquet Lois had made, I dodged marble markers, crossing the uneven ground to Oliver's gravesite, where I put the flowers next to the casket.

The turnout for the service was small — thirty adults and his two grandchildren. The minister was frail and had to be helped across the rough ground to the grave. His hands trembled, but his voice was firm.

"From Second Corinthians, chapter nine, verse six, the Good Book says, 'But this I say, He which soweth sparingly shall reap also sparingly; and he which soweth bountifully shall reap also bountifully.'"

The minister closed his Bible and lifted his head. "We have evidence of Oliver's caring for others right here in this cemetery. He kept the graves mowed and trimmed, without pay. He planted trees and flowers in memory of those who have gone before us. Oliver sowed bountifully, but it us who have reaped the benefit of his compassion, his love, and his charity. Let's bow our heads in prayer."

Eddie seemed composed and in control during the brief eulogy. Once the final prayer was said, his jaws clenched. I'd been watching him because I knew what was coming. Oliver's spade leaned against a tree.

The casket was lowered. The vault lid moved into place. Eddie reached for the spade, taking the handle in a firm grip. For a second or so, he stood with his head bowed. It was a poignant moment — not a dry eye among us.

The funeral director moved a piece of green carpet aside, exposing the soil that had been taken from the grave. Eddie stooped and picked up a clod. As he crumbled the lump, he shook his head. "This stuff won't grow nothing." He sighed. "But then I guess it don't have to."

He stood and plunged the spade into the dirt, then gently sprinkled the dirt over the vault. "Bye, Dad," he said quietly before turning to his family. "Son?" he asked, holding out the spade.

Both of Oliver's grandchildren took a turn, as did Molly, Eddie's wife. Then he offered the spade to me. "Bretta?"

I didn't hesitate. My fingers wrapped around the wooden handle. It hurt to move my shoulders when I lifted the scoop of soil. In the past, I'd heard the comment about "planting" someone and thought it unfeeling and crude. But in this case, planting Oliver was exactly what we were doing — as an act of love and respect for a man who'd earned both.

After mourners had been given the opportunity to place dirt on Oliver's casket, all meandered toward their cars. I hung back so I could have a private word with Eddie. He saw me waiting and came over.

"It was a nice service," I said. "Your father would have approved."

"I think so. Anyhow, it felt right. When Mom died, my kids were too small to hold the spade. I was proud of them today, but I never thought about others wanting a turn." He chuckled. "Dad would've gotten a kick out of prissy Mrs. Dearborne handling a spade."

"Dearborne? Lydia Dearborne? Which one is she?" I asked, craning my neck.

Eddie scanned the area. "That's her," he said, pointing. "The red-haired woman getting into the car parked nearest the exit."

"I want to talk to her, Eddie. I'll see you —" I took a step, but the heel of my shoe had sunk into the sod. I stumbled. If I hadn't been stiff and sore, I might've regained my balance, but my reflexes were slowed by strained muscles. Eddie made a grab for me, but I went down on one knee.

"Bretta, are you all right?"

"Help me up, but do it slowly."

He took my arm. I tried not to wince, but he'd grabbed a tender area. I got to my feet as quickly as I could to relieve the pressure. Rubbing the spot, I looked around for Mrs. Dearborne. "She's gone?" I asked.

"Lydia? Yeah." He dismissed her with a wave of his hand. "I'll be at your place this afternoon. I've lined up some guys to help remove the tree limbs. The weatherman forecasts showers for the weekend. I'd like to get the area cleaned up so I can do a controlled burn of the thatch —"

I'd been inspecting the grass stain on the knee of my panty hose. "Rain?" I said. "*This* weekend?"

Eddie grinned. "I see it as poetic justice for the witch. I hope it rains like hell on her parade."

"That's not nice," I said. "Don't forget I'm part of that parade."

We visited a while longer about my garden. I got directions to Lydia's house, then crawled into my SUV and headed down the road.

I knew I wouldn't like Lydia Dearborne from the moment I set eyes on her property. Eddie had called her prissy, and if her yard was any indication, the word was apropos. The house was pristine white. There wasn't a flower or a weed in sight. The grass had been given a crew cut — no blade longer than an inch. Branches had been lopped off trees so they resembled lollipops spaced in tidy rows.

I knocked on the front door, but received no answer. The clatter of a metal bucket drew me around to the back of the house. Lydia didn't see me, so I watched her in fascination. The smell of ammonia perfumed the air as she scrubbed the trunk of a tree.

The chore itself was unique, but the woman had tackled the job dressed in white slacks, a green blouse, and matching green shoes. Not your average tree-trunk-scrubbing uniform. But then, scrubbing trees was hardly your average person's idea of garden work. Rubber gloves encased Lydia's arms up to her elbows.

She walked around the tree, inspecting

her endeavors. That's when she spotted me. "Oh," she said. "Mrs. Solomon. You startled me."

"Have we met?"

"Not formally, but my friend Darlene's daughter works for you." Her expression turned to pity. "How is poor little DeeDee?"

The hairs on the back of my neck bristled like the brush in her hand. "She's doing wonderfully. I couldn't ask for a more competent housekeeper."

"I'm surprised. She was such a shy, delicate child."

"She isn't a child."

"No, of course not." Lydia lifted a shoulder. "Oh, well, at least she's doing something appropriate." She clicked her tongue in distaste. "My, my, the things women do nowadays are amazing. I had my car serviced last week and a woman dressed in filthy coveralls took care of it. Just a little while ago, when I came home from Oliver's funeral, a lady was here from the Gas Service Company."

Lydia frowned. "We didn't talk long because I was in a hurry to change out of my funeral clothes. She seemed familiar, but I don't know anyone who'd have her job. She crawled under the house without a qualm. Came out with cobwebs in her hair and dirt under her fingernails."

I could have said a number of things in reply, but I plunged into another topic. After her comment about DeeDee, I happily employed the shock method of questioning. "Did Claire act like a woman about to be murdered?" I asked.

Lydia blinked. "How does such a person act, Mrs. Solomon? She was Claire. Talking and laughing while she curled my hair."

"She told us in the park that she had a hot piece of gossip she hoped you'd confirm. What did she ask?"

"She didn't ask anything. We just visited."

"She said if she phrased her questions right you wouldn't know what she was after." I smiled coolly. "Since you don't have a clue, I guess she was good."

"I'm not a fool, Mrs. Solomon. I know when I'm being pumped for information." She gave me an arch look as she stripped off her gloves and laid them on a chair. "Claire and I talked about the passage of time. How people move away and you lose track of them. I told Claire I've always been lucky to have caring neighbors. Oliver's land connects with mine on the west.

I've heard that someone is interested in the property that lays to the east. There isn't a house anymore, but the site would make a lovely place to build a new home."

"Do you think Claire was interested in buying that land?"

"Not at all. Why would she want property out here when her business was in town?"

I hadn't heard anything that could be termed a "hot piece of gossip." My frustration made my tone sharp. "You must be forgetting something. Claire expected you to tell her a piece of important information."

"Don't be snippy, Mrs. Solomon. Since Claire's murder I've had a difficult time. I haven't slept without medication. My sister and my daughter came to stay with me, but they left this morning to go back to their lives. Now I'm coping alone."

"I didn't realize you and Claire were such close friends."

"I wouldn't call us friends, though I saw her once a week. She began doing my hair when I won a contest she held at her shop. My name was drawn as the winner of a wash and set, though I never registered for the prize. Hadn't stepped foot in her shop."

"How did she get your name?"

"I never win anything, so I didn't ask. She was excellent with my hair. I told my friends about her work, and they switched to Claire." Lydia touched her henna-colored curls. "I'm going to miss her. She was clever. Have you seen the mural on her ceiling?"

"Yes. It's very nice."

"Claire did the work herself. A month or so ago, I was tilted back in my chair, and she told me she'd been thinking about painting a picture on the ceiling. She asked my advice, and we tossed ideas back and forth. Claire hit upon the idea of a woman with flowers sticking out of her head like hair."

"Is the girl on the ceiling a real person?"

Lydia started to speak, then stopped. After a moment she mumbled, "Now, isn't that strange?"

"What's strange?"

"I haven't thought about that family in years."

Totally confused, I said, "What family?"

"Shh," she said sharply. "I'm thinking."

I watched Lydia, who was acting more than weird. When she finally looked at me I said, "Well, what's going on?"

A sly smile twisted her lips. "That's my secret."

"There aren't secrets in an ongoing murder investigation. If you have information, you have to give it to the authorities."

Lydia sniffed. "Which you are not."

From the stubborn twist of her lips, I could see I wasn't going to convince her to talk to me, so I switched gears. "What about the flowers?"

Lydia lifted a shoulder. "Claire said that by painting Missouri wildflowers on the ceiling she might be able to achieve a total state of . . . uh . . ." Lydia stopped and thought. "Now, what was that word?" Her face brightened. "That's it — a total state of catharsis."

"Catharsis?" I murmured, studying Lydia. "What did Claire mean?"

"I couldn't tell you." At my look, she snapped, "Because I don't know, Mrs. Solomon. When Claire was in one of her analyzing moods, she'd quote her ex mother-in-law, who in turn quoted this Aristotle." Lydia shook her head. "Seems silly to me. What did Aristotle Onassis ever say that was so profound?"

Chapter Fourteen

I turned my head to hide my amusement. How could I expect Lydia to know about a Greek philosopher who had believed in logic and reason? Where was the logic and reason in the idea that a woman's place was only in the home?

I mumbled something about getting back to the flower shop and went around the house and climbed into the SUV. After I'd cranked over the engine, I smiled at the powerful sound. I'd never owned anything remotely like this vehicle. I zipped down the drive, whipped out onto the road, and then applied the brakes. A sheriff's car was headed my way.

Sid pulled alongside me. He gave my new wheels a sharp study and grunted. "Looks like a rich father has its dividends. Why red?"

"Why not? Any news on who rammed Bailey's truck?"

"Nothing on who, but a red SUV was found abandoned out near the River City waste plant. It was reported stolen from a strip mall. The owner went into a store to get cough syrup and left the motor running. Our suspect got in and drove away. No one saw who it was, so we don't have a description. There's damage to the left front fender complete with flecks of black paint."

"What about my car? Did you find anything?"

"Not much. It was beat to hell with a baseball bat. I read in the officer's report that you called that wad of wilted flowers on the floorboard a tussie-mussie. I saw it. Looked like a bunch of leaves and dead blooms to me. Why do you think it was put there?"

"I told the officer that each leaf, each flower, even the placement of them, is important. It contains a message, and it isn't good."

"A message?"

I explained about the language of flowers, but Sid lost interest. When I took a breath, he said, "I hear you're a regular visitor to Monroe." He reached down beside him and held up a plastic bag. "Here's the personal items that were in the truck — CDs and the ring of keys that were in the ignition. We kept the notebooks and papers for a closer inspection. I'd give this stuff to his family, but so far they haven't been located. His daughter is on some cruise ship with her grandmother." He passed the bag out the window.

I took it, placing it on the seat next to me. I hadn't thought about Bailey's having children. "What's his daughter's name?" I asked, trying to keep my voice casual. "How old is she?"

"Jillian Monroe is all I know. I didn't ask for her life history." He stared at me. "I heard he bought the cottage next to your house." He raised an eyebrow. "That's convenient."

I wasn't going to discuss my relationship with Bailey, so I asked, "Are you on your way to talk to Lydia?"

He studied me a moment, then said, "Yeah. I assume that's where you've been. Did you get anything out of her?"

"Nothing much."

Sid's eyes narrowed. "I'll be the judge of that. What'd she say?"

I shrugged. "Changing attitudes of neighbors. The property to the east of her place is for sale. Claire herself painted the mural on her beauty shop ceiling." The devil in me added, "She's keeping something to herself, and I think it has to do with the painting."

"Is it important?"

"I don't know, but she says it's her secret. She was snooty about it. Lydia also said that Claire painted Missouri wildflowers so she could achieve 'a total state of catharsis.' "

Sid's eyebrows zoomed up. "Aristotle's theory of catharsis? Interesting."

When he saw my mouth hanging open, he said, "Don't look so damned surprised. I read more than deputies' reports. Philosophy exercises my brain in other areas."

He drummed his fingers on the steering wheel. "Aristotle believed that pity and fear were the extremes of human nature, and for a person to attain virtue these emotions should be avoided. According to him, by viewing a tragedy there could be a kind of purgation or purification from these feelings — a catharsis."

"I'm impressed. But wasn't Aristotle talking about a tragedy represented by a stage enactment, not real life?"

"If you're scared you look for comfort anywhere you can find it." Sid tilted his cap back and scratched his head. "But I don't see how flowers painted on a ceiling could be called a tragedy, unless she was an artist with my talent."

"Claire's ex-husband, Howie, told me she was scared about something, but I didn't get that impression when I talked to her.

She seemed more excited than frightened." Sid's expression stopped my palavering.

His chin dropped, and he glared. "When did you talk to —"

Kaboom!

Lydia Dearborne's house exploded into a fireball, altering the bright yellow sunlight into a surging, unnatural, orange glow. The concussion slammed me into the steering wheel before the SUV's suspension rocked me like a baby.

"Holy Mother of God," said Sid.

I twisted around in my seat and stared in horror. The upward escalation had blown the house debris sky-high, where it maintained a sort of suspended animation. Hunks and chunks appeared to burst into flame against the blue background. As gravity took hold, charred bits of unidentifiable materials slammed to earth. Ashes floated on air that was thick with black smoke. Where the house had been, flames leaped and danced like demons intent on total destruction.

While Sid called in the emergency, I thought out loud. "She has to be dead. She couldn't have lived through that explosion even if she was outside scrubbing trees."

"What?" shouted Sid.

I raised my voice. "Lydia must be dead,

but shouldn't we check?"

Sid shot me a disgusted glare. "Which part of her are we gonna look for? That was either a bomb or a gas leak. See how the flames are roaring straight up? They're being fueled by something. I've called the gas company to come turn off the main valve. Until they do their job, we're gonna sit tight."

Gas company.

With my eyes on the fiery scene, I said, "Lydia told me a woman from the gas company had gone under her house for an inspection." I glanced at the dashboard clock. "That was approximately an hour ago."

Sid looked at the house and then back at me. "Holy shit! Are you thinking this was intentional?"

"Carl never liked coincidences. It's more than a fluke that after an inspection the whole house would go up."

His mouth pressed into a grim line. "If you're right — and I'm not saying you are — tell me what Mrs. Dearborne knew that would make her a threat."

"I think she knew something, but she didn't know she knew it."

"Double talk," said Sid. "I hate it. Be clear."

"In the park, Claire said she wanted

218

Lydia to confirm a piece of information. When I saw Lydia just now her hair was freshly curled. When I was in the beauty shop I smelled fresh perm solution. A permanent takes time to complete. They chatted. Claire maneuvered the conversation and got what she wanted. Lydia didn't have a clue until I asked her some questions. She started thinking, and up came this 'secret,' which she wouldn't share with me."

I thought a moment, then added, "I bet the killer has been waiting for a chance to kill Lydia, but delayed the deed until Lydia's company left."

"Why? If you've killed once and plan on killing again, what's a few more bodies?"

I didn't have an answer. Fifteen minutes later a group of rural volunteer firefighters arrived. Sid jumped out of his car and motioned for me to move on.

"I know where to find you," he said.

I put the SUV into gear and drove back to River City, meeting emergency vehicles on my way. As each one passed, I shook my head and murmured, "Too late. Much too late."

Bailey had been moved out of the Critical Care Unit into a private room, but he hadn't regained consciousness. I'd been told his vital signs were good and the swelling to his brain was going down.

A nurse had patted my hand and said it would only be a matter of time before he opened his eyes. When I pressed her to be more specific, she had smiled and said, "He'll come around when the time is right."

"Time?" I grumbled as I dragged a chair up to Bailey's bedside.

What was time, anyway? We gain time, kill time, do time, are behind the times, or pass the time of day. Old folks look back and say they had the time of their life. Young people want to be ahead of their time. There are instances when we'd like to turn back the hands of time. And sometimes, we're simply out of time.

When Lydia went to Oliver's funeral, she probably thought she had plenty of time left. She'd been scrubbing tree trunks, for God's sake. Surely if she'd known her time was almost up, she would have done something more worthwhile.

I picked up Bailey's hand and tenderly wrapped his fingers around mine. "Open your eyes," I said quietly. "It's time."

No one would've been more surprised than I had Bailey done as I'd directed. But he didn't, and I wasn't. I sat with his hand in mine and talked.

"This really sucks. I can feel your warmth, but you aren't here with me." I leaned closer. "I have a major problem. Well, I guess it isn't really my problem, but Claire did call me. She thought I could help her. I have all these thoughts waltzing around in my head. Help me, Bailey. Help me figure this mess out.

"If I start with the park where I met Claire, then I have to consider Oliver's dying words — 'Bretta — Spade.' I'm not sure if they belong with the rest of the scenario. Oliver had a heart attack. Claire was murdered. Both were in the park. Both knew Lydia Dearborne. Oliver heard Claire say Lydia's name. Before Oliver's heart acted up, I noticed he had his head cocked to one side as if he were concentrating on remembering something. He said, 'So long ago.' He had his spade in his hands. Earlier he'd told me 'whenever I touch this wood, memories of bygone years flash into focus.' "

I rested my cheek against Bailey's hand. "Bygone years. Claire and Lydia talked about neighbors and how times change." I grimaced. "Dana said, 'Time's supposed to blur the memories —' There's that word again. *Time.* My father believes that time heals all wounds. He seriously thought, when he left all those years ago, I'd get over the pain. That I'd simply forget him and go on with my life. I did to a certain extent. I married a man I adored and who adored me. I started and maintained a successful business, but at odd moments I'd think about my father and wonder what he was doing. And more importantly, I wondered if he ever thought of me."

I sighed deeply and sat up. "You're not helping, and I'm getting off track. I wanted to talk to you about this murder case, and here I am going on about my personal life."

I glanced over my shoulder. "Before someone comes in and tells me visiting hours are over, I want you to hear the latest development. Lydia Dearborne's house blew up. It was murder, Bailey. I'm sure of it. When Sid questions the Gas Service Company, he'll find they didn't send an inspector out to Lydia's house.

"Lydia has had someone with her since Claire's murder. She's been on medication, too. This very morning her family leaves, and Lydia feels well enough to go out — out where she could talk. About what, I'm not sure, but our killer feared she had something to say. If I'd stayed another five minutes, I'd have been blown to bits." I shuddered. "I left her house in the nick of time."

I sat quietly, thinking, then said, "Lydia told me it was a woman inspector and that she seemed familiar. Why didn't I ask for a physical description?"

I snorted. "Because at that *time* I didn't know it was important. *Time.* That word sure does crop up — time after time. It's time for me to go. Time for you to wake up."

I stood and leaned over Bailey so I could whisper in his ear. "What's it going to take to bring you back to me? A hug? A kiss? I can supply both, but you have to ask."

I'd have been thrilled with a muscle spasm, but Bailey lay quietly. Tears threatened, but I winked them away, forcing a bright note in my voice. "You think over what I've said. I'll drop by later to hear your theories."

Before I left the hospital, I called the flower shop to check in with Lois. "How's it going?" I asked.

"Manageable. Where are you?"

"At the hospital." Anticipating her next question, I added, "Bailey isn't conscious, but he's improving."

"That's good news. I have three messages for you. One is from DeeDee. She says the cleaning crew is at the house, and they're doing a wonderful job, but your father is wandering around the estate like a lost soul. Eddie called. He and his crew are hauling brush out of the garden." Lois heaved a sigh. "I've saved the worst for last. Evelyn was by."

"Do I want to hear this?"

"Probably not, but *I* had to listen to her. She has too much time on her hands. While looking through some bridal magazines she saw a picture of an arch made of twisted grapevines."

I heard paper rustling. Lois said, "She left the picture with me. If we had another month, we could do it, but we've got four days. I told her no way. She told me to give you the message."

"Message received. Now, forget it. I'm not adding another thing to this wedding. As it is we're going to be hard-pressed to get everything done and delivered and set up. Eddie says it's going to rain."

"It wouldn't dare."

"I'll be at the house if you need me, but don't tell Evelyn. I'm almost out of antacid tablets and patience."

"Speaking of patience. How do you feel about hiring Kayla to do odd jobs here at the flower shop? I can't give her money outright, but I could give it to you, and you could give it to her."

"Sounds complicated. Can we talk about

it after this wedding?"

"Yeah, sure. I want her under my thumb for a while. If this escapade had gone on her permanent record, it could haunt her for the rest of her life."

I shook my head. "It was a turtle, Lois. A year or so down the road, what possible difference could it make?"

"I don't know, but some people could view her as a troublemaker. She trespassed into the principal's office. She had a disregard for someone else's property. If she was up for a job and her prospective boss called the school to ask what kind of student she'd been, would that boss hire her if he or she found out she'd been in trouble?"

"Depends on the trouble. A turtle is pretty tame compared to some of the pranks kids pull."

"I suppose, but she's so young. Here comes a customer. Gotta go."

I hung up the receiver and walked slowly out of the hospital. On automatic pilot, I started the SUV and left the parking lot. Dana had said, "We were so young and full of —"

Full of what? Hopes? Dreams? Plans for the future? Somehow I didn't think she'd been talking about aspirations and goals. When I'd tried bamboozling Sonya about what had happened all those years ago, I'd been left with the impression that I'd touched a nerve.

I drove to River City High School with the idea of probing for that nerve ending. Sid had said Claire didn't have a police record. But there were other paper trails.

My inquiry into obtaining information from the school's permanent records hit a brick wall in the form of a Mrs. Florence Benson, secretary. When I walked up to her desk, she smiled pleasantly. Her hair was gray, eyes blue. She looked like someone's sweet little grandmother, the kind that bakes sugar cookies and never forgets birthdays.

After I'd made my request, she said, "I'm sorry, Ms. Solomon. This isn't a public library. Our records aren't part of a free-reading program. Besides, I'd need maiden names. Do you have those?"

"I can get them."

She glanced at the clock on the wall. "My break is in thirty minutes."

I raced down the hall to the 1966 display. Hunting and mumbling, I searched out Dana, Sonya, Kasey, and Claire's last names. Kasey Vickers had never married, so that was simple enough. Claire had returned to her maiden name, Alexander.

Dana Simpkin Olson. Sonya Darnell Norris.

Huffing and puffing, I arrived back at Miss Benson's desk. I'd used five minutes of my allotted time. "Alexander. Vickers. Simpkin. And Darnell. Now will you help me?"

"Up to a point."

I expected her to click some computer keys on the machine next to her. Instead she got up from her desk and frowned at the clock before disappearing down a back hallway. I waited and waited and waited. Finally, when I'd decided she'd sneaked out a side exit, she came back with a stack of ordinary folders.

She tapped them. "If you'd been looking for students who'd graduated in nineteen sixty-nine, I could have brought the names up on the computer. But since we're talking nineteen sixty-six, I had to find them in the vertical files. What do you want to know? You have twelve minutes."

"I'm not sure. Something they all had in common."

She raised her eyebrows. "Could you be more specific? Same classes? Same bus route? What?"

"Did they get into trouble?"

"Trouble? What kind of trouble?"

"That's what I'm looking for."

She sat down and opened the first folder. Running a finger down the page, she scanned and muttered. I strained my ears but couldn't make out a word. She took another folder off the stack and gave it the same perusal. When she reached for the final report, she slid me a glance, and I knew she'd found something.

I waited as patiently as I could until she'd flipped over the last sheet. I asked, "What did they do?"

"Is this the Claire Alexander who was murdered a few days ago?"

I nodded.

Mrs. Benson pointed to a yellow tab stuck to the folder. "Her file has been flagged, meaning she had trouble while in our River City school system. Claire's career as instigator goes all the way back to kindergarten. From that time, and including eighth grade, her teachers attached personal notes to her record outlining different capers, fights, and disruptive behavior."

"What kind of disruptive behavior?"

"The usual kid stuff. Picking on others. Cutting in line. Chewing gum in class. Arguing with the teacher." Mrs. Benson tapped the folder. "It wasn't until high school that she found her niche."

"And that would be?"

"Agitator. I realize it was the sixties and everyone was protesting everything, but the way her file reads, Claire Alexander jumped on the bandwagon with both feet. She organized boycotts, strikes, and demonstrations about too much homework, bad school lunches, and the right to wear miniskirts. From what I get here, most of her demonstrations were orderly, not violent. Minor annoyances to the administration. Claire and Kasey Vickers are named as the founders of the Botany Club, which is still in existence today. In fact, all four girls were members."

Mrs. Benson scanned Claire's file again. "Claire and her cohorts picked the wrong person to tangle with when they upset Ms. Beecher — God rest her soul. The home ec teacher had taken enough of Claire's foolishness."

Mrs. Benson chuckled. "Kids can find the strangest ways to get into trouble. Claire and her three friends were denied taking part in the photo sessions for the school's yearbook because — here's the corker — they stole four bottles of lemon extract from the home ec kitchen."

That explained the girls' absence from the club pictures. But why would four high school girls want bottles of lemon extract?

Chapter Fifteen

When I pulled up the lane to my house I wasn't sure where to park. Three vans with "River City Cleaning Company" painted on their sides blocked my entry into the garage. Four trucks piled with brush were lined up caravan-style, headed down the drive. My father had apparently been watching for my arrival. He limped out the front door and down the steps, waving me to a space near the veranda.

I nodded and brought the SUV to a stop in the shade. Before I climbed out, my father launched a conversation through the closed window. The only words I caught were "— stay close to home until this maniac is caught."

I opened the door. "Are you talking about me staying close to home?"

"Of course, daughter. Your safety is my concern." He gestured to his dusty clothes and green-stained fingers. "I've spent the day investigating your gardens, searching for plants and flowers that would match those of the tussie-mussie. In your personal library I found a book on the language of flowers. I've got it nailed down."

I assumed he hadn't nailed the book down, so he must be talking about what the tussie-mussie represented. I was skeptical. "You've figured out the message?"

"Damned straight, and it isn't good. Someone is hell-bent on bringing you grief. Come into the dining room; I have it laid out."

He took off for the house. I followed more slowly. Since I had the sketch in my purse, I couldn't quite believe that my father had found each leaf, each blossom, and put it together from memory. But the project had kept him out of trouble. That by itself deserved a few minutes of my attention.

DeeDee met me at the door. Her eyes sparkled with excitement. "The c-cleaning crew is d-doing a great job. The boxes of p-plaster chunks are gone. The d-dust has been s-sucked up. They're f-finishing in the b-ballroom." She leaned closer. "It's g-gonna cost you a f-fortune."

I grimaced. "It's money well spent if the dust is gone." I stood in the foyer and looked around my home. Above me, the crystal prisms on the chandelier sparkled. All the wooden surfaces gleamed from a recent polish. Each riser on the horseshoe-shaped staircase glowed as if lighted from an inner beauty. The air had a clean, lemony fragrance.

I sighed softly. "Money well spent, DeeDee. Tell the foreman to bring me the bill before he leaves, and I'll write out a check."

"He s-said he'd mail you a s-statement."

"Whatever." I nodded to my father, who shuffled his feet impatiently in the dining room doorway. "Have you seen what he's been doing?"

"E-earlier this morning, we m-moved his s-stuff into a bedroom. While I made his b-bed, he took a walk around the es-estate. When I b-brought him lunch, he was m-messing with a b-bunch of weeds on the d-dining room t-table."

"Weeds." I shook my head. "That's what I'm afraid of, but I'll still have to be appreciative."

"And nice, Bretta," she added softly. "You're always p-patient with me. Give h-him the s-same respect. He is your f-father."

I winked. "My, aren't you the little pacifist? Make love, not war. Next thing I know you'll be wearing flowers in your hair reminiscent of the sixties."

"Flower power. I've heard about that."

She giggled and raised her hands above her head. "Flowers sticking out to h-here. I'd l-look like a b-blooming idiot."

"Or the painting on Claire's ceiling," I said.

A buzzer went off in the kitchen. "Gotta go," DeeDee said. "Th-that's my timer."

Flower power. Someone in history had once said, "Knowledge is power." While in high school, Claire had organized strikes, boycotts, and demonstrations. All represented acts of power. She'd told Lydia that by painting Missouri wildflowers on the ceiling of her beauty shop she might be able to achieve "a total sense of catharsis."

Wouldn't that be power, too? A power over what had been troubling her? She'd dyed her hair green — which, according to Dana, meant Claire was bothered by something.

"Bretta," called my father. "Please come into the dining room. I want to show you what I've discovered."

I moseyed across the foyer, my mind trekking on Claire. Lydia had said she hadn't registered for the prize she'd won from Claire's shop. Had Claire made up the contest so she could meet the woman? Why? What had Lydia known?

My father gestured to the dining room

table. I dropped my gaze but didn't focus on the items. Going back to this catharsis business. If Claire needed catharsis she was looking to be purified — which translated to me that *she'd* done something wrong. But if she were the culprit, then why had she been killed?

"Don't you see it?" demanded my father.

I squeezed my eyes shut. "I'm trying."

When I'd been in Dana's kitchen, she'd said that Claire had "this natural radar when it came to wickedness." Whatever had happened had been in the past. Kasey, Dana, and Sonya had been Claire's friends in high school. If something were about to come out, would one of them try to stop Claire from telling it? The girls had gotten into trouble for stealing four bottles of lemon extract. So many years later, why would it matter?

"If you're not interested, just say so," said my father in a disappointed tone.

Reluctantly, I abandoned my thoughts and stared at my father's labors. As I took in the assembled tussie-mussie, I gasped. "Where did you get this? Is it the one that was in my car?"

"Nope. Made this one myself. Do you still have my sketch?"

I pulled the paper from my purse and

laid it on the table next to the small bouquet of leaves and flowers. My gaze Ping-Ponged back and forth. "Damn," I said. "This is excellent." I bent and sniffed. "It even smells the same as the interior of my car."

"I worked my way through your garden using my nose and my eyes." He touched some dark green fernlike leaves. "This is tansy."

"What does it mean?"

"Before I get to that, let me say I had a heck of a time finding a source for negative meanings. Like you said, flowers are supposed to convey a message of happiness, flirtation, and love. This bouquet is a deadly warning, daughter. The tansy is an herb and was put in coffins in ancient times because of its strong odor and its use as an insect repellent. If the leaves are crushed, they release a scent that reminds me of pine. According to the book I used, the tansy means 'I declare against you.' "

"I'm not surprised. I told you in the alley that the tussie-mussie hadn't come from an admirer. I knew that as soon as I saw the dried white rose."

Dad touched leaves that were elliptical with slightly toothed edges. "This is pennyroyal. It's part of the mint family and was also used as an insect repellent. It means 'You had better go.' "

I touched a leaf that had a patent leather feel to it. "This looks familiar. It isn't an herb."

"No. It's from a rhododendron bush. It means, 'Danger. Beware. I am dangerous. Agitation.' "

"There's evidence of that. This other is a milkweed flower. What does it mean?"

"Let's skip that for the moment. I want you to notice that the bundle is tied together with a vine, not twine as you first thought."

I leaned closer and saw a bright orange cord about the size of a stout thread with hairlike tendrils. "What is that?"

"I had to ask Eddie. I described what I'd seen by flashlight." He pointed to his sketch. "I put those little hairs on my drawing because I'd noticed them, but I didn't know what I was seeing. Eddie told me the plant is dodder. He'd seen it attached to some weeds at the back of your property. I went hunting and was amazed at how it grows. It's a member of the morning glory family. It doesn't have leaves, roots, or chlorophyll, but has these special suckers that draw nourishment from its host. 'Meanness' is what the book tells me it represents."

"And now the milkweed?"

My father scratched his head. "That's the odd part. I've spent the last hour thinking and thinking, but I can't figure out how it fits into the rest of the message."

"What is it?"

"Milkweed means 'hope in misery.' " He motioned to the tussie-mussie. "After all the threats — death, danger, beware, meanness, I declare against you — this seems out of place. If you remember, the milkweed flower was right on top, above the dried white rose. As you said, placement is as important as the plants. So if that's the case, it's almost as if the giver was saying the milkweed flower negates the rest. 'Hope in misery,' " repeated my father. "If he's miserable, then why continue?"

Slowly, I answered, "Because *she* has hope that her plan will succeed. Perhaps she is suffering but has an urgent need to finish what she started." I closed my eyes and whispered, "A type of catharsis — a purging of the soul."

My brain was overworked. I needed fresh air. I went out the terrace doors to have a look at the garden. A smile of appreciation came easily to my lips. Having those old decayed trees gone had made a huge difference in the landscape. Eddie had made a wonderful start on the renovation, and I moved in his direction to tell him. He was alone, a notebook in his hands and a faraway gleam in his eyes.

I recognized that look. He was plotting my garden, letting his imagination soar over the mundane details. If he concentrated only on the necessary work, what was needed to complete the project, he'd get bogged down. But to stand back and visualize the final results brought a fresh vigor and anticipation to the job.

Eddie had buried his father that morning. He needed this time alone. I quietly went back into the house. I told DeeDee I was leaving for a couple of hours. I wanted to check on Bailey, but I also wanted to go to the park. Eddie's big job was my garden. My big job was the Montgomery wedding. Maybe if I went back to the park I could recapture the enthusiasm I'd first felt when Evelyn had outlined her plans.

As I drove into town, I made a conscious effort to put Claire's and Lydia's deaths out of my mind. I lowered the windows and turned up the radio just as a meteorologist gave his weather report: "The Ozarks are ten inches short on rainfall for the month of June. And folks, it looks like we're going to miss a good shot at precipitation for the weekend. Highs will be in the eighties, with lows overnight in the sixties. If you have plans to go out on our many lakes and streams, take plenty of sunblock."

"Sorry, Eddie," I said with a smile. "No rain on Evelyn's parade."

I pushed buttons until I found a song I liked, then settled back. I didn't know Nikki, but she was a woman in love, about to marry the man of her dreams. The shipment of flowers had arrived in excellent condition. The weather was cooperating. I could count on Lois and Lew for assistance. My heart gave a little skip of confidence. I had the ability to bring my part of this wedding off with panache.

Twenty minutes later, I strolled down the path the bride would take. Seeing the shrubs Eddie had planted reminded me that I had to order several cases of gold paint so I could spray the foliage. Just the thought of doing this ridiculous chore made my blood pressure skyrocket again.

Quickly I dismissed the foliage from my

mind and let the serenity of the park soothe me. After a few minutes the colorful mental pictures that frolicked in my head reaffirmed my conviction. I would do my best to make this a gorgeous wedding. My mood had mellowed, so I even felt a bit more benevolent toward Evelyn. After all, she was the mother of the bride, and she obviously loved her daughter.

I stopped in the area where the guests would be seated, and squinted at the gazebo. I'd learned early on in my career that for an event to be impressive, the senses — taste, sight, smell, hearing, touch — had to be titillated. The brass and copper baskets would catch the last rays of sun. Five hundred flickering candles would add to the ambience. I didn't like the idea that my fragrant flowers would have to compete with Dana frying shrimp, but the food-preparation tent was some distance away from the main festivities.

I pondered each point of the wedding. Taste, sight, and smell would be well covered. Evelyn had hired a woman to play the harp. The lilting music would calm any frayed nerves. I frowned. Touch was the one impression left undefined.

"What can we do for touch?" I murmured, walking toward the gazebo. Then I spotted an unlikely vision. I hadn't seen Evelyn crouched on the steps. She hadn't heard me because she was crying. The sight of this arrogant, self-possessed woman weeping was disconcerting.

"Evelyn?" I said. "What's wrong?"

She jerked upright and dashed a hand across her eyes. "I'm a mess. I never thought anyone would be here this time of evening."

"I was thinking about the wedding and wanted to have another look."

"Me, too, but I let my guard down."

"Nikki is okay?"

"Oh, yes. She's fine. As far as I know, everything is falling into place. I should be happy, but what will I do when Saturday is over? I've dedicated so much effort to planning and anticipating this day that once the candles are lit, it's the beginning of the end."

I leaned against the railing. "I know what you mean. There's a letdown after you've come through a big event. You want to relax, but you're still pumped, and there's nothing left to do." I paused. "Maybe it will help if you keep in mind that once our duties are over, your daughter will be starting a new life as a married woman."

Evelyn sighed. "I lose sight of that sometimes. I keep thinking of what I need to do
to make it perfect for her."

"It will be perfect."

Briskly, Evelyn stood up. She smoothed
her dress and tucked a stray black curl behind her ear. "Now, about that grapevine
arch. I hope you've had the chance to
study the picture I left with your employee.
I think we should —"

My earlier feelings of benevolence for
Evelyn dissolved into a mist. Nothing had
changed. She was still as irritating as bird
droppings on a freshly washed car.

Chapter Sixteen

The coroner released Claire's body the next morning. By ten thirty, Harriet Mitchell was at my front counter, placing an order for a spray of flowers to grace her ex-daughter-in-law's casket.

"Claire had no family," explained Harriet. "Her mother died when she was a baby. Her father drank himself to death a few years ago. Claire was always kind and thoughtful to me. Giving her a decent burial seems the right thing to do. My son is throwing a fit, but that's his problem."

"Why should he care?"

"Money. I have a little nest egg set aside. He has his eyes on it. Claire's funeral expenses will deplete the balance by several thousand dollars."

"It's very generous of you. I've gotten the impression, from things people have said, that Claire admired you. She quoted you often."

Harriet blinked. "Quoted me? Whatever did I say that was noteworthy?"

"Maybe not you per se, but Aristotle."

"Oh, yes. I tried to help her. She had a burden on her heart. She wouldn't talk about it in specific terms, but occasionally she tossed out odd comments. Her most recent observation has stuck in my mind, given the way she died. Claire admitted she didn't think there's a God because He allows evil in our world."

"In my line of work, I deal with bereavement on a daily basis. Nothing is more heart wrenching than to help a family choose a suitable memorial for a child who's been killed or a young mother who has died from cancer. Evil people continue to live and wreak havoc on others, and yet the good die young."

Harriet's eyes sparkled. I could see the Scout leader in her emerge before she opened her mouth. "Aristotle believed that reason is the source of knowledge. Each time we see or hear of evil, we use our ability to reason, to use logic to evaluate the situation. If this world were perfect, if everyone lived long, wonderfully productive lives, then where's the challenge? By allowing us to see others make mistakes, God has given us the chance to learn and grow. As each generation comes along, the lessons learned by the previous generation are passed on."

"But what can we learn from the death of a child?"

"Each tragic event in our life makes us stronger. Are you familiar with the word *heterosis?*"

I shook my head.

"It's a phenomenon resulting from hybridization in which offspring display greater vigor, size, resistance, and other characteristics than the parents. A properly developed hybrid will have any weaknesses bred out and optimum values enhanced."

"I get the gist of what you're saying, but where does Claire's death fit in? What have we learned from her murder?"

Impatience threaded Harriet's voice. "You're expecting a revelation from one circumstance. You have to view Claire's death from a general outlook. How her life touched others. How her death affected those around her. How she lived. Where she lived. What she did."

"And this will give me insight into God's plan?"

Harriet laughed. "Not at all, but it will make you question. We can't begin to understand the why, but to grow intellectually we have to question, to reason, and to think logically. Events from our past shape the people we are today. If Claire had been raised with a functional mother and father, would she be dead today at age fifty-four? Is this cause and effect? When her parents passed away was Claire's fate sealed?"

My brain was spinning. "It's too early in the morning for this conversation. I'm out of my depth."

"Not at all. You have a logical mind, and being a florist augments your capabilities to reason through a situation."

"I don't understand." •

"It's another of Aristotle's theories. He defines the imagination as 'the movement which results upon an actual sensation.' As a florist, you're attuned to receiving sense impressions. You see details that others might overlook or ignore. You listen carefully to what is needed and use your talents to deliver."

Last night while in the park, I'd had these thoughts about the senses, but had been stymied by one. Curious, I asked, "How does touch come into play with respect to my being a florist?"

"I'm sure you've physically comforted someone by giving them a hug. However, to advance my theory, I'd substitute feel for touch. You *feel* the pain of others. You *feel* the need to be involved."

She cast me a smile. "You also have good

taste. Claire liked bright colors. I'll leave the choice of flowers to your discretion. Send me the bill." She turned and walked away.

"Wait," I called. "There are five senses. You left out smell. Is it obvious?" I waved my hand to our surroundings. "Flowers have a scent?"

Harriet cocked her head and studied me. "And good cigars have an aroma. Skunks have an odor. All can be smelled, but a sensory perceptive person will categorize rather than make a blanket analogy."

I watched Harriet leave the shop. My forehead puckered with thought. I fingered the lines, smoothed away the ridges, but my mind rippled, stirred by Harriet's theories.

I was especially struck by the phrase "cause and effect." I squeezed my eyes shut so I could recall her exact comment: "Events of our past shape the people we are today."

If my father had stayed home, would I have turned out differently? I credited my mother and Carl as having the biggest influence on me. My father's absence had shaped my life, too. But which had the most effect on me? His leaving or his staying away? I had no way of knowing for sure, even though his abrupt departure had been as traumatic as a death. But even death doesn't end a relationship. Memories, often scarred and battered from constant use, plague the mind and the heart.

I opened my eyes. The first thing my gaze landed on was the plant display by the front window. A dracaena had missed getting a drink of water. The leaves were limp, the plant wilted. From experience I knew once it received moisture it would revive, but there was a good chance the leaves would develop brown tips. I could trim away the damage, but the plant would never be the same. Cause and effect.

"That was quite a conversation," said Lois.

I grimaced. "The one in my head or the one with Harriet?"

"Both. The way your mind works has always been a mystery to me." She nodded to the door. "I had a hard time following what she said. I liked the part about a florist using her senses, but she lost me on the scent, aroma, and odor thing. What did she mean about 'blanket analogy'?"

I glanced at Lew to see if he was going to jump in with a lengthy explanation. He widened his eyes at me in a fake innocent stare. Well, fine. I'd give this philosophy a shot. If I got it wrong, I was sure he'd bull-doze in to correct me.

"Okay. Here goes," I said. "Scent, aroma, and odor are categories of smell. Most people only smell." I giggled. "You know what I mean — use their noses. They don't consciously apply the correct word. Harriet says that as florists we classify things more specifically."

I thought for a moment. "She's right, you know. Take, for instance, how we distinguish color. To some, brown is simply an earth tone. As florists we categorize by fine-tuning — cocoa, toast, toffee, and fudge. When I named each one, didn't you have clear mental pictures of each color?"

Lois nodded. "I get it, but it sounds to me like you need a snack."

I waved away her suggestion as excitement throbbed through my veins. It was as if I'd exchanged a low-watt bulb for a brighter one. It's funny how an image or an idea changed when a speck of knowledge or a new perspective came into play.

"Claire was an artist as well as a beautician. She was creative. She painted that mural on the ceiling of her shop and called it a way of achieving 'a total sense of ca-tharsis.' Doing the work might've been re-warding, but I'd lay you odds it was the picture that was important and suited her purpose."

"And that would be?" asked Lew.

"She used Missouri wildflowers for the hair. The girl looks sweet, innocent. Her eyes are closed as if she's sleeping. But I can't figure out where the tragedy fits in." My mouth dropped open. "Oh, my gosh. She's not asleep. She's dead."

Lois gasped. "Claire painted a dead girl on her ceiling? That's morbid."

"Not that kind of dead. She looks angelic." I bit my lip. "I have to see that painting again."

"How?" asked Lois. "According to the story in the newspaper, Claire didn't have a partner or any family. The shop will be locked up. It's a crime scene." Her eyes narrowed. "You aren't thinking about breaking in?"

"Of course not." I fluttered my eyelashes. "I have more *sense* than that. If I was in jail, you and Lew would have to do this wedding by yourselves."

"God forbid." Lois sighed. "I suppose we could do it, but I'd probably end up your cellmate. I'd kill the woman."

"Evelyn isn't so bad," said Lew. "I feel sorry for her."

"Why is that?" demanded Lois.

He lifted a shoulder. "We've had extra people help at holidays, and they make mistakes. Evelyn walked in the door, watched me take an order, and took five more without a problem. She thrives on challenge. Once this wedding is over, I think the woman will fall apart."

I nodded. "She said as much to me last night when I saw her in the park. In fact, she was crying."

"That's just great," said Lois. "When a woman cries, that means someone's gonna pay. You just wait. It'll be us. Before this day is over, Evelyn will be in here wanting to add something totally off the wall to this wedding."

I went to the phone. "That's an excellent reason for making myself scarce. I talked her out of the grapevine arch. But if she has another brain cramp, tell her she'll have to discuss anything new with me."

"Are you calling Sid?" asked Lois.

"No way. I don't want him glaring at me while I study that painting. Besides, he's county. I'm calling River City's police chief, Jean Kelley. She'll be a bit more tolerant." I crossed my fingers. "At least, I hope she will."

Once Chief Kelley was on the line, I said, "This is Bretta Solomon. Would it be possible for you to meet me at Claire Alexander's beauty shop?"

"What for?"

"I want another look at that painting on the ceiling. I've had a couple of thoughts."

"And they would be?"

Her indifference gave me an inkling as to how the conversation I hoped to initiate would be received. She might not be as blunt with her contempt as Sid, but I doubted she would be enthusiastic at the idea of exploring Claire's sensory perception.

Beating around the bush, I asked, "Could this wait until I've had another look at the painting?"

Reluctantly, Chief Kelley agreed, and we settled on a time. After I'd hung up, I dialed another number. When Eddie answered, I said, "This is Bretta. Can you meet me in half an hour at 3201 Marietta Avenue? I need your expertise in identifying some Missouri wildflowers."

"Guess I can. That's down in the old part of town. I don't remember any garden plots."

"This is a painting."

"Hell's bells. I don't know nothing about art."

"But you know flowers, and that's what I need."

Eddie grumbled and groused. I cajoled and cajoled until he finally agreed to meet me. I hung up the phone and said, "Boy, the things you've got to say and do to get a little cooperation really bite."

Lois pointed to the front of the shop. "I see a familiar white BMW pulling into a parking spot." She huffed on her fingernails and polished them on her shirt. "Golly, I'm good." She leaned across the counter, peering intently. "Oh, hell. Evelyn is carrying another magazine."

I sprinted for the back door.

Chapter Seventeen

"This better have some bearing on the case, Bretta," said Chief Kelley, getting out of her car. She crossed the sidewalk to the door of the beauty shop. "I've got a pile of paperwork that needs my attention."

"I think the painting is important, I'm just not sure how."

"Well, that's encouraging," she said, inserting a key in the lock. She turned the knob. "I'd hate to think you had all the answers."

"Not even close." At her hard look, I added, "But I've got a couple of theories, if you'll be patient."

She pushed open the door and motioned me in. "Not one of my virtues, but I'll walk the walk." Looking past me to the street, she said, "I see a man headed this way. From the expression on his face, I'd say he's as happy to be here as I am. Who is he? What's going on?"

I made the introductions, then asked, "Can Eddie come in with us? He's here to identify the flowers in the painting."

Chief Kelley agreed. We moved into the

shop and stood under the painting, studying the artwork in silence. The picture was as colorful and distinctive as I'd remembered. When I'd first seen it, I'd concentrated on the flowers. Today that was Eddie's department. This time I focused on the girl. As I stared at her I kept thinking she looked familiar, but was it merely a scrap of leftover memory from when I'd first set eyes on the painting?

The face was a smooth, unblemished oval. Thick, dark lashes fringed her closed eyelids. Her lips were slightly parted, as if she were about to speak. Tiny hands were folded in prayer; the tips of her fingers rested against her chin. She appeared to be wearing a robe. Soft brush strokes had created the effect of draped material that flowed gracefully.

What made me think that Claire had depicted her as being deceased was the strange aura that surrounded the portrait. I'd seen the same dramatization used when the subject had a religious theme.

Chief Kelley said, "What's the deal with the radiating light? Is she supposed to be an angel?"

"A girl who has passed away."

"Who was she?"

"Lydia Dearborne knew but wouldn't

tell me. I have a feeling her identity is important." I turned to Eddie. "Do you know who she was?"

"No, but then I probably wouldn't recognize my own mother if her face was two feet wide, painted on a ceiling, and had flowers sprouting out of her head."

"Okay. How about the flowers? Do you know their names?"

"Sure. You would too, if you took a book and drove down a country road." He pointed. "That pink daisy is echinacea — coneflower. Pink evening primrose is curled around her ear. That huge bloom is from the rose mallow family. Elderberry is the cluster of white. Orange butterfly weed. Goldenrod, purple asters, and over to that side are ironweed and milkweed."

"Milkweed?" I murmured. "Hope in misery."

"How's that?" asked Chief Kelley.

"Just thinking out loud." I pointed to the one blossom Eddie hadn't mentioned. It stood above the others as if Claire had given it preferential treatment. The cluster consisted of eight flowers and was yellow-green, tinged with purple. The individual flowers had five tubular hood-shaped structures with a slender horn extending from each.

"What's the name of the yellow-green flower up at the top?"

"I'm not sure. I'm thinking it's in the milkweed family because of the shape of the leaves and blossoms, but the color is off. I've never seen anything like it around here."

Chief Kelley was losing interest. "Maybe Claire got a wild hair to be inventive."

Eddie said, "Why would she do that? All the other flowers have been painted accurately, complete with stamens, pistils, and sepals. I have a book in the truck that was Dad's. I'm gonna get it."

Uneasily, I watched Eddie leave. With just the chief and me in the shop, I knew what was coming. I felt her gaze and tried to ignore it, but she wasn't having that.

"All right, Bretta. What is it about this painting that made you ask me down here? Something has put the wind in your sails. Give it over." She flashed me a wicked smile. "Or would you rather tell Sid?"

That was a threat if ever I heard one, but I wasn't alarmed. Fact was, now that I'd seen the painting, I wondered if Sid might've been the better choice over Chief Kelley. Sid had known about catharsis, but the chief had accommodated me by letting me into the beauty shop. I owed her an explanation. Whether she understood or believed me was up to her.

I gave it a shot. "Claire painted this picture because it represented a tragedy. By giving form to whatever was bothering her, she hoped to be purged — a catharsis."

Chief Kelley glanced at the ceiling. "You're saying that girl died tragically."

"That's my guess."

"So we need to match her picture to some fatal event that happened — how long ago?"

"I think you'll need to look back to nineteen sixty-six."

"Nineteen sixty-six? You've lost me. If Claire needed to be purged, why'd she wait so long?"

"The painting is new, but Claire's needs weren't. From all accounts, she spent her entire life looking for acceptance. She tried finding it with men, but had five failed marriages. She donated her talents as a beautician to help others, but that probably wasn't enough. In her younger days, Claire changed her hairstyle if she wanted to make a point. Dyeing her hair outrageous colors and using those weird contacts were ways of disguising her appearance."

The chief perked up. "She's been hiding

out from someone?"

Slowly, I nodded. "Yes, but not the way you're thinking. She's been hiding from herself. Something traumatic was bugging her. When she looked in the mirror she saw the person she had been, so she invented a new image."

"I don't understand how dyeing her hair green would make her feel any different, but I'll give it thought. Let's skip on to the flowers coming out of the girl's head. What does that mean? If she died tragically, did she eat something poisonous?"

"I suppose that's possible, but you're being objective, thinking only about what you're seeing — the flowers. Try being subjective — look beyond the painting to Claire's thoughts and feelings. The flowers are important. I'm just not sure why. Claire put this girl's image on the ceiling because Claire regarded her as the heart of the problem. Up there, in plain sight, she was a daily reminder."

"Of what? Guilt?"

Eddie banged the door shut. "I've got it, Bretta. And I was right. It is in the milkweed family." He put the open book under my nose. "See? *Asclepias meadii*. Mead's milkweed. According to this, the plant is listed as endangered by the Missouri Department of Conservation and is classified as threatened by the U.S. Fish and Wildlife Service."

"Really?" I looked from the picture in the book to the painting on the ceiling. It was an excellent rendition. "Why is it endangered?"

"This article doesn't say, but the Mead's milkweed's natural habitat is grassy prairie. From that I would guess agriculture and residential development have eliminated it. You know how it goes. Heavy machinery comes in and plows up native ground. Plants are destroyed. Once concrete is poured any roots or seeds that escaped the excavation are history — and, on that note, so am I. I have to get to work."

Once Eddie had left, Chief Kelley turned to me. "What does this extinct milkweed have to do with your theory?"

"It fits, but I'm not sure where. Someone said something to me about extinct, but I can't remember who or the context of the conversation."

"Well, if you remember, give me a call. In the meantime, I'm sending a photographer over to get a shot of this painting."

"What for?"

"I don't have time to search back to nineteen sixty-six for a might-have-been tragedy. I'll cut to the chase and run the picture in the newspaper. If that girl is local, someone might recognize her if the painting is accurate. It'll be like a composite drawing. Something about the girl might give us a lead." The chief motioned toward the door. "Let's go," she said. "I have work to do, too."

I gazed up at the painting. If Chief Kelley followed through with her plan, River City residents would soon stare into that angelic face. It didn't seem right for her to be on public display. And yet, here she was on the ceiling of a beauty shop. But only Claire's clientele had seen her. Once her picture was printed in the newspaper, she'd be fair game for any and all observations.

Half an hour later, I was seated at Bailey's bedside, trying to explain what was bothering me. "It's just a painting," I said, picking up his hand. "But something about it has caught my heart. She looks so defenseless. I feel as if I should protect, not exploit, her, but that's exactly what will happen. Once her photo hits the paper, there will be speculation. If she's recognized, her whole life will be opened up. I hope her memory can take the scrutiny."

Massaging each of his fingers, I said, "I've never told anyone this, but after Carl died, I'd hear his voice in my head." My cheeks felt hot. "Don't think I've lost my mind. Carl and I were close. When he was alive, I knew what he was going to say before he said it."

My throat tightened so I could barely speak. "Once he was gone, I was lonely. It was as if a part of me had died, too. Most of the time I went about my life as usual, but other times, especially if I was alone, I'd lose it."

A tear rolled down my cheek. In order to wipe it away, I tried to pull my hand out of Bailey's, but his grasp was tight. I leaned closer. "You can hear me, can't you?"

His fingers tightened around my hand.

"Are you playing possum so you can be privy to all my tawdry secrets?"

No answering pressure.

I chuckled. "Ah. You already know them, right?"

His fingers moved.

I should have hunted up a nurse or a doctor, but for a moment I wanted to keep Bailey's improvement to myself. "I wish you could talk to me. In the last two years when I needed insight into a problem, Carl would speak to me, but I haven't heard his voice for weeks."

I sat up straight. "I haven't heard Carl's voice since I met you in Branson. Do you think there's a connection?"

His fingers moved against mine.

"Oh, Bailey." I moaned quietly as it registered how deeply I cared for him. "I think I'm falling in love with you. I love the way you hold me. The way you touch me. The way you kiss me. But I loved my husband. Can you love two people at the same time?"

His fingers moved.

"What's wrong with me? It's only been two years since Carl's death. That doesn't seem like enough of a trade-off for twenty-four years of marriage. Shouldn't I still be grieving?"

I tugged my hand out of his and stumbled to my feet. "I have to go."

I left the hospital in a rush, hoping to leave my confusing thoughts behind. But they hung around like an unwanted guest, invading my space. I was amazed at how easily I'd fallen in love with Bailey. We'd had a few conversations. We'd shared a kiss, a touch.

"How could I substitute Bailey for Carl?" I asked aloud.

"Babe, he's there. I'm not."

The unexpected sound of Carl's voice made me jump. I jerked the steering wheel and ran off the pavement. Horns blared. I quickly gained control. "Carl?" I whispered. "I'm scared."

"No wonder. Driving like that would terrify anyone."

"Don't be silly. This is serious."

"What you feel for Bailey doesn't take away from your love for me. I might be gone, but I'm not forgotten. I'll always be in your heart, Babe."

Perhaps it was my imagination, but instant warmth enveloped me. It was as if I'd been gathered close by a pair of loving arms and given a hug.

I wiped the tears from my eyes. "Stay with me, Carl," I said quietly. "I'm going detecting, but my questioning technique needs work. I've had good results in the past, but this time everything I do seems purely amateur. I'm not getting much when it comes to hard facts."

"I don't believe that. I trained you. You just aren't putting everything you know in the right order. Think it through, Babe."

I turned into the high school parking lot. "I'll do that later. Right now I want to talk to the botany teacher. Maybe he or she can fill me in on the extinction of the

Mead's milkweed plant."

"And if you're lucky the teacher will be a fossil who'll remember Claire and her cohorts from their younger days."

"That would be too much to hope for, Carl," I said as I walked through the school's front door. And it was.

Miles Stanford was seated at his desk when I knocked on his classroom door. He motioned for me to come in. In the first few minutes of our conversation I learned this past year had been his virgin voyage into academic employment. He was fresh-faced and self-conscious of a huge pimple on his chin. He kept a hand over it as we made polite chitchat.

I'd only given him my name, so maybe he mistook me for an interested parent. With an enthusiasm that exhausted me, he outlined his plans for the upcoming school year.

"As I teach my students about plants, their structure, growth, and classification, I'm learning right alongside them. Not the botanical information, but how to get under their skins." He rubbed the pimple and winced. "Each class, each student, is a personal challenge. I spent too much time this year on botanical names. I won't do that next year."

He used his free hand to flip a stack of papers. "I have here a syllabus that will interest even the most unresponsive kid. I want to raise moral consciousness about the world around us. If I have my way, no one will leave my room without having gained something that will make this planet a better place to live."

Was I supposed to applaud? I was tempted. It sounded like a portion of a speech he might have delivered — or was he practicing on me?

I smiled politely. "The reason I'm here is to get information on an extinct plant. The Mead's milkweed."

"Really? That's interesting. It's been on the endangered list for years. Is this the local club's new project?"

"What local club?"

"The Missouri Save the Wildflowers Association. You need to speak with Kasey Vickers. She's the chapter's president."

"I know Kasey. I might give her a call, but since I'm here, do you mind telling me about the plant?"

"There's nothing particularly impressive about it. It flourished in most of Missouri, but erosion, herbicides, and overgrazing threatened its existence. Baling hay in September would've allowed the Mead's milkweed time to disperse its seeds. Manipulating the land could've saved the species, but then human intervention was originally the plant's downfall."

"Is it valuable?"

"Only from an ecological point of view."

"Did it grow around here?"

"Yes. Mead's milkweed is native to dry prairies and igneous glades of the Ozarks."

"Igneous?"

"Formed by volcanic action." He grinned. "I don't suppose you want a lesson in geology, so suffice it to say that from the molten slag, rocks solidified and over time were covered with a thin topsoil. Mead's milkweed found a home. Here, let me show you."

He walked to a laminated map of Spencer County that hung on the wall. "See this area?" He pointed to the southwest corner of the map. "If your group is planning a field trip, I'd start here. The rock formations and the open prairie are prime locations. I doubt that you'll find the plant, though stranger things have happened."

I leaned closer, squinting at the tiny printing. My heart thudded with excitement. The tract of land he indicated was east of Lydia's house on Catalpa Road.

Stranger things, indeed.

Chapter Eighteen

I wanted to zip on out to Catalpa Road and do some looking around, but I wasn't dressed for hiking through igneous glades and grassy prairies. I went home to change out of a dress and hose.

There was no sign of my father, but DeeDee was in the kitchen. The food channel blared from the television in the corner of the room. Lined up on the table were bottles of rum, whiskey, and vodka.

"Hey-ho," I said, eyeing the liquor. "What have we here? A party for one?"

DeeDee whirled around. "I-I didn't h-hear you come in."

I adjusted the sound on the TV. "I'm not surprised. What are you doing?"

She nodded to the television. "Earlier this m-morning th-there was this program about f-flaming f-foods. It was f-fantastic." She moved away from the counter, and I saw three saucers. Each contained six sugar cubes piled in neat triangles. "I t-tried wine, but the f-flame wasn't b-blue. I went to the l-liquor s-store and bought a variety so I c-can experiment."

"I hope your mother doesn't hear about your purchase. She'll have your suitcase packed before we can say Harvey Wall-banger."

"Who is h-he?"

"It's the name of a very potent drink." I walked to the counter. "What are you flaming besides sugar cubes?"

She took a deep breath and spoke slowly. "I'm checking to s-see which liquor works best. A b-blue flame is the most elegant when making a presentation. I can add the liquor to b-bananas, grapefruit, anything I want."

I made a face. "Roasted grapefruit. That sounds divine."

DeeDee giggled. "I've got more imagination than that. I'm d-doing Cherries Flambé served over low-fat vanilla ice cream. I f-found some s-silver goblets in the attic. At our n-next d-dinner party, I'll lower the l-lights and —" She flung out her hands. "Ta da. You'll be impressed at the s-sight."

I touched her shoulder. "I'm already impressed that you drove your car to the liquor store and bought the stuff. How did that go?"

"Great. I p-picked out what I w-wanted

and took the bottles to the cashier. She asked to s-see my ID."

I laughed. "Cool. That hasn't happened to me in years."

"Do you have t-time to watch me compare which liquor p-produces the p-prettiest f-flame?"

"No. I'll leave you alone. Just don't hurt yourself or set fire to the kitchen."

DeeDee pointed to a small fire extinguisher. "I w-went to the hardware s-store, too. Martha says to be p-prepared."

Martha Stewart. I rolled my eyes. At the flower shop, customers were always quoting her. I was tired of hearing the name, but DeeDee was one of Martha's faithful followers. I kept my comment to myself, but DeeDee saw my expression.

"Sh-she has great ideas. Tomorrow she's g-going to show how to s-sculpt a block of ice into a bear using a piece of nylon fishing line and a chain saw."

Chain saw? Yikes!

I quickly left the kitchen and went upstairs to change clothes. I was proud of DeeDee. A few weeks ago I couldn't get her out of the house. Now she was going to a liquor store and buying booze.

I grimaced. Not exactly what I might have wanted, but at least she was showing a degree of independence. I couldn't fault that. Maybe I should look into enrolling her in a gourmet cooking class. It would broaden her horizon beyond the television, and she'd have a chance to meet people who shared her interest.

Dressed in blue jeans, a T-shirt, and sneakers, I went downstairs and peeked into the kitchen. DeeDee was carefully spooning rum over a pile of sugar cubes. The fire extinguisher was close at hand, but so was a box of wooden matches. I cringed, but didn't say anything. She wasn't a child, but she was a bit naive. Could I walk out the door and leave her alone? If she was to gain maturity I had to hope for the best and let her learn.

I started to step away, but she reached for the matches. I had to know that she was all right. I waited. She struck the match and applied the flame to the mound of sugar. I heard a soft *poof,* and the cubes burned blue.

"Hot damn," said DeeDee, her stutter gone. "I did it." She turned, caught sight of me, and grinned. "I'm fine, Bretta. Watch this." She picked up an aluminum lid and put it over the saucer, smothering the flames. "See? I'm prepared."

★ ★ ★

I drove into River City, stopping in at the flower shop to see if I was needed. I found my father seated on a stool. He was entertaining Lew and Lois with a story from my childhood. All were enthralled, and my entrance from the alley went unnoticed. I stood in the doorway and listened to my father.

"— made Bretta crazy because that mother cat had hidden her kittens. Bretta was about five, maybe six, and I'd told her she couldn't go up in the hayloft, but that didn't stop her. As soon as my back was turned, she was up that ladder, poking among the hay bales. If I'd told her an old black snake made his home up there, she'd never have gone."

"Bretta doesn't have a high regard for snakes," said Lew.

Lois chimed in. "She had a narrow escape with one not long ago."

My father nodded. "I read about it in the paper. Anyway, she climbed up there looking for those kittens."

I knew what was coming, and so did the others. I shivered as I remembered the sly rustle of movement over the hay. I had leaned down, expecting to see bundles of silky fur. Instead, I'd come nose-to-nose with that old snake.

"— screamed like a pig stuck in a fence," continued my father. "I don't think her feet touched a single rung of the ladder as she came down. She tore past me, slipped in a pile of manure, and landed flat on her back." He shook his head. "Lord, but she was a smelly mess. She was crying and reeking when I took her to the house to get cleaned up."

I waited for him to finish the story, but he stopped and Lew swung into a remembrance from his life. I stared at my father's profile. That moment when I'd entered the house, all those years ago, was as vivid as if it had happened only yesterday.

My mother was at the sink. I'm sure she heard my bawling before she saw me. Perhaps it was fear that I'd been mortally wounded that prompted her to place the blame for what had happened on my father. Her verbal rebuke had been delivered in a soft tone, but as I recalled her words, I flinched.

"Alfred, your carelessness will be the death of our daughter."

My father hadn't replied. He'd hunched his shoulders and walked quietly from the room. While my mother cleaned the poop off me, I'd asked her what "carelessness" meant. She'd said, "Having no thought for the safety of others." I worshiped my father and had taken up for him in my typical outspoken way. My mother didn't approve of "talking back." My punishment had been to pick green beans until supper.

Mom had never screamed insults. She'd spoken quietly, but the words — *careless, ineffective, wasteful, imprudent,* and *head in the clouds* — had been applied often to my father. For a child they'd meant nothing because my mother never raised her voice. Mom was just talking, and Dad was just listening.

I felt a chill as the implication of what I was thinking registered. When spoken on a daily basis the constant belittling would be intimidating and devastating to a person's self-esteem. I studied my father. I saw the proud tilt of his head. The confident way he carried himself. He had dignity and seemed self-assured.

A small voice inside of me murmured, Only because he got away.

I gasped and everyone looked my way. "Hi, all," I said, trying to smile. "Just dropped in to see if I would be missed if I took time off." My glance slid over my father's face. "Dad, if you aren't busy, I'd like for you to come with me."

His smile went from ear to ear at my invitation. It was a simple gesture on my part, but the fact that my father showed overwhelming delight reminded me I had some serious holes to mend in our relationship.

Lois said, "Tomorrow is Thursday. Are we going to start on the wedding?"

"We have no choice. We can't leave everything until Friday. The next three days are going to be horrendous. That's why I'm taking the rest of the day off." I motioned to my father that I was ready, and we went out and got into the SUV.

My father patted the dashboard. "Now that you've been driving this beauty, how do you like her?"

My first impulse was to downplay my feelings — be reserved. But I stopped myself and was totally honest. "It's a helluva machine. I love it."

If he'd had a tail it would have wagged. "Good, good. I'm glad I could give it to you." He glanced at me. "But more importantly, I'm glad you accepted the gift."

"It wasn't easy. I'm used to working for everything I get. It still doesn't feel right, but I'm not giving it back."

"I don't want it back. Just enjoy."

We were silent for a few blocks. I kept

asking myself how I was going to broach the subject of my mother. I finally decided to use the story my father had told to Lois and Lew. After all, that had been the source of my enlightenment.

"I heard you telling about that old snake in the hayloft."

"As a child you didn't get addlepated very often. It's one of my favorite memories."

"I'm surprised you remember it fondly, considering how Mom blamed you."

"She was right. I should have watched you more closely."

"I was pretty strong-willed. I thought those kittens were in the hayloft. Come hell or high water I was going to check."

"Even if I'd told you about the snake?"

"I'd have taken a hoe with me, but I'd probably have gone up there."

"Yeah. You're probably right."

I swallowed my nervousness. "Mom did that often, didn't she? Blamed you for stuff that did or didn't happen."

His gray head swiveled in my direction. "I had faults that irritated your mother. Let's leave it at that."

"Not this time, Dad. Because you and Mom never argued or had rousing shouting matches, I thought you got along.

But your marriage was too silent. When Carl and I had a dispute, we'd get vocal. We'd air our problem, make up, and move on. As I remember, Mom did all the talking. You listened or walked away."

"She was usually right."

"I don't think right or wrong has anything to do with it. I think you took her abuse as long as you could and that's when you left."

"Abuse?" His eyes widened. "Your mother wasn't abusive. She was an exceptional woman. We were just mismatched. She had her way of doing things, and I had mine. It's funny how the very traits that attract you to a person can turn out to be the most frustrating. Your mother was strong of spirit and firm in her convictions. When I first fell in love with her, I admired the way she always seemed to know what was right. I always seemed to make the wrong choice. She had no patience with my ideas. I liked to make changes, try something new, even if it failed. She wanted everything to stay the same."

"Such as?"

He thought a moment. "The vegetable garden comes to mind. She was pregnant with you and as big as a barrel when it came time to plant. I worked and worked that soil until it had the texture of flour. I sowed the seeds, putting the corn near the pig lot. I thought that as the corn grew tall it would hide the dilapidated building. When we sat on the porch we wouldn't have to look at it. I admit it was an aesthetic concept, but what difference would it make? The ground was the same in both places."

"Mom didn't want the corn there?"

"Hell no. She got so upset she nearly went into premature labor. She said the hogs would smell the corn ripening and would tear down the fence to get to it."

"Did she raise her voice?"

"Of course not. That wasn't her way."

"But you were made to feel inferior. That you'd screwed up, right?"

"I had."

"No, Dad. What you did wasn't wrong. What Mom wanted wasn't wrong, either. It was just a difference of opinion."

"We had those differences often, daughter. After a while, it gets to where you can't trust your own instincts. You begin to question whether you have a working brain. I'd had this cattle-branding-tool idea spinning around in my head for years. I'd tried talking to your mother, but she wouldn't listen. She only saw the here and now, not what could or might be. Those months before I finally left were hell. Nothing I did suited her, so I took off."

I turned onto Catalpa Road and slowed the SUV. "I can better understand now why you left, but what about me? You sent a yearly check, and Mom deposited it into an account for me. After she died you started sending me a birthday card and a box of grapefruit at Christmas. Dad, I don't even like grapefruit."

He stared at me. "Well, I'll be damned. I didn't know that."

"There's so much about me you don't know. Mom's been dead for over fifteen years, but you waited until last Christmas to come see me. Why?"

"How did I know if you'd want to see me? I didn't really think your mother would speak ill of me to you. Fact is, I figured once I was gone she'd simply never mention me again. But I couldn't be sure. Time has a way of slipping by. Before I knew it you were grown. You had a life here in River City. You had a husband, who from all accounts was kind and loving to you. Then when I read Carl's obituary in the paper, I thought of returning."

"Thought must have been all you did.

He's been dead for two years."

"Give it a rest, Bretta. I'm weak. I'm shy. I'm old. I'm scared. Take your pick. I didn't feel I could intrude on your grief. I came at Christmas because DeeDee called and said you needed me. *You needed me.* I got on the first plane. We spent a few days together. I went back to Texas, but I wasn't satisfied. I wanted more."

"More what?"

He whispered, "I wanted revenge."

"On whom?" I squawked.

Wearily, my father said, "Let's drop this. I've said too much."

"No. No. I think we're finally getting somewhere."

He stared out the window. "I wanted revenge on your mother. I wanted to prove her wrong. I'm not a fool. I'm not lazy. I have amounted to something. In this world, money spells success. I have money, and I've made it using my abilities, my imagination, and my skills."

"You don't have to prove anything to me. I credit you with my creative talent, my imagination, and my penchant for 'what if.' Mother's influence grounded me so I give it some thought before I go off the deep end. I got the best from both of you, with my own personal quirkiness tossed in to keep life interesting."

I topped a hill, and my lips turned down in a frown. Sid Hancock stood in the middle of the road at the end of Lydia's driveway, waving me to a stop. "And if my life gets too humdrum, I have Sid to annoy the hell out of me."

I slowed the SUV, pulled alongside him, and put down the window. His pale complexion was blotchy from the sun. His eyes shot sparks when he saw my passenger.

"Take your joyride somewhere else, Bretta," Sid said, keeping his gaze off my father. "We're working a crime scene."

"So Lydia's death wasn't an accident?"

"Nope. Murder. There was no gas inspector. The fire marshal says the gas line was tampered with. Gas leaked and filled the house. When Lydia flipped the switch for the kitchen light, the spark triggered the explosion. You've got your information, now buzz off."

"I'm *buzzing* on my way to the property east of here."

Always suspicious, Sid demanded, "What for?"

"I'm looking for a flower."

"A flower? Don't you have a shop full of them? Now you're out scrounging the fields and ditches." He shook his head.

"Jeez. You can do the damnedest things." He waved me on, but hollered, "If you haven't passed back by here in half an hour, I'm coming to look for you."

"Be still my heart," I muttered under my breath, but I put up a hand to show I'd heard.

My father chuckled. "That was quick thinking about the flower."

"It's the truth. I *am* looking for a flower, but not because I'm a florist. On the ceiling of Claire Alexander's beauty shop is a painting of a girl. Among the flowers surrounding this girl is a bloom that's been identified as Mead's milkweed."

"Milkweed? Like what was in the tussie-mussie?"

"Same family, but an extinct cousin. From what I understand, it grew in this area. An area where Oliver and Lydia used to live."

My father glanced over his shoulder. "So we're investigating the murder right under the sheriff's nose? I like that. He's entirely too arrogant."

"Forget Sid," I said, pulling into the first driveway that was east of Lydia's place. The lane was rutted, grass and brush waist-high. "This is as far as I want to take the SUV, Dad." I glanced at his neatly creased trousers, knit polo shirt, and dress shoes. "There's rough terrain ahead. You might want to wait here."

"Not a chance, daughter. I'm with you on this mission."

"Sid gave us thirty minutes. Let's make the most of it."

We got out and pushed our way through the thicket. I tried not to think of ticks, chiggers, and other creatures hiding in the grass.

"Where are we going to find this Mead's milkweed?" Dad asked.

"In an igneous glade," I said, then explained what the botany teacher had told me. "I doubt we'll find the plant, but I want to see where it could have grown. I'm not sure if that's important, but something about this area is."

Dad stopped a few feet ahead of me. "Here's what's left of a foundation," he said. "It was either a shed or a very small house."

"Lydia said there used to be a house here." I pointed. "Look at those old trees. They're ancient. Wonder how come they died?"

Dad squinted, then moved so the sun wasn't in his eyes. "Dutch elm disease swept this part of the country and took plenty of victims. But I don't remember the trunks turning black like that."

Dad wandered on, but I stayed where I was. Parts of the concrete foundation had crumbled until it was no more than a pile of rubble. Saplings as thick as my arm had taken over the area. A plump toad hopped out of the grass and scuttled into hiding under the rocks. Mother Nature had reclaimed this spot as her own, rubbing out nearly all traces of human inhabitance. The trees, their trunks rotted hulls, stood like decrepit sentries. I gazed at them, wondering what they were guarding.

Off to my right, my father shouted, "Bretta! You have to see this." He motioned to me.

"I'm coming," I said, but I didn't move. I kept staring at the foundation. Carl had said I needed to put everything in the right order. I knew that Claire had been a rebel. The sixties were a time of revolution — of social reform. People were looking for answers. They wanted to preserve and often took up causes.

"Bretta?" called my father.

I hurried forward and stopped at his side. He flung out his arm and stared at the ground. "Would you look at that? Can you believe it?"

I looked and saw a tangle of plants. He picked a leaf, and after he'd bruised it with his fingers, held it under my nose. The aroma was powerful, and memorable.

"Tansy?" I asked.

"And that's pennyroyal," he said, pointing. "Over there are rhododendron bushes. And unless my eyesight is failing, I see orange dodder wrapped around those weeds yonder." He turned again. "There's the milkweed. Everything needed for the tussie-mussie that was left in your car."

"Except for the white rose," I said.

"Are you going to call the other River City florists and ask them —"

I shrugged. "What? Did they sell a single white rose in the last day or two? Why would they remember that?"

"I guess you're right."

I turned and stared at the grassy prairie, and heard Carl's voice in my head.

"Put it together, Babe. Use logic and reason to figure it out. If the Mead's milkweed was the cause, then what was the effect?"

Chapter Nineteen

Early the next morning, I called the hospital to check on Bailey. A nurse told me he was stirring, and mumbling, but he hadn't opened his eyes. Next I searched the newspaper for the picture of the girl from Claire's beauty shop ceiling. No mention or photo in today's paper. I drank another cup of coffee, and then gave it up. There wasn't any way around it. I had work to do.

I drove to the flower shop, but I dreaded going inside. I hadn't slept well. My mind had tossed and turned all night long, running over and over what I knew about Claire. As I unlocked the shop door, I squared my shoulders, prepared for battle. Murder investigations would have to be put on hold. I was a florist, and the wedding adventure was about to begin.

Sometimes it's nice to be the boss, but today I just wanted to be an employee. I knew that by the end of the day I'd be sick and tired of my name.

"Bretta, where's the ribbon?"

"Bretta, what do you want me to do now?"

"Bretta, is this arrangement too big?"

"Bretta, how many roses should we save for the bride's bouquet?"

I couldn't blame my help. On a big job everyone wants reassurance that they're doing the right thing. No one wants to screw up. But to whom could *I* turn? Who was going to tell me if I was making the right decisions? And each judgment call had to be made off the top of my head. We didn't have guidelines.

During my floral career, I'd never undertaken an event that involved so many picayune details. For each section of the Tranquility Garden either a unique bouquet or a display had to be fabricated from the tools of my trade and one hell of an imagination. This last was my department, too. Lois and Lew would offer suggestions, but once again the final decision would be mine.

By quarter till nine my crew had gathered in the workroom. Lois and Lew knew what to expect. The three women I'd hired were oblivious. They'd helped us out on Valentine's Day, when the Flower Shop had been a madhouse, but that holiday would be nothing compared to what was ahead of us.

Besides doing the wedding work, we had

our regular duties. Evelyn might think River City would come to a halt for her daughter's nuptials, but that wasn't the case. We had Claire's funeral flowers to do. Lydia's memorial service was pending. Then there were the usual assorted hospital, birthday, and anniversary bouquets to design.

I'd worked out a game plan for what needed to be done and when. I'd assigned specific tasks to each person, leaving myself free to gallop around the shop, available to be at their beck and call, while doing my own work.

By noon we were honking on. Twenty Boston ferns had been cleaned of any dead leaves and repotted into brass containers. The morning deliveries had been made. I thought everything was coming along, but apparently I had a touch of hubris. My pride took a beating when Lois finished a prototype of the wreath that was to float on the reflection pool at the base of the gazebo.

She bellowed from the back room. "Bretta, you gotta see this."

I went to the tub of water and stared at the drowned flowers and candles.

"It sank like a stone," she said, trying not to snicker.

On paper the plan had seemed feasible. The ring of Styrofoam had floated when I'd given it a test run, but the added weight of the flowers and candles was too much for it to remain buoyant.

"Hell and damnation," I muttered. "Now what?"

"Bretta?" called Lew from the workroom. "How are you going to attach this tulle to the gazebo?"

I'd bought one hundred yards of white gold-shot tulle. The netting was to frame all six of the gazebo openings and hang in gossamer folds like a tent under the peaked roof. According to Evelyn, I had to achieve the impression that Nikki was taking her vows among wispy clouds.

I turned to Lois. "Should we use ribbon to tie the tulle to the posts? Or tendrils of ivy and wire?"

"I don't know. What are we gonna do about this sunken treasure?"

"Bretta?" said Gertrude. "There's a woman here to see you. She says the mother of the bride wants preparation photos. You know what I mean? Some behind-the-scenes candid shots."

I peered around the doorjamb and saw Kasey at the front counter. Her blond hair was limp. She looked thinner and more retro sixties than she had at the park on Saturday. Her camera was focused on Lew.

I'd given him the job of measuring the tulle into accurate lengths for each of the six gazebo openings. He was such a perfectionist, I knew he'd get the numbers correct, but he wasn't used to working with the flimsy material. The hundred yards of tulle had slipped and slid into a filmy lake on the floor. He'd gathered it up in his arms but had succeeded in draping his body diaphanously. The man looked totally inept.

"Don't take that picture," I said, but I was too late.

Click!

Kasey spun in my direction with the camera aimed at me. "Don't even think about it," I said sharply.

Click!

I was seething. "Dang it, Kasey, don't take another picture."

Click! Gertrude picking her teeth.

Click! Eleanor eating the last jelly doughnut.

Click! Marjory turning over a vase of roses.

In four quick strides I was at the front counter. "What do you think you're doing?"

"My job."

"No. Not here. Not now. We're under enough pressure. We don't need this distraction."

"Evelyn wants photos of Sonya, Dana, and you at work."

"I don't care what she wants."

In a low voice, Kasey said, "How does it feel?"

"How does what feel?"

She brought up the camera and took my picture. "To not get what you want. Sonya and Dana both asked you to back off from Claire's murder investigation, but you keep asking questions. You keep snooping and prying into things that aren't any of your business."

My eyes narrowed. "Is that what this is about?" I waved a hand. "Fine. Take your pictures — and while you're doing it, let me ask you this. In your environmental work have you come across any Mead's milkweed?"

Kasey's lips parted in an *O* of astonishment. She stared at me for a full minute, then picked up her equipment and walked out.

"Whatever you said to her really worked," Gertrude said. "She hightailed it out of here like a duck in a hailstorm."

"Let's get back to work," I said. "Lew, we're using wire and ivy. Eleanor, help him get that tulle under control. Marjory, you missed a puddle of water over by that table leg. We don't have time for an emergency run to the hospital if someone should slip and fall. Gertrude, please answer the telephone. It has rung three times."

"And me?" called Lois from the back room. "What about this floral submarine?"

I gritted my teeth, stared into space, willing an answer to come to me. Finally, I said, "We'll double the ring of Styrofoam. I bought spares. Attach another under the one you already have. If you need to, add a little more greenery so the extra thickness doesn't show."

"Can do," she said.

I glanced around the workroom. Everyone was intent on his or her tasks. Maybe I'd have five minutes to concentrate on what I had to do. I consulted my notes. Two massive bouquets set on pedestals were to flank the reflection pool. I filled the copper containers with water and grabbed the bucket of flowers I'd reserved for the arrangements.

White larkspur for height. I used my florist knife to barely cut the stem end. I needed as much stalk as possible. My bouquets would be in competition with the twilight canopy. And yet, I had to keep in mind that once these bouquets were completed, they had to be hauled in the delivery van to the park. I'd considered making the arrangements on-site, but there would be enough to do on Saturday.

The rest of the day passed without incident. I finished the two bouquets and the arrangements for the reception tables, then called a halt at six thirty.

"We'll have to work later tomorrow night. Let's go home." I didn't have to say it twice. Before I could draw a breath, Gertrude, Marjory, and Eleanor had grabbed their handbags and were out the door.

"I'm pooped," said Lois, dropping into a chair. She eyed me. "You don't look like you have the energy to drive home."

"I'm tired," I admitted, "but the show is just starting. Tomorrow we have to make the corsages, the boutonnieres, and the bridal party flowers. And I can't forget that I have to go to the park and spray the shrubs gold before everyone gets there for the rehearsal." I had a heart-stopping thought. "Those cases of paint were delivered, weren't they?"

"Yes," said Lew. "Three big boxes. Talk about your environmental hazard. All that aerosol paint fogging the air can't be good. Do you have a mask to wear over your nose and mouth?"

"I'll figure out something," I said. "I'm scheduled to paint the shrubs before the rehearsal. Paint the shrubs? Gosh, I can't believe the things I do."

Lois struggled wearily to her feet. "By the way, what did you say to Kasey to make her 'hightail it out of here like a duck in a hailstorm'?" Her eyebrows drew down in a frown. "Are ducks afraid of hail?"

I grinned. "I haven't a clue as to what ducks like or dislike, but Kasey wasn't pleased when I asked her about Mead's milkweed."

While we turned out the lights and gathered up our belongings, I brought Lois and Lew up to speed on what I'd discovered. When I'd finished, both were too tired to offer more than a feeble "Good night."

As I drove home, I wondered if we were getting too old for this stuff. If we were exhausted now, how would we make it through two more days?

I woke up Friday morning to the smell of smoke. I tried to leap out of bed but I'd done too much lifting and stooping yesterday. Shuffling across the floor like a decrepit woman, I peered out the window. It was early, not even light yet, but I didn't need the sun. I had flames.

"Omigod." I gulped. "The garden's on fire."

I grabbed my robe and struggled into it. I made two tries to find the belt, then realized I'd put the robe on wrong side out. I didn't stop to change it. I stuffed my feet into a pair of loafers and hurried downstairs with my robe flapping about me like the Caped Crusader.

"DeeDee!" I shouted. "Dad! Come quick. The garden's on fire."

I didn't pause, but headed out the terrace doors and nearly took a fall when I tripped over a rubber hose. I traced it to the water faucet at the side of the house.

"Bretta?" called someone from the shadows.

I thought I recognized the voice. "Eddie, is that you?"

"Yeah. Sorry about the drifting smoke. The wind has shifted, but now that I've started the fire, I don't want to put it out until I get this controlled burn finished."

My heart eased its rapid beat at the word *controlled*. "You set this fire on purpose?"

Eddie said, "Jerry, keep a close eye over

here. I don't want heat anywhere near this old ginkgo tree."

I watched Eddie walk toward me. He had a small tank strapped to his back. A black hose with a perforated nozzle was connected to the receptacle.

Once he had joined me on the terrace, he said, "I told you we had to get this heavy thatch out of the way. A rapid fire will burn the grass but won't damage the plants underneath. I should be able to start moving soil tomorrow."

I nodded. "Now I remember, but the smoke woke me from a sound sleep. I panicked when I thought my garden was on fire."

Eddie grinned. "It is, but it's under control. I told the fire department and the Missouri Conservation Department that I was doing a burn. I didn't want your neighbors calling in an emergency." He pointed to the hose. "We have water close at hand. I have three men with shovels and wet burlap to smother any flames that spread farther than I want."

My father opened the terrace door, and he and DeeDee stepped out. I told them what was going on.

Dad asked, "Why so early? The sun isn't even up."

"For exactly that reason," said Eddie. "Any wayward spark will be spotted in the dark."

Dad nodded. "Makes good sense."

Now that my eyes were accustomed to the dusky light, I saw Eddie's men. They wore heavy overalls, long-sleeved shirts, and stout boots, but none of them had a tank like Eddie's. "So what's this?" I said, pointing to the apparatus on his back.

"Propane tank." He turned away from us and twisted a valve. I heard a clicking sound, a roar, and flames flashed from the nozzle.

DeeDee said, "W-wow. I wonder if M-Martha has one of those. You could brown a h-hundred m-meringue pies at one t-time with that b-baby."

Eddie touched the flame to some blades of grass growing in a crevice of the sandstone terrace. The blades shriveled and dissolved into ash. "Petroleum has too much vapor that can lead to unpredictable explosions," he explained. "It's too combustible. Kerosene or diesel fuel leaves a residue in the ground. Since I'm planting this area, I don't want that. This propane torch gets the ball rolling. If I see a spot that needs added heat, I only have to touch it and — *poof* — the thatch is gone."

"Eddie," shouted one of the men. "The fire is almost to the southwest corner. You wanna check it out?"

"Gotta go," he said. "I'll be around all day to make sure everything is saturated with water. We don't want any flare-ups. I hoped it would rain tonight or tomorrow, but I guess that isn't going to happen."

The sun popped over the horizon, showering the landscape with flecks of gold. Looking at the light, I said, "I can't forget to paint those shrubs in the park."

Eddie snorted. "Better you than me." He took a couple of steps, stopped, and hollered, "Jerry, I said I didn't want the fire close to that tree. Put your eyes back in your head and pick up a shovel."

I looked at Jerry and saw him staring at me. Under my breath, I said, "Wonder what his problem is?"

DeeDee giggled. "B-baby doll p-pajamas show p-plenty of leg."

My father said, "We have enough heat around here, Bretta, without you adding to it."

Embarrassed, I wrapped my robe around me and marched into the house. What a way to start the day.

Chapter Twenty

Friday was a repeat of Thursday with two exceptions. The morning paper ran the girl's picture from Claire's beauty shop ceiling. The photo was less imposing in black and white and only the width of two columns. I asked Lois, Lew, and my three extra helpers if they recognized the girl. None did. I thought about calling Chief Kelley to see if the picture had generated any new information, but didn't. As Avery, my lawyer friend, had said, I had "enough on my plate" with this wedding.

At four o'clock, the hospital called. Bailey was awake and asking for me. Tears of relief filled my eyes, but my heart was heavy.

"Go see him," urged Lois. "According to your schedule, we're doing fine."

"I can't."

"Why not? While he was in a coma you visited him. Now that he's awake, don't you want to be there?"

I sighed. "I do, and I don't."

Lois grabbed my arm and hauled me to the back room for a private grilling. "I'm not getting this," she said. "What's going on? I know you like the man."

"That's the problem. I don't just *like* him. I think I may love him."

Lois rocked back on her heels. "Well, I'll be damned. You finally admitted it. I'm impressed. I thought it would be at least another six to eight months before you figured that out."

I made a face. "Are you saying I'm slow?"

She grinned. "No, just conservative, and loyal to Carl's memory, and timid, and scared, and you think too much, and —"

I held up my hands. "Stop. Stop. I get the picture. I'm a neurotic mess, but only where Bailey is concerned. He boggles my mind."

"Everyone should be so boggled. What's the problem?"

"I miss Carl, but I'm adjusting. I like my life the way it is. I have DeeDee. Dad is here, and our relationship is progressing. Bailey could complicate everything. I don't know what he expects. He said he's interested in me. He bought the cottage." I gave her a meaningful look. "He might want *more* than I'm ready to give."

Lois knew me well and tracked my thought explicitly. "Bretta, the man just

woke up from a coma. I doubt that he's recovered his libido this quickly."

"I don't know. He's danged sexy."

Lois rolled her eyes. "If he has that kind
of stamina, hook him and reel him in. He's
a keeper."

Grumbling, I said, "I never was much of
a fisherman, but I'll think about it while
I'm spraying the shrubs. Help me load
those boxes of gold paint into the SUV. I'm
going to the park. Can you keep everyone
in line while I'm gone?"

"On the straight and narrow," she said,
hefting the first box. "They won't know
you've left the building."

Painting foliage was a mindless chore.
Shake the can, aim, and press the nozzle. A
light first coat. Another application and a
final touch-up. Move on to the next bush.

Ho hum. This area of the park was quiet
and secluded. In a few hours the wedding
rehearsal would begin. I wanted to be done
with this painting and out of here, but if I
could be a leaf on a tree, I'd stay. I wondered if Evelyn would order her daughter
around like she'd ordered us.

Another ho hum. I could think about
Bailey, but what was the use? I could plan,
and dream, and fret, and stew, but until I

faced him, I didn't have a clue how I should act. A small part of me wanted to rush to his side and fling myself into his arms. But I wasn't the flinging type. Carl used to tease me that when it came my time to pass on, I'd have it planned down to my last breath.

I couldn't help it. I had to think everything through to what I thought might be the correct conclusion. I called it "covering my ass." I didn't have to be right, but I had to use my brain.

I hadn't always been like this. The flower shop had changed the way I approached life. Every hour of every day I had to anticipate any eventuality. Should I order extra flowers? Would people want red roses this week or yellow or pink? Most of the time it was guesswork based on experience, but I still had to plan, to think, to reason.

I tossed another empty paint can into the box and uncapped a fresh container. My arm moved steadily back and forth, giving the foliage the Midas touch. The motion was hypnotic, and I was tired. My eyelids drooped. I jerked upright. Or maybe I was sucking down paint fumes. I giggled. Good thing I wasn't a smoker. If I lit up, I might *poof* like the sugar cubes DeeDee had saturated with liquor.

I eased my finger off the spray button. *Poof!* In my mind I saw Eddie's torch burst into flames and burn the blades of grass.

I shook my head to make the thought clearer. When that didn't work, I put the paint can on the path and walked away from my work. I went to the gazebo and sat on the steps. Taking deep breaths, I concentrated on that fragment of thought.

Liquor. Alcohol. *Poof!*

Cause and effect.

Mead's milkweed.

I put my elbows on my knees and cupped my chin in my hands. Staring at the ground, I ordered myself to concentrate.

Claire had been the activist. Sonya had won honors in the Debate Club. Dana had cheered her team to victory. Kasey had been president of the Botany Club. In fact, all four girls had been members.

The preservation of our natural resources would have interested Kasey. It would also have made a good debate topic for Sonya. From past information, Claire had been hot and ready to take on any and all causes. Dana would've tagged along because that's the kind of person she is.

Was the Mead's milkweed extinct back in the sixties?

I sat up straight. Howie, Claire's ex-husband, had been the one to use the word *extinct*. I closed my eyes so I could remember his exact words: "History has a way of biting you in the ass. Everything can't be saved. It became extinct just like she is."

"Everything can't be saved," I said out loud. During the sixties groups were formed to save the whales, save the rain forests, save the — flowers?

Had the girls tried to save the Mead's milkweed? How? Eddie had said a rapid burn would get rid of the thatch but would leave the plants underneath unharmed. Had the girls tried a controlled burn? Eddie used a propane torch to set the fire. What would the girls have used as an accelerant to set fire to an entire glade?

Something combustible. Gas? Diesel fuel? Kerosene? No. All were environmentally unsafe, and would have gone against ecological preservation.

My eyes binged open. "I'll be damned." It had to be the lemon extract. Wasn't it made up of alcohol? Wouldn't it burn?

"Bretta, are you all right?"

I jerked around. Dana, Kasey, and Sonya stood off to my left.

Dana said, "Bretta, you're pale. Are you sick?"

"Inhaled too many paint fumes," I said, getting up from the steps. I brushed past their united front, then turned and asked, "What brings all of you to the park? Kind of early for the rehearsal, isn't it?"

"There isn't going to be a rehearsal," said Sonya.

I looked from one to the other. "Why? What's going on?"

"Evelyn says the ballet company has been held over in St. Louis for an encore performance."

I shook my head. "I bet Evelyn is fit to be tied."

Sonya said, "She's handling it well. She says Nikki is an intelligent woman. She can find her way to the altar."

"I'm glad Evelyn is confident. I haven't liked this tight schedule since the first time I heard about it." I looked at the women and repeated, "So what brings you to the park?"

Sonya seemed to be the trio's spokeswoman. "Dana called the flower shop and was told you were here. We've tried talking to you one-on-one, but that hasn't worked. Perhaps if we're together, we can persuade you to leave Claire's memory intact."

I raised an eyebrow. "Claire's memory or your reputations?"

The women traded looks. Sonya said, "You obviously have something on your mind. Say it, and let's be done with it."

I wasn't ready to speak my theory aloud. There were still too many leftover pieces of the puzzle. But I couldn't let this opportunity pass. I felt my way along. "Something was bothering Claire on the day she was murdered. She hinted at a secret while we were here at the park. Later she called me. Why me? Why not one of her friends? Unless she knew none of you would help her."

"That's not true," said Dana. "We would have done anything for Claire."

"I'm sure you would. Right down to stealing four bottles of lemon extract from the high school's home ec kitchen."

Sonya laughed. "That was a long time ago. What does a childhood prank have to do with Claire's murder?"

"You tell me."

Kasey started to speak, but a look from Sonya silenced her.

I nodded. "Okay, if that's the way you want it. As you said, it was a long time ago, but not if the memory of what happened plays in your head daily. The mind keeps events fresh, and the pain doesn't go away, especially if you continue to probe it. I think that's what Claire did. She was the organizer of your little group. She decided to take the lemon extract, but only after Kasey expressed an urge to preserve the Mead's milkweed plant.

"I'm assuming you learned about the plant's extinction in botany class. Perhaps you took a field trip and saw it growing in its natural habitat, which is out on Catalpa Road."

Sonya scoffed, "I don't see what you're driving at. We used the extract to make lemon squares."

I shook my head. "No, you didn't. You set fire to that glade. You wanted to do a burn. Get rid of the heavy thatch of grass so the Mead's milkweed would have a chance to survive."

Sonya looked at her two friends, then turned back to me. "This is all very interesting, but again I'm asking, what does it have to do with Claire's death?"

I didn't answer right away. I sensed a change in the trio facing me. When they'd arrived at the gazebo, I'd felt the tension in the air. Now they seemed more at ease. In fact, the longer I'd talked the more relaxed they'd become. That meant I was missing something. What?

Softly I recited, "You can boil me in oil. You can burn me at the stake. But a —"

The tension was back. Sonya's spine stiffened. Dana's knuckles turned white as she clenched her hands.

"No!" shouted Kasey. "Stop it. Don't say another word."

"Why does that poem upset all of you so much?"

Sonya took a step in my direction. Her eyes were narrowed. "I'm telling you for the last time to drop it, Bretta."

I was fully aware of my vulnerable position. I was in a secluded area of the park with three women, any of whom could be a murderer. In my head I heard Carl whisper, "Use the buddy approach, Babe, and if that don't work, run like hell."

I softened my tone. "Your childhood friend has been murdered. A killer is walking around free. Doesn't that bother you? If any of you knows something, you need to tell me."

Sonya said, "We don't have to tell you anything. I'm leaving, and if you ladies have any brains, you'll come with me."

Without hesitation, Kasey went to Sonya's side. I looked at Dana. She was my best bet for information. I waited hopefully, wondering if she'd meekly follow Sonya's lead.

Dana licked her lips and fought back tears. "We aren't bad women, Bretta. We weren't bad girls. We most surely aren't murderers."

Her words and tone touched me, but if I believed her, then who had killed Claire and Lydia? Who had driven the SUV that plowed into Bailey's truck? Who had constructed the deadly bouquet that had been left in my car? Who had the most to gain by bringing the past into the present?

Chapter Twenty-one

Nikki Montgomery's wedding day had arrived. It was Saturday, and the ceremony was to begin at eight o'clock that evening. My crew and I were in the park by ten a.m., ready for some intense decorating and beautifying. We wouldn't bring the flowers until later in the day, but there was plenty of preparation to do before we set the bouquets in place. My SUV was packed with everything I'd need — hammers, nails, tacks, florist knives and nippers, wire, tape, a ladder, and a box of Band-Aids.

Lois would stay at the flower shop until twelve, when the store closed. She had several sympathy arrangements to make for Lydia's memorial service, which was scheduled for two o'clock this afternoon. Gertrude was answering the phone, doing whatever needed to be done. Once the shop was locked, both women would join us in the park. I'd left money for them to buy us lunch. By noon we would be in need of sustenance.

I had begun my day by tackling the tulle. Working with the filmy material was like fighting a phantom opponent. My nerves were already shredded. I'd spent another sleepless night, worrying and wondering. I'd juggled thoughts of the wedding with the murders until I thought I'd go bananas. Bananas had made me think of food. I'd raided the refrigerator. At the very back of the freezer, I'd found DeeDee's stash of Blue Bunny ice cream — tin-roof sundae, my favorite. I'd eaten half the carton, and had indigestion the rest of the night.

Lew, Marjory, and Eleanor unpacked the twenty Boston ferns from the delivery van. Each person was armed with a sketch I'd made that showed where the bouquets, ferns, hanging baskets, and displays were to go.

From my roost on the ladder I watched the goings-on in the park. Kasey and Evelyn were outside the reception tent. Both women were smiling, which was a good sign. In another section Sonya played ringmaster, directing her twelve helpers with clear, precise orders. She caught me watching and gave me a curt nod.

In the far corner of our arena, Dana and her group were unloading supplies into another smaller tent that would serve as the food-preparation station. For easy entry into the tent, the side flaps were up. I watched Dana set an ice chest on one of the tables, then rub her stomach.

I was on intimate terms with that gesture. Dana had a belly full of nerves. Maybe I should offer her one of my antacid tablets. I'd brought along a new supply. I could share, and perhaps ask a question or two.

I started down the ladder, saw the tulle in a wrinkled wad on the gazebo floor, and went back up. First things first, old girl, I said to myself.

For more time than I cared to think about, I folded and looped, wired and tied the tulle into a floating, gossamer gob of shimmering clouds.

"Bretta, that is absolutely fabulous," said Evelyn from the gazebo steps. "It's just the way Nikki and I had it pictured. Thank you."

I rubbed my neck, trying to get rid of the crick. My legs and feet ached from climbing and standing on the narrow rungs of the ladder. It helped ease my pain that I'd accomplished what I set out to do, and the work had been approved.

"How's everything going?" I asked.

"Wonderful," said Evelyn. She glanced at her watch. "Nikki and the rest of her bridal party should be here in another few hours. I can't wait."

"She's cutting it pretty close."

"I know. I spent a horrible night last night. But things are going to work out just as I've planned. I'm leaving in a few minutes to check on the hotel rooms. My guests will need snacks to help them recuperate. I want them to have whatever they need."

"Will they be coming out here?"

"Not right away. The limo will deliver them to the park later this evening."

I started to say that they ought to get a feel for the garden, but at this point I didn't care. I just wanted my part done.

"Did you see the shrubs?" I asked.

"I'm glad you brought that up. I saw them, and they aren't shiny enough."

"Really?" My eyes narrowed. "What would you suggest?"

"I have a case of aerosol lacquer in my car. It's on the backseat. The doors aren't locked. Have your man unload the box and give each bush a quick touch-up. I want those leaves to gleam in the candlelight."

My jaw dropped. Before I had recovered, Sonya called, "Evelyn, could you come over here? This lamp oil has an unusual odor."

Evelyn touched my arm. "You're doing an excellent job, Bretta. Now, see to those shrubs." To Sonya, she said, "I've checked the oil. It's what I ordered. Nikki loves the smell of clematis blossoms. I had the oil specially blended even though the cost made me blink twice."

I'd never noticed a scent from the blossom of a clematis vine. I started toward the group so I could have a whiff, but my path crossed Lew's. I explained about the case of lacquer in Evelyn's car.

"I'll get it," he said, "but you might want to go to the hospital. I have my cell phone with me, and Lois called from the shop. Mr. Monroe is pitching a fit. He wants to see you immediately."

"Bailey?" My heart skipped a beat. "Why? What's wrong?"

"Haven't a clue, Boss. I'll go get the lacquer, and I suppose you want me to do the spraying?"

"Yes. You, Marjory, and Eleanor spray the shrubs. The rental company has finished setting up the chairs for the guests. Now I can attach the satin bows. After that, I have to do the display by the entrance into the reception tent. White satin is to cover the wire stands that are to be at different heights for the bouquets."

I thought a moment. "Did I put that tall pedestal in the SUV? Yeah. Yeah." I nodded. "I remember taking it out of the closet." I shrugged. "Anyway, by the time we finish these jobs, it'll be after twelve, and Lois and Gertrude will arrive with lunch and the helium for the balloons. For the rest of the afternoon, you'll be trundling back and forth from the park to the shop hauling bouquets. Our extra helpers will be inflating balloons."

"What about Mr. Monroe?"

I raised my chin. "What about him?"

"Are you going to the hospital?"

"I just gave you a rundown on what I'm doing. Did I mention leaving the park?"

Lew pursed his lips. "Fine. I'm turning off my phone. If he should get my number, he might call me. I don't need to be harassed by a man I've never met. I have people closer at hand doing an excellent job of that."

I grimaced. "I'm sorry. Don't you feel the pressure we're under? Am I the only one worried about details?"

A wail of displeasure rose from the food-preparation tent. Lew cocked his head in that direction. "Sounds like another nervous Nellie. Marjory, Eleanor, and I will be spritzing bushes if you need us."

The conflict in the tent subsided quickly. I went over anyway, and met Evelyn as she was leaving. She brushed past me without a word, headed for the parking lot. I stepped into the tent and saw Dana kick an ice chest. Instantly, she dropped to her knees and lifted the lid to see if the contents of the chest had been harmed by her temper.

"What's going on?" I asked.

Dana spoke over her shoulder. "That woman and I don't jive. Nothing I do suits her."

"It isn't an exclusive club. I'm a founding member. What's her problem now?"

Dana stood up and moved to a cart that held a huge deep-fat fryer. "She doesn't want me to start frying the shrimp until eight o'clock, when the ceremony begins. That gives me thirty to forty-five minutes to have everything ready for the guests. I told her if there's one glitch, then everything will be thrown off this tight schedule. Evelyn has assured me there *will not* be any glitches."

I shook my head. "I have problems, too. Maybe we need a break." I looked at the boxes, sacks, and ice chests sitting on the tables. "Have you got anything to drink?"

"Nothing cold, but I have a thermos of coffee. Want some?"

"Oh, yes, if you have enough to share."

She nodded, got out some Styrofoam cups, and filled two. As she handed mine across to me, she said, "I'm telling you upfront, I'm not discussing Claire's death. We can chat about other things but not her murder."

I led the way to a table near the front of the tent. We sat and sipped. It was an effort, but I didn't say a word. After a while, Dana began to talk. I hid a smile. When something is on your mind, it's hard to keep still.

"I hit my stride in high school," said Dana. "I was forty pounds lighter. I was a cheerleader. I was dating three guys at one time. I thought I had the world by the tail. I could do anything, be anything I wanted." She glanced at me. "I didn't care about the extinction of a stupid milkweed plant. But I liked stealing the lemon extract from Ms. Beecher, the home ec teacher. She was such a crab. Said my cooking lacked skill and finesse."

I laid it on thick. "This Ms. Beecher should see you now." I sniffed the air. "It smells wonderful in here. You're a true professional, Dana."

Dana looked pleased, but demurely said, "I don't know about that."

"I *know* you ladies need to get into gear," said Sonya. "You don't have time to sit and gossip."

I stood and faced Sonya. "I'm well aware of my responsibilities. If you'll excuse me, I have to attach satin bows to chairs." I walked off but glanced over my shoulder. I expected to see Sonya giving Dana hell for talking to me, but Sonya had moved on and Dana had gone back to work.

I tied the bows to the chairs. I inspected the shrubs, which now looked artificial with their sheen of lacquer. I positioned the wire stands for the display by the entrance into the reception tent, then draped the stands with white satin cloth.

Lois and Gertrude arrived with food and the helium tank. After we'd eaten, I put the three extra helpers to work inflating the latex balloons, then I sent Lew to the shop for the first load of bouquets.

Finding a spare minute, I sat on the gazebo steps and said to Lois, "I'm exhausted. Remind me of this day when I'm asked to do another wedding."

Lois leaned against the railing and grinned. "You wanted the kudos. Can't get them without showing your talent."

"I feel more like a pack animal than a florist. Do you have any idea how many trips I've made to the SUV for tools and materials?"

"Nope. Have you made any trips to the hospital?"

"Don't even start on Bailey."

"I talked to him. He doesn't understand why you won't come see him."

"Did you tell him I'm busy with this wedding?"

"Yes, but we both agree you could find the time to make a quick visit."

I glared. "I don't need you siding with him." I waved a hand, dismissing the subject of Bailey Monroe. "I'm not discussing him. Let's talk about something else."

Lois curtsied. "What's your pleasure, madam?" She raised an eyebrow. "Murder?"

My tone was dry. "That's a safe topic." But I couldn't resist filling her in on the conversation I'd had yesterday in the park with Sonya, Dana, and Kasey. "Those girls set fire to that glade using lemon extract as an accelerant. Can you believe that?"

"I not only believe you, but I remember that fire." Lois shook her head. "Damn, Bretta. How have they lived with this all these years? At least with Kayla's prank, the only things destroyed were fish. What a horrible tragedy." She frowned. "But as I remember it, nothing was reported about the fire being arson."

"What's so tragic about a field burning? And why do you remember that particular fire?"

"Because I was pregnant and emotional. The idea of a woman and her child trapped in their house was terrible. They burned to death. The family had nothing. One grave, one casket; they were buried together. A neighbor supplied the cemetery plot and the grave marker."

I closed my mouth when I realized that I was staring at Lois like a slack-jawed idiot. This news changed everything. No wonder the tension had disappeared as I talked to those women in the park. I'd merely scratched the surface of their juvenile high jinks when I'd accused them of setting fire to that glade.

I had a hundred questions, and there was only one person I could think of who might crack if I exerted a bit of pressure. "I need to speak to Dana," I said, staring at the food-preparation tent.

"It better be a speedy conversation," said Lois. "Here comes Lew with the first load of bouquets."

Lois took off for the van. I got up from the steps and went in search of Dana. I found her stacking a wedding cake layer on pillars. Once she had the cake safely in place, I didn't waste time with subtlety.

"A mother and her child died in that fire the four of you set."

Dana whirled around. She met my gaze full on, then crumpled like a wet dishcloth. "Go away, Bretta. Please."

"I want to hear what happened."

"But I don't want to talk about it."

"I don't understand how you could have kept it a secret. Wasn't there an investigation into their deaths? Were none of you suspects?"

Dana held up her hands. "I'm trembling so badly I won't be able to pipe icing onto these cakes. Why are you doing this now?"

"Clear your conscience, Dana. Maybe then you'll find peace."

"Peace?" She tried to laugh, but it was a feeble effort. "That would be wonderful, but I doubt that telling you will bring me peace."

I kept still.

Dana closed her eyes. When she spoke her voice was low, and I had to lean closer to hear. "When the fire spread to the prairie, it went like the speed of sound through that dry grass." She blinked away tears. "We were shocked, but there wasn't anything we could do to put it out. We got in our car and left. It wasn't until the next morning that we learned the woman and her daughter had died."

Dana took a shaky breath. "Everyone thought of the fire as a tragic accident. That's the way it was reported in the newspaper. The glade was used back in the sixties like Make Out Point is today. It was a hangout for the kids. There was talk of dope smoking. A dropped cigarette, but nothing more."

My blood boiled. "Which one of you rammed Bailey's truck?"

Dana frowned. "Who's Bailey?"

I studied her puzzled expression. Her confusion seemed genuine. Impatiently, I motioned for her to continue.

"The day before Claire died she called me to talk about what happened the night of the fire. I cut her off. Hung up on her. When I saw her green hair in the park the next day, I knew we were in trouble. Then she said that horrible rhyme. We made it up before the fire. It was our credo. We were 'on the make,' upholding our rights as citizens. When that woman and her daughter died, we swore never to utter those words again. I thought Claire was being mean, reminding us of our secret. But I never dreamed she'd die."

"She was murdered, Dana. What happened in nineteen sixty-six might have been an accident, but Claire's death was homicide."

Dana licked her lips. "In our own way we've tried to atone for what we did that night. We were young and scared. The mother's name was Alice. The fifteen-year-old daughter was Erica. According to reports, the house went up like cardboard. Neighbors saw the blaze but couldn't pull them to safety. If the younger daughter, who was ten, hadn't spent the night away from home, she'd have died too."

"I doubt she took much comfort in that. Her mother and sister were dead. What happened to her?"

Dana lifted a shoulder. "I heard she went to live with relatives. After a year, Claire tracked down her address and sent a gift. A few months later, Claire sent another."

"Did she write the girl a letter explaining the reason for the presents?"

Dana stared at me. "Gosh, no. She'd never do that." A look of uncertainty crossed her plump face. "Or would she?"

"Claire might," I said. "The girl must have wondered why someone was sending her presents. Did Claire hear back? Get a thank-you card?"

"No. Claire couldn't be sure the girl had even gotten the packages, but they weren't returned. A couple of gifts could hardly make up for the loss of her family, but Claire felt she had to make contact in some way."

Dana rubbed her arms and spoke quietly. "After Sonya, Kasey, Claire, and I graduated, we went our separate ways. We'd see each other around town, but our friendship wasn't the same. We never talked about what happened that night, but in our own way we each tried to compensate for what we'd done. Kasey has her environmental work. Sonya spends all her free time volunteering in the pediatric wing at the hospital. My being a clown and making children laugh at birthday parties isn't much, but even if we'd come forward with our story, the woman and her daughter would still be dead."

"But Claire might not," I said quietly. "For years she was able to go on with her life. Then all of a sudden she needed catharsis. Why? What happened? What was the gossip Claire needed confirmed by

Lydia Dearborne?"

"I don't know, but I think she's the lady Claire got the little girl's address from."

"But you said that was a year after the fire."

Dana nodded. "I've told you all I know. The others are going to be furious with me. Please don't say anything to Sonya or Kasey until after this wedding. We're already stressed enough as it is."

I left the food-preparation tent without making any promises. I wanted to find a quiet corner to mull over what I'd discovered, but the hustle and bustle around me was too distracting. I couldn't concentrate.

The next hours passed in a final flurry of frustration. While unloading one of the massive gazebo bouquets, Lew broke the tallest flower head from its stem. I did some finagling — tape and wire are a florist's best friends. We checked lists, checked bouquets, and checked twinkle lights. We smoothed tulle, smoothed satin cloth, and smoothed ruffled feathers. Finally, at six o'clock, I called a halt. We'd done what we'd been paid to do.

Evelyn hadn't arrived, so I hunted up Sonya to tell her the exact location of the bridal party flowers. I found her fighting to keep her composure. Her power suit was rumpled and smudged. Her eyes held a "help me, Lord" expression.

Was the wedding getting to her? Or had she learned that her past had finally caught up to her?

I asked, "Have you talked to Dana?"

"Why?" Sonya squawked, craning her neck. "What's happened now? She forgot the oil for the deep-fat fryer and her husband had to bring the jugs from home."

"Nothing like that," I said. "I just wanted to tell you that the corsages and boutonnieres need to be kept in the ice chests until time to pin them on. We've labeled each, so there shouldn't be any confusion as to who receives which one."

Sonya nodded. "Evelyn called. You're to leave the helium tank."

"Why?"

"She has a special heart-shaped balloon she wants inflated to tie to the limo."

"This has gone way beyond ridiculous. Have you met any of the wedding party yet?"

"No."

I flipped my hands, absolving myself from the event. "I've had it. No rehearsal. Everything on a schedule. I'm out of here."

Sonya looked longingly at the path that would take her away from Tranquility

Garden. Deliberately, she looked away from freedom and squared her shoulders. She asked, "You aren't coming to the wedding?"

"No. I've seen enough. I'm taking a hot bath and going to bed."

"Evelyn assumes you'll attend."

"I'm not under that obligation. I've done my work. You're the coordinator."

"I'm surprised you don't want to see and be seen. It's good advertising for your shop. This wedding will be the talk of River City for weeks and months. Anyone who is anybody is coming."

I looked around at the serenity and beauty. Soon this place would be filled with River City families. The previous Saturday, when we'd met in the park, Sonya had said the mayor was attending, as well as doctors, lawyers, and councilmen — the elite of our society.

A twinge of unrest caught me by surprise. I tried to analyze the feeling, but I couldn't get a handle on it. I finally told myself it was because my part in this gala was finished. After the candles were lit there would be no turning back for Nikki and her groom.

I chewed my lower lip. Evelyn had said something along those lines. I searched my brain for her exact words: "Once the candles are lit, it's the beginning of the end."

Sonya asked, "What's wrong? Have you changed your mind about attending the wedding?"

I ran a hand wearily through my hair. "You've made valid points for me to stay, but I'm tired. When I get tired, I get cranky. The best place for me is home."

It might have been the best place. But thirty minutes later, I found myself in the hospital parking lot.

Chapter Twenty-two

I didn't analyze why I'd come to Bailey. I only knew that I had to talk to someone. I couldn't shake the feeling that I was on the edge of a precipice and any wrong move could be disastrous. Since I'd left the park, my chest ached with anxiety. I was antsy — filled with apprehension. I needed professional feedback. But I couldn't face Bailey until I was able to relate the facts in a rational manner.

I paced the parking lot, pondering what I knew, filling in the blanks with what I suspected.

Events of our past shape the people we are today.

In 1966, four girls had the righteous idea of saving a plant from extinction. Their good deed had resulted in the deaths of two innocent people. Lois had said, "One grave, one casket; they were buried together. A neighbor supplied the cemetery plot and grave marker."

I was sure Oliver had been that neighbor. Before he'd suffered his fatal heart attack, he'd seemed confused. Perhaps in his befuddled state, he'd thought the park was the cemetery, hence his question: "Where are the markers?" As for the "Bretta — Spade," I could only guess at what had been in the dying man's mind. Eddie had said that whenever anyone close to Oliver had passed away, he used his spade to sprinkle soil on the grave. If Oliver had donated the cemetery plot, I had to assume he'd cared about that mother and her child.

The puzzler was — what had prompted him to have that particular thought at that particular time?

I blinked. One grave. One casket. One little girl's family wiped out. I ran my fingers through my hair. One daughter had been spared. That child had been ten years old.

Everyone who'd been in the park the morning Oliver died had been involved in some way or other with that fire. Everyone except Evelyn. I grew still, staring, visualizing, and remembering.

I'd been so caught up in the details of this wedding that I hadn't considered it anything more than an extravaganza brought about by an indulgent mother doing a bit of River City social climbing. Now I wasn't so sure. My theories were conflicting, but my gut feeling said something wasn't right.

Who was Evelyn Montgomery? What did we know about her? Why had she chosen River City for her daughter's wedding?

I'd thought it strange that an environmentalist was taking the wedding photos. I'd thought it odd that Dana had been given the entire responsibility of such a lavish banquet, when her expertise was birthday parties and anniversaries.

Was the choice of the women — Kasey, Dana, Claire, and Sonya — a coincidence? Or was it an elaborate scheme to get all four women together in one place at one time? River City had other caterers, other photographers, but none of them were linked to a terrible secret — a fire that had killed a mother and her daughter.

Oliver hadn't met Evelyn until she came into the park. Had he seen a glimmer of the child she'd been but couldn't quite make the connection? He had made the association with a grave marker. But wouldn't that traumatic episode supercede any gentler memories of this orphaned child?

I pictured Tranquility Garden, and my agitation grew stronger. The hurricane lamps set at strategic spots around the gazebo, five hundred candles strewn throughout the area, specially blended oil for lighting. Paint and lacquer on the shrubs, delicate wisps of tulle, a helium tank, and a deep-fat fryer to be used at a specific time.

Was I way off track? I took a deep breath. It was time to air my theory.

I charged into the hospital and punched the button for the third floor. On the ride up, I added everything together, and I came up with a four-letter word: *fire*. What better way to seek revenge for your mother's and sister's deaths than to bring all the guilty parties together for one big . . . *burn*.

The elevator came to a stop. I stepped off the car and turned toward Bailey's room. But why would Evelyn choose her daughter's wedding for such a dastardly act? This was the conflict. This was why I needed to talk to Bailey.

I pushed open the door to his room and found my father seated at Bailey's bedside. They were visiting compatibly. My father had one leg crossed over the other. Bailey's smile was a welcome sight. Emotional tears filled my eyes. I couldn't control the sob that worked its way up my throat and past my lips.

"Bretta?" said both men at the same time. My father came to his feet, grabbed his walking stick, and limped toward me. "You're as pale as a turnip, daughter."

"Sweetheart," said Bailey. "What's wrong?"

My fears were unleashed by their concern. In a torrent of words, I said, "Evelyn was in the park. She heard Dana's comment about the hot piece of gossip from Mrs. Dearborne. Oliver's overworked heart couldn't take the strain. He was stressed trying to remember. Add in Evelyn's and Eddie's argument and Oliver keeled over. Three people are dead. I think more victims are to come."

I grabbed my father's arm. "I don't know what to do. Maybe I'm wrong, but what if I'm right? Five hundred guests are supposed to attend that wedding."

Bailey patted the side of his bed. "You're not making sense, Bretta. Sit here and tell us what's going on. Start at the beginning."

"I can't sit." My gaze went to the clock above his bed. "Soon those candles will be lit. Evelyn said it was the 'beginning of the end.' "

My father put his arm around my waist. "We'll do whatever you say, but you have to calm down so we can get the gist of your worries."

Talking to myself, I muttered, "Evelyn said she had the lamp oil specially blended with the fragrance of clematis blossoms. Dad, when you looked up the meaning of those flowers in the tussie-mussie, did you come across clematis?"

"Yeah. Recognized the name right off. When we lived on the farm your mother had a vine growing up the clothesline pole."

"What does clematis mean?"

"Artifice — deception and trickery. Lousy definition for such a beautiful —"

I broke out of my father's grasp. "I've got to go back to the park. I don't know what I'll do, but I've got to do something."

Bailey called, "No, Bretta, don't —"

But I was already on my way. The stairs were closer than the elevator. I figured I'd have to wait for a car, so I took the steps, thinking this route might be quicker. I clopped down three flights, and then wound my way through a maze of corridors until I finally made it out of the building and across the parking lot.

Irritated at the delay, I revved the SUV's engine and headed for the exit. My father stepped from behind a parked car, and I nearly clipped him with my bumper. Tires squealed as I slammed on the brakes. I unlocked the door and watched him climb in.

"I don't know about this, Dad. Maybe you should go home."

"Don't talk. Drive."

There wasn't time to argue. I stepped on the gas and asked, "How did you get down here so quickly?"

"The elevator was still on the third floor. I got on, pushed the button, and here I am. No mystery there, but I am mystified by what you think might be happening at the park. Can you explain while you drive?"

"I can try." Grimly, I began, "Evening weddings normally have candles, but this ceremony is teeming with flammables. Back in nineteen sixty-six —"

While I talked, I took advantage of the SUV's power. I ignored yellow lights, and when the intersections were clear, I crossed against red. I prayed for an officer to appear, but none did. The trip seemed to take forever, but according to the clock, we were making good time. I drove by instinct — braking and accelerating as the need arose.

The exit ramp I wanted loomed ahead. I switched lanes and decreased my speed, but only until I was on the road leading to the park. I took the sharp curves at an excessive rate. When we got to the park entrance, I slowed to a crawl.

"Good Lord above," said Dad. "Look at the cars. You say Evelyn only came to River City eight months ago. How'd she get such a following of people so quickly?"

"Money, is my guess. A donation here, a donation there. She's lovely to look at. She can be charming. I myself tried to please her because she was the mother of the bride — and paying big bucks for my service."

I edged my way past the cars, knowing there wouldn't be a legal place to park. As we drew closer to Tranquility Garden, I put the SUV's windows down. I didn't hear anything except the rustling of leaves in the treetops. It was getting dark early. The gathering clouds had blocked the setting sun's rays.

"A front is moving in," said Dad. "The wind has changed. It's blowing from the north."

With one hand on the steering wheel, I leaned out the window. The faint, lilting notes of the harp drifted on air currents. I almost smiled. "Music," I said. "Maybe I'm wrong."

The words were barely out of my mouth when I saw the path that led to Tranquility Garden. Where was the limousine? Where was the bridal party? Where was the bride?

I slammed the SUV into park and left the vehicle blocking traffic. Jumping out, I said, "Dad, stay here in case you need to move my car. I have to see what's going on."

I sprinted across the tarmac, my gaze on the path. I didn't see Evelyn until she stepped from the shadow of a tree. She wore a flannel shirt, jeans, and boots. I tried to be calm, gesturing to her informal attire. "Has the theme of this elegant wedding been changed?"

"Don't come any closer, Bretta," Evelyn warned softly. "You're not going to stop me."

No need for pretense. "You're Alice's daughter. Your sister was Erica. Both were killed in a fire."

"You've been busy."

"Evelyn, think about what you're doing. Think about Nikki."

"There is no Nikki. It's a hoax."

"But why a wedding?"

"Because Sonya, Claire, Dana, and Kasey's professions made that seem the most workable solution. If they'd been nurses, teachers, secretaries, I'd have made their acquaintance, then planned a huge party toward the same end."

"How did Claire figure out you were the sister of the girl who died?"

"Family resemblance. I think Oliver saw it, too, but he died before he could say too much. He was kind to my sister and me. He taught us the meaning of flowers and showed us how to plant an herb garden. But most of all, he helped me get through the funeral by letting me —"

"— use his precious spade to put dirt on their grave?"

Evelyn nodded. "I feel bad that Oliver died. As for Claire, I didn't go to the beauty shop with the intention of killing her. I only wanted to find out what information she hoped to get from Lydia Dearborne. But Claire made me furious. She pointed to my sister's picture on her ceiling and told me she'd painted it because it was cathartic — a way of purging her past indiscretions."

Evelyn's voice rose in outrage. "That woman classed the deaths of my mother and sister as an indiscretion."

"And you killed Lydia because —"

Evelyn regained control and spoke quietly. "She was a loose end from the past. I couldn't be sure what Claire might have told her. I wanted to go to Lydia's house immediately after I'd killed Claire, but you

338

came into the shop. I had to see what you were up to. By the time I got to Lydia, her sister and daughter had come to visit. They were innocents. I couldn't kill them. So I took a chance and waited until Lydia's company had gone away."

"Did Claire come right out and ask if you were the daughter who'd escaped the fire?"

"Not in so many words. For weeks now, she'd tried to trip me up. She asked hundreds of questions, but I always had pat answers. Many times I thought I'd thrown her off my trail by talking about this bogus wedding. But Claire kept prying and prying. I'd drop into her shop every so often, just as I did with you and the others. The rest of you were oblivious, but Claire was different. All those years ago, she sent me gifts. Once she even called, to see if I was happy and settled in my new life."

Evelyn stopped to look at her wristwatch. "I was a child, but as I grew older, I'd think about the woman in River City who had seemed so concerned but wouldn't tell me her name other than Claire. In her letter she said she was graduating high school with three of her closest friends. I kept the letter because it was a tie to River City and to the family I'd lost."

Evelyn glanced at her watch again and said hastily, "Last year my aunt passed away. As I was going through her belongings and mine, I came across the letter. When I read those words with adult eyes, I had this horrible feeling that Claire's concern was motivated by guilt. I had to know the truth, so I made the decision to move to River City. From the first time I met Claire, she said I looked familiar. Then she painted my sister's picture on the ceiling of the beauty shop. Putting my sister's image up there was cruel."

"Why cruel?"

"Because Claire was my sister's killer."

"It was an accident, Evelyn. Those girls were burning off the field to preserve an endangered plant."

Evelyn laughed bitterly. "Save the plant. Kill my family. It was a lousy plan."

I waved my hand to our surroundings. "All this work, all the money you've spent, was for revenge?"

Evelyn nodded. "Yes. To bring grief to the girls who killed my mother and sister. To wreak havoc on a town that didn't care enough to investigate the deaths. I've looked at back issues of the newspaper. Do you know my family's murder didn't rate more than a tiny story at the bottom of the front page? They were dead. My life was forever changed. But this town didn't care."

Evelyn bent down and carefully picked up an open container. "Tonight, River City will care. They'll see the light."

Before I could draw a breath, she hurled the can under a cedar tree. I saw the arc of liquid. I smelled the gasoline vapors. She struck a match.

"Nature's own bomb," Evelyn said, tossing the flame.

The gas ignited with a whoosh. The fire leaped up the cedar tree, found dry tinder, and exploded into an inferno. Sparks leaped and whirled on the rising wind. With choreographed precision, the blaze spread to the shrubs I'd painted and Lew had touched up with lacquer. The natural moisture trapped in the leaves was no contest for this heat. The flammable material combusted and the shrubs were aflame.

In horror, I said, "Are you insane?"

Evelyn shook her head. "Not at all. I'm well aware of what I'm doing." She cocked her head. Screams came from the area where the guests had been entertained by the music.

I started in that direction but glanced back at Evelyn. She was on the move. With everything else so well planned, she would have to have an escape route. But Evelyn didn't head for the parking lot. She took off into the woods.

In the midst of this heat, an icy finger of fear crawled up my spine. Evelyn had years of hatred bottled inside. Was the wedding in the park her only scheme? Did she intend to burn all of River City?

I ran after her.

I wasn't sure where we were headed, but I crashed into the underbrush about twenty yards away from the wedding fiasco. This part of the park hadn't been tamed. I caught a shadowy glimpse of Evelyn ahead of me, off to my right. I angled that way and found a hiker's path. Picking up speed, I gained on her, but the climb grew steeper. Before long I was huffing and puffing.

The fire raged at my back, but off in the distance I heard sirens. Damage control was headed for the park, courtesy of Bailey or my father. However, Evelyn was still on the loose. I hoped my being on her trail might keep her from committing another horrendous act.

I've run for my life before, but I've never been the aggressor. I wasn't comfortable with the role. What would I do if I caught up to her? What was her strategy? I believed she had one. She'd plotted an entire wedding, down to the minutest detail, with the thought of achieving this devastating finale.

Fear forced me to put one foot in front of the other. Behind me, in the direction of Tranquility Garden, was a series of explosions. I assumed this was the specially blended oil for the hurricane lamps.

I quickened my pace, and the trail began to level out. I looked up and saw Evelyn silhouetted against the night sky. She posed there briefly, seemed to stare straight at me, then she disappeared over the horizon. I plugged onward until I came to the spot where she'd vanished.

I turned and saw Evelyn hadn't been staring at me but at her handiwork. Fueled by an insatiable appetite, the fire leapfrogged from treetop to treetop. Sparks sprinkled the earth, igniting the underbrush. Like ground troops, the flames advanced at a rapid rate, energized by the rising wind.

I started down the hill, lost my footing, and made the journey on my butt. My ungainly passing raked up moldy leaves. The musty odor mixed with the acrid smoke made my eyes water. When I hit the bottom of the gorge, I wiped my eyes on my shirttail. With my vision cleared, I searched for some landmark that would tell me where I was in relation to the park.

The night seemed brighter, and I thought the moon had come out. But it had a surreal glow. I looked up at the ridge. The fire had spread at a heart-stopping rate. It was above the gorge. I blinked, and the flames swooped toward me. Stumbling to my feet, I wanted to shout — *I'm not the enemy* — but this army knew no friend or foe. It would take no prisoners. Its mission was death and destruction.

I ran down the gorge, unsure of where I was going, but I didn't have a choice. I couldn't see what lay on the other side of the embankment. I couldn't see what was ahead of me. Suddenly the terrain changed. Waist-high blades of grass grabbed at my jeans, sliced into the flesh of my arms. My feet sank into spongy soil.

I stopped in my tracks to take stock of where I might be, and saw Evelyn. I'd temporarily put her out of my mind in my haste to get away from the fire. She was huddled at the base of a giant tree. Her eyes were closed.

I fought my way over to her. "Evelyn, the fire is headed our way."

"I know."

"Let's go."

She opened her eyes. "This old tree looks like the ones that used to stand near our house. My sister and I played for hours under their branches. I'll die here."

Evelyn spoke so calmly, I didn't immediately grasp her meaning. When I did, I was infuriated. "You led me on this merry chase so you could die at this spot?"

She stared at me. "I didn't invite you to follow me."

"What would you expect me to do? Let you escape?"

She didn't answer, but closed her eyes. Her posture was that of a martyr — a Joan of Arc in blue jeans.

Well, fine. Let her stay. I was leaving. I took two steps past the tree. I couldn't do it. I swiveled on my toe and grabbed her arm. "You're coming with me."

Evelyn jerked away. "I'm tired. I've done what I set out to do. Just let me die."

Grimly, I stooped until we were nose to nose. "Not on your life." I pulled her upright. "Let's go."

She stared at me. "Why are you doing this? Why should you care what happens to me?"

I didn't answer, because I didn't know.

She'd killed twice. Her fate should be to burn in hell, but that was for a higher court to decide. I tightened my grip on her arm.

Evelyn sighed and stood up. "At this point, I really don't care what happens to me."

Encouraged but not completely convinced of her change of heart, I kept hold of her arm, and we loped down the gorge. The tall grass and the mushy ground were a hindrance. The fire was about fifty yards behind us. I could feel the blaze of heat breathing down my neck.

The cattails in our path were a surprise. The tall marsh plants with their fuzzy, cylindrical flower spikes batted us about the shoulders and face as we forged on. I kept moving, but Evelyn tried to hang back. I demanded, "What's your problem?"

"The lake is straight ahead. I don't know how to swim."

"The lake?" I said. "If we can make it to the lake, we can jump in —"

"Not me," said Evelyn.

I nodded behind us to the wall of fire. "And you're afraid of drowning?" I didn't give her a chance to reply. I towed her along, but finally had to let go of her arm. It took all my energy to get through the jungle of cattails. Evelyn limped next to me, mumbling about the water.

I glanced over my shoulder. The damp ground and green foliage had slowed the raging fire, but we were being attacked from a far greater danger. The slopes of the gorge — or, as I now knew, the spillway from the lake — contained driftwood, decayed trees. The wind whipped up the flames, making the dried wood burn like a funeral pyre. If we didn't hurry, the fire would edge past us and cut off our escape.

I needed more energy, more stamina for this dash to safety, but I floundered. My chest ached from sucking in the smoke. Each breath I took seared my lungs. The soggy ground tugged at my feet, slowing my progress. We were getting closer to the lake. But out of the corner of my eye, I saw the flames.

Embers rained down on us. Sparks showered us with pinpricks of pain when they landed on our flesh. In a dead heat, we raced the fire. For every step we took, the flames advanced two yards. Tears filled my eyes. We weren't going to make it. I thought of DeeDee. I thought of my father. I thought of Bailey.

I took another step and sank into knee-deep water. The cattails thinned out. We were at the lake's edge. There wasn't time for hesitation. I took Evelyn's arm and said, "I can swim, but you can't fight me."

She nodded, and we took the plunge. My lifesaving skills wouldn't win an award. My swimming technique wouldn't get me into the Olympics. But at least we were out of the fire's deadly grip.

Behind us, there was a thunderous crash. I glanced back and saw a flaming tree had fallen across the spillway. Fiery projectiles splattered the water, sizzling on contact.

I didn't try to identify the tree's exact location. At some point I'd been in its path. My immediate problem was how to contend with Evelyn's stranglehold on my shirt. She kicked her feet ineffectually. I ordered her to stop. "Take a deep breath and float," I said. "We aren't going far."

The lake covered three acres. I had no intention of crossing it, but simply prayed for enough strength to get us to the closest shoreline. The will to live drove me through the inky water. I might be a smaller size than I was two years ago, but I've never been in good physical shape. My body had taken a severe beating when I'd chased Evelyn over hill and dell. Towing her through the water was almost more than I could endure. Sheer exhaustion forced me to stop swimming. I couldn't paddle another inch. I straightened my legs under me and felt the lake bottom.

I could barely get the words out. "Evelyn. Stand up. We're safe."

She knelt in the shallow water and stared across the park. "Safe from what, Bretta?" she asked softly.

I followed her gaze. A patrol car with flashing red lights barreled toward us.

Epilogue

It had been five days since the fire in the park. Evelyn had been indicted on two counts of homicide — Claire and Lydia — as well as arson, public endangerment, and a few other charges. There were multiple civil suits filed against her by wedding guests, citing pain and suffering and mental anguish. Evelyn had been denied bail and was awaiting trial in the River City jail. I'd thought about going to see her, but I was a witness for the prosecution. Besides, what would I say if I saw her?

I was at the Flower Shop, watering plants, watching the clock. Bailey was being discharged from the hospital at noon. DeeDee had helped his daughter, Jillian, clean the cottage, making it ready for his homecoming. I'd stayed away. Jillian seemed like a pleasant young lady. She was twenty years old, full of youthful thoughts and ideas, and extremely possessive of her father.

Tipping the water can spout over the dracaena plant, I was happy to see it had survived its wilting episode without any visible sign of damage. I'd escaped the fire with only a few minor cuts and blisters. Since that night, I'd thought about cause and effect in relation to my father, and to Evelyn, and to life in general. I'd even bought a book on philosophy, trying to get a perspective on human morals, character, and behavior.

I was still waiting for enlightenment, though the words of Aristotle played often in my mind.

The quality of life is determined by its activities.

After my close encounter with death, I figured I'd better curb my pastime of detecting. I revised that thought once I'd done some soul-searching.

Where would be the quality of life if I didn't care enough to get involved?

If I didn't make a difference in my corner of the world?

If I minded my own business?

About the Author

With the Bretta Solomon series, which includes *Roots of Murder*, *Murder Sets Seed*, and *Lilies That Fester*, Janis Harrison has combined her career as a florist with her love of writing. She and her husband live near Windsor, Missouri, where they operate their own greenhouse business.